'Like *Room*, where parenthood is at once your jail and your salvation, it is almost claustrophobic – but in the most glorious way' Lisa Taddeo

'Instantly engrossing. Sonya's emotional interiority is fascinating and compelling, and I really cared about her and Tommy – they felt very real to me' Marian Keyes

'Sonya is a gorgeously rendered character. Her struggle with identity and control and the corrosive effects of dysfunctional family dynamics, childhood trauma and skewed expectations is told with such empathy and flair' Donal Ryan

'Lisa Harding is a vivid and original stylist and a gifted storyteller – this is a fabulous novel' Kevin Barry

'A gripping, atmospheric and deeply truthful novel from a writer whose work I love' Joseph O'Connor

'Unputdownable; infuriating, nerve-wracking and hugely enjoyable' Roddy Doyle

'A fearless, fully compelling and illuminating look at one young woman's journey through addiction towards a greater understanding of herself and the richness of parenthood. I was both shaken and completely absorbed' Jane Urquhart

'Startling, urgent and intimate' Lisa McInerney

LISA HARDING is a writer, actress, playwright and the author of one previous novel, *Harvesting*. She lives in Dublin.

BRIGHT BURNING THINGS

LISA HARDING

BLOOMSBURY PUBLISHING

LONDON · OXFORD · NEW YORK · NEW DELHI · SYDNEY

BLOOMSBURY PUBLISHING
Bloomsbury Publishing Plc
50 Bedford Square, London, WC1B 3DP, UK
29 Earlsfort Terrace, Dublin 2, Ireland

BLOOMSBURY, BLOOMSBURY PUBLISHING and the Diana logo are
trademarks of Bloomsbury Publishing Plc

First published in Great Britain 2021
This edition published 2022

A catalogue record for this book is available from the British Library

ISBN: HB: 978-1-5266-2446-8; TPB: 978-1-5266-2447-5; PB: 9-781-5266-2448-2;
EBOOK: 978-1-5266-2444-4; EPDF: 978-1-5266-4291-2

2 4 6 8 10 9 7 5 3 1

Typeset by Integra Software Services Pvt. Ltd
Printed and bound in Great Britain by CPI Group (UK) Ltd, Croydon CR0 4YY

To find out more about our authors and books visit www.bloomsbury.com
and sign up for our newsletters

One fire burns out another's burning,
One pain is lessen'd by another's anguish.
William Shakespeare, *Romeo and Juliet*

And all my mother came into mine eyes
And gave me up to tears.
William Shakespeare, *Henry V*

1

There she is, lethal and irresistible, my high-kicking sidekick, and there goes that minx of a song, 'Impossibly Beautiful', and there is the sky so high and the light so bright and the sand warm velvet beneath the soles of my bare feet, and here comes the rush, an intense feeling of connection with all that is right and good in this world: my son's sticky hand in mine as he stares at the sky, my dog trotting alongside, his black coat glinting in the sunlight.

'Don't look directly at the sun, sweetheart, it burns your eyes.'

'But Yaya, you do it too.'

I bend to kiss him on the forehead, over and over as he laughs and pretend-wrestles me away. We look like everyone else as we skip down Sandymount Strand; dogs and kids, a mark of normality. No man, but then that's not unusual these days. Tommy breaks free and he careens like a drunk – no, that won't do, push that one away – runs unsteadily towards the surf, the frothy tongues of water that lick the sand. 'Go, Herbie, go – mind Tommy!' The dog bounds after him and the two of them frolic at the water's edge and I feel wave after wave of delicious things, my body vibrating with them, fingertips electric, heat pulsing its way through me.

The fever builds and I find I'm stepping out of my trousers and pulling my T-shirt over my head, dropping them in a puddle at my feet before I sprint towards my boys. My imp is waving, beckoning me into the shimmering water. *Hello, Elation, you spangly bitch.* I'm in my bra and knickers, but that's ok because it's hot and others are in their swimsuits and my underwear could pass for a bikini, so this is fine this is fine this is fine. Herbie is barking wildly. He'd have been put down in a week's time, they said, if I hadn't taken him then. Who rescued who? – the thought rises as I am submerged, the cold a tingle, adding to all the other tingles of the day, and my head is under and it's silky salty down here.

My body feels strong as I push through the surge of water, the sunlight refracted like so many tiny stars, until my lungs are burning, and my heart is thrumming in my throat. I turn on my back and float, staring directly at the concentration of light. When I close my eyes a carnival of colours and shapes explodes behind my lids. Oh, Mr Sunshine's working his magic alright! I crane my neck to see my boys, but there's a stranger, bending down to talk to Tommy. A distorted version of the happy song of moments before burrows and grooves. Now the stranger is picking him up. Not ok. Strike at the sea with sharp, staccato strokes, fluid sloshing in my ears and mouth. As soon as my feet hit the shallows I sprint, pushing the body of water away as if it were mere air.

'It's ok, it's ok, sweetheart, I'm here now, I'm here,' I say, or I think I say, my voice warped and bouncing in my ears as I open my arms to gather him up.

'You really shouldn't leave a little one alone like that,' the stranger says, an old woman who's cradling Tommy too close. 'Here,' and she reaches into her bag to hand me a towel. 'Where are your clothes?'

I don't like the aura of authority about this woman who still hasn't let go of my son. Start to shake with anger and cold, purple patches breaking out on my arms and legs.

'It's ok, Herbie,' I say as I pat the dog on the head.

'Oh, that poor creature belongs to you? I thought it was a stray.'

The woman's voice sounds like a swarm of something biting and black, with wings. Static builds up inside my head, so I have to shake it.

'Are you alright, dear?' falls out of the woman's mouth, and it stings.

'Jesus, I'm fine, perfectly fucking fine. Now just give me back my boy and we'll be out of your way.'

The woman's grip on Tommy tightens. 'Perhaps you should dry yourself off first?'

Shaking with something else now and it's rocking me deep inside. My voice is huge and swallowed and I'm scared of what might happen if I release it. Breathe: in, out, in, out.

The woman sucks in her cheeks, biting down on them, making her appear cadaverous, as if she might spirit Tommy away to another dimension. 'Is there someone I can call?' Her voice a hag's voice. I knock the phone out of her hand and grab my son from her arms, which are stick-thin with loose swathes of skin. Feel repulsed by this old woman: her proximity, her bossy intrusion into our happy, happy world.

The woman calmly bends to pick up her phone, which makes my reaction seem all the more extreme. Even when I can see myself like this from the outside, I still can't stop the tornado whipping up through me: a 'child thief', a 'kiddy twiddler', a 'dirty old bag', 'witch/bitch/crone/cunt' rip out of me as I run, a bawling Tommy clasped tight to my sopping bra, Herbie in step. Sprint to the car without stopping to pick my clothes up off the sand; people are staring – let them stare, they have nothing better to do. I throw Tommy in the back with Herbie – whose hair on his back is standing up, his Sid Vicious act – before I turn the key, which I left on the front right-hand tyre (a trick Howard taught me, as I was forever losing my keys – good for something, the prick). Rev the engine and move away from the packed car park on to the congested road, my bare feet slipping on the pedals.

I put the heater on full, willing my old banger on, humming one of Tommy's favourite tunes: *Mary had a little lamb, little lamb, little lamb…* Usually when I hum he sings, his cartoon-angel-like voice high and pure, but this time he just sticks his thumb in his mouth and sucks on it hard, as if worrying it might make the other thoughts go away. 'Ok, little man?' I say in the rear-view mirror and smile, giving him the thumbs up. Nothing. Try again: 'Ok, big man?' I stick my tongue out, roll it so the two sides touch off each other, which would normally make him chuckle, then roar with laughter, but he just squeezes his eyes shut and sucks more intently. 'Ok, Mister Man, we'll be home soon, and we can have some fishy fingers and jumping beans, ok?' I turn on the radio and Ravel's *Bolero* blasts from the speakers.

As the car heats, fog forms on the windows. I draw a heart on the windscreen, keeping one hand on the steering wheel, and write 'Mummy loves you' inside it. 'Tommy, look.' I trace the letters with my fingertip, reading aloud. He opens his eyes, squinting, leans into Herbie, tries to hug him, arms only reaching a third of the way around his wide girth. The dog moans, a happy contented sound. 'Good boy, Herbie, best boy.' His thick tail thumps on the tatty nylon seats. 'My best boys, what would I do without you?' At the next traffic light there's a man beside us who nods madly, winds his window down and shouts: 'It's not every day. Lucky day. Lucky me. Alright, darlin'?' I ignore him until the traffic lights shift to green, when I give him the finger as I speed off, tendrils of his voice hanging in the air: 'Yup, I'd like that alright...' My adrenalin spikes as I realise he's following me, or is he, or is that mad imp deluding me? 'Not too long now,' I say to my two boys in the back, who are still cuddled into each other. I turn to the right, checking the mirror, and see him still, but then, no, it's not him, he was just having his fun, harmless fun, it's ok it's ok it's ok. My heartbeat slows down as I think of the promise waiting for me in the fridge. I'm glad I had the foresight to do that: chill it. It's hot in the car now and it's still warm outside.

Pulling up at the row of tiny terraced red-brick cottages, I pray that none of the snoops are lurking behind their half-slatted blinds. That Mrs O'Malley, always butting in, dropping in home-made bread for 'the little mite'. I know how to make Tommy happy with his orange food: his cornflakes and marmalade and baked beans and fish fingers and Cheddar cheese. Meat is dead animal flesh; I had to tell him that. Not the fish, though, I don't tell him about the fish being hooked and whacked over the head. He won't eat anything remotely resembling green – something to do with mould. He's not undersized or anything, but then I don't know any other four-year-olds. I cover myself as best I can with the skimpy towel and run up the tangled path to the front door, painted a shocking pink by my own hand, sploshed and botched. 'Let yourselves in,' I shout as I tear into the one bedroom we all share. I rip off my wet under-wear and open the top drawer, a jumble of socks, bras and knickers, manage to locate a clean pair, before finding myself in the kitchen in just my pants in front of the fridge.

'Yaya, you've no clothes on.' Tommy's voice is at the kitchen door. I hear his footsteps padding into the front room, the tip-tapping of Herbie accompanying him, then the sudden burst of noise as the TV blares. 'Too loud,' I shout. He doesn't lower the volume – maybe he didn't hear me, or maybe he's trying to annoy me. I twist the top off the bottle and am tempted to glug from the neck – need to cool, to soothe – but force myself to open a cupboard and get a glass. A mark of staying civilised, even with no one to witness me. Particularly with no one to witness me. This delicate white deserves a glass, the space to aerate. Pour, sip daintily, then throw my neck back and drink the whole thing in one go. Instantly I relax. How tense that woman made me feel, that man in the car – *other people, fuck them* – and I pour myself a second glass. A faint burning in my stomach, a mellow warmth spreading in my chest. By the third I find I can swallow, breathe, swallow, breathe. Like swimming.

I turn the grill on to 180 degrees, open the freezer to take out the fish fingers, and find there are none. I rummage through the cupboards, locate two cans of baked beans and one open can of dog food, a bit rank, but should be ok, Herbie eats anything. Stick the beans in the microwave and slip my frilly apron over my pants, an ironic moving-in gift from Tina, back when we shared a flat in London: 'To my favourite Domestic Goddess!' I see my old pal, grinning, off her face pretty much all the time on anything at all. The beans are hissing and spitting, jumping out of their skins. The microwave is spattered with bright orange sauce. Later. I'll clean that later.

'Anything good on?' I place the dog's plate on the couch beside him and Tommy's plate on his knees.

'Where are the fishies?'

'Don't start, Tommy. Remember the starving children in Africa?' The moment I say it I wish I could force the words back inside. The kind of shit my father used to spew at me. 'There was none left. We'll get some tomorrow, ok?'

Tommy nods and lifts a spoon to his mouth.

'Ouchy.'

'Too hot, darling?' I go to his plate and blow. 'There now, see… Yummy?' Lift the spoon and make an airplane noise as I bring it towards his mouth, which is clamped shut. See my hand moving of its own accord, slamming the spoon against his lips and forcing them to open. The clang of metal as the spoon falls from my shaking hand on to the floor. Hyper imaginings, never a good sign. 'Ok, not to worry, you'll eat when you're hungry.' I manage a jaunty wink before finding myself back in the kitchen, the bottle to my mouth, to hell with decorum, *be still my banging heart*.

The bottle emptied, a space opens up and my head feels liberated, as if I've just removed a too-tight elasticated band from my hair. Glide into the living room and flop down between my two boys, Tommy feeding Herbie the rest of his beans by hand: what a sweet, caring boy. I'll make sure he eats later. Settle against the warmth of their bodies, feel mine softening, falling.

Sometime later an acrid smell of burnt cheese on toast from yesterday fills the room. I sit up too fast, head banging, dots dancing in my eyes. Black smoke is billowing under the kitchen door. Move as if in a trance, groggy, but pulse racing – is this another of my night hallucinations? Open the grill door, reach in, grab the handle, flames are leaping, drop the pan on to the floor – *fuck, be still my walloping head*. Wrap my hand in a soggy tea towel and lift the pan into the sink. Under the tap, and whoosh, the flames burst and die, black charcoal in their place. I lined the grill with baking paper instead of tinfoil, stupid stupid stupid woman. I see my son in the doorway, eyes huge and glassy. 'Ok, Tommy, everything's alright now.'

He smiles, his mouth tight and tilted, an exact replica of his grandfather, and says, 'Beeootiful. Hot and slinky like the sun.'

Herbie whines. My hand is hot and scalded.

'Water, Yaya.'

I smile at him, my little oracle, and hold my hand under the cold tap.

Every window will need to be opened. Every part of me is jangling. Feel myself crashing, falling into the pit. Should've known when I first saw her there on the beach, shimmering, irresistible, that this was the way it would go. Grab the full bottle, turn my back, undo the screw top with my teeth. Tell myself that what Tommy doesn't see can't hurt him.

2

The windows are wide open and I'm naked except for the apron, no sign of another body in the bed. The clock says 9:10 – what, morning already? The TV is blaring and the house stinks of burnt charcoal overlaid with bleach, making my hot, scratchy eyes water. 'Tommy? Tommy, darling?' I lie back on the pile of tussled pillows, exhausted by the effort, and stare out the window at the grey overhang of cloud. One day of sunshine is all I deserve. My body is heavy yet my brain is racing, careening against the inside of my skull. Need to get up, shower, get dressed, go to the supermarket, make lunch, tidy the mess from the beans, scrub the charcoal off the blackened walls, buy some polish, spray the house, maybe get a bunch of flowers, tulips, brightly coloured, need to wash Tommy, clothe him, feed him, walk Herbie, find the lead – where's the lead? – must pick up after him, need to remember to do that, bring the poo bags, get my son into the fresh air, make sure he eats. Close my eyes, drained by the effort of imagining the day's activities. Everything feels parched: tongue, gums, lips, eyes, eyelids, fingertips. Will Tommy think to bring me in water? – he should know to do that by now.

When I wake again it's a quarter past one in the afternoon. Push myself to sitting, look at the low, lumbering clouds, full and heavy like swollen cows' udders. Nausea rises. 'Tommy?' My voice skips and scratches. 'Listen, Tommy…Mummy's got her witch's voice today!' No response and the TV is muted. Force myself to stand, the ground beneath my feet shifting – a whole-body seasickness.

The kitchen has been scrubbed, sparkling. Did I do all this last night, or this morning? When? My boys? Wait – 'Tommy? Herbie? Tommy?' Breathe, Sonya, breathe, breathe, breathe. Pull on my jeans and a warm hoodie, fight the acid reflux by swallowing manically, fight the spins by holding on to any hard surface to hand. Keys? On the hook by the door. Another gem that Howard drummed into me. Slam the door behind me, the whole house shaking, and run to the green, adrenal glands in overdrive. There are three little children and a dad, someone I don't recognise. 'Excuse me, have you seen a big black dog and a little boy?' The man looks at me like all men ultimately look at me, like I'm a strange creature that's just crawled out from under a rock: should he stamp on me or run? This man grabs his three children and herds them away. *That's right, run away, you always do in the end.* Rain starts to gather in the heavy clouds overhead. An image of my boys, lost and scared, rises up and slams me, winding me with the force of it. Where else would they go? The beach? The shops? I run to the corner Spar. 'Have you seen a little boy and a big black dog?' The boys behind the counter shake their heads, then snigger. 'It's not funny, you assholes, a little boy is missing…' They stop laughing. 'Haven't seen him, missus.' Run on to the main road searching for a flattened black coat, insides trailing, blood oozing, all worst-case scenarios playing out. 'Herbie? Good boy, Herbie, good boy.' My voice is ripping from me. Herbie would never let anything happen to Tommy, as long as the stupid mutt hasn't stepped out into oncoming traffic. Everything else he instinctively understands, except for that one kink, where he'll see a car and barrel into its path. I run back to the park and perch on the swing, pushing it into motion with my feet, hearing Tommy's voice in my ear: 'High, higher, highest.' The movement helps offset the mounting sense of panic. Lift my face towards the sky, the lightly falling drizzle cooling my hot cheeks. How long has Tommy been missing? An hour, five? Who could I call? My father? The thought is swiped as soon as it surfaces. Howard? He'd say this was bound to happen. The guards? – but what kind of a backlash might come from a call like that?

My feet take off, slipping in my flip-flops on the wet tarmac as they run towards the house directly opposite ours, with its clipped hedge and planted borders, front door an innocuous brown, in keeping with the rest of the street. Why didn't I think of this in the first place? I knock politely, three times, wait, then knock again and again, louder and louder, fuck *propriety*, until the door opens a crack. 'Have you seen Tommy?' Mrs O'Malley points behind her into the kitchen, where Tommy is sitting at a table, a book in front of him, Herbie at his feet. Rage rips through me. 'Didn't you stop to fucking think I might be worried?'

Mrs O'Malley pulls the door behind her and steps outside. 'Not in front of the child. You didn't get the note, then?'

Note or no note, how dare this woman go into my house and take my boys?

'Your front door was wide open this morning. You had me worried.'

Breathe, swallow, restraint. 'Yes, I can see that.' I bring my thumbnail to my mouth and tear the quick with my teeth. Need to pull this back. 'It won't happen again. I'm sorry.' This last word visibly softens Mrs O'Malley, who opens the door wider so Tommy is fully visible, so beautiful, lost in his own world, dunking biscuits and drinking milk. 'Such great concentration.' She speaks low and nods in his direction. Have I missed something? 'It's the *Encyclopaedia Britannica* and he's enamoured with Australia and the marsupials.' Has she told him about bushfires burning them alive? And why is my son allowing himself to drink milk from another animal? Have I not told him often enough? Why have I not run to him and engulfed him in one of my hugs, squeezing the breath from him? Mrs O'Malley gestures at me to come into the living room and sit on the rustling couch, which looks like it's still wrapped in the plastic covering it was delivered in decades ago.

'Tommy was very hungry this morning, Sonya.'

I nod solemnly like I'm giving this some consideration. Need to present some level of respectability and remorse.

'I had a migraine last night.'

'You certainly were out cold this morning.'

I blow on my scalded palm.

Mrs O'Malley gets up to plump the pillow on the single armchair, then trails her fingertip over the mantelpiece, collecting imaginary dust. The room is dimly lit, various shades of brown, stifling, redolent with an old-lady smell of TCP, stale potpourri.

'I'm happy to mind the boy and the dog for as long as you need. I have spaghetti bolognese for later.'

'Tommy doesn't eat animal flesh.'

A crease on Mrs O'Malley's forehead actively furrows deeper, a worm making a groove in the centre of her already deeply lined face. Smoker's slits frame her thin mouth, which is outlined in a plum pencil, made to look bigger than it is. Powder is catching in all the ravines, her rouged cheeks giving her the appearance of one of my childhood Pierrot dolls, which used to come alive at night, dancing and whispering diabolical instructions that I could never quite remember the following morning, although a feeling of being complicit lingered. My father kept putting them back in their 'proper place' on the shelf in my bedroom after finding them stuffed in pillowcases under the bed, face down. He told me they were my friends and how could I do that to my friends?

'He told me you don't let him have milk.' Mrs O'Malley interrupts my musings.

'Cow's milk? Disgusting. What mother in her right mind…? The calves cry themselves hoarse.'

She flicks a crumb off her forearm. 'What does he eat? He's small, isn't he?'

'I'm small,' I say, my voice anything but, as it bounces off the walls, amplified.

'Yaya?' Tommy comes hurtling into the room and throws himself into my arms, Herbie a pace behind him, his whole body wriggling from the force of his big tail walloping side to side. Mrs O'Malley clears the tiny porcelain figurines within reach.

'Hey, I missed you guys. Don't ever go anywhere without telling me again.'

The old bag butts in: 'Sonya, you need help.'

A mist forms in front of my eyes. There is no anger, only a calm sense of purpose as I gather my boys and close the door behind me. I congratulate myself on not slamming it, on not losing it. My earlier use of the F-word won't be forgotten, but then nor will my neighbour creeping into my house, breaking and entering, and stealing my son, yes, stealing him from under my roof when I was sleeping.

We walk towards the car. My boys look a bit dejected, in need of an adventure.

'Who fancies walkies on the beach?'

Herbie howls and Tommy nods excitedly.

'Mr Fresh Air will blow all the cobwebs away, Tommy.'

'Clean in the head, Yaya!'

'That's the idea, Mr T!'

Need air and water, lots of water. Mouth dry and head banging. Never again.

'Tommy, you're never to go anywhere without telling me again, ok?'

'Sorry, Yaya.'

'Don't say sorry, beautiful boy. You've nothing to be sorry for. Just don't do it again.'

3

The beach is cold and grey, in contrast to the golden scene of yester-day. I retrace my steps but can't find my clothes anywhere. Maybe the old crone took them, for identification purposes. Shake my head, which is excruciating, attempting to empty it of the build-up of static. Tommy is paddling, licking his ice cream, and Herbie is running along the edge, barking at the waves, which are wilder today. The hypnotic hiss and suck as the water pulls back from the shore, leaving sleek, polished pebbles in its wake. I bend to pick one up, a flat-edged 'skimmer' perfect for frisbeeing along the surface of the sea, out beyond the breakers. 'See, Tommy, this is how you do it.' Father's face is looking down at me, smiling. I was always very good at skimming stones. Tommy can't seem to get the knack, and after three attempts gives up, instead launching himself on to Herbie, who looks like a lumbering bear with his long coat all wet and matted. 'Giddy-up, Hewbie Howsie!'

'Tommy, you're getting too big,' I shout, as Herbie miraculously picks up speed and gallops off down the beach. Abruptly I sit, and just as abruptly I cry. This is all part of it: my 'condition', as diagnosed by Howard. He said it was what made me such a great actress: extreme and electric. The moods crashed through me then, never really landing, never really taking hold, but since stopping acting and having Tommy, alone, and the tiredness and the feeling of being judged by the voices, and now the old ladies of the world, they have taken up permanent residence. How old would my own mother have been?

My son's warm body clambers on top of me.

'Why's Yaya crying?'

I wipe the wet from my cheeks and hug-wrestle him to the ground. 'Yaya's not crying. It's just sea spray in my eyes.' His worried face looks unconvinced. 'Salt makes your eyes water, Tommy.' Then I tickle him until he's writhing and hitting back at me, tears flowing from his own eyes. 'See, Tommy, you're crying now, and you're happy. Tears don't always mean you're sad.'

'But I don't like so many tickles, Yaya. It hurts.'

I pick him off the ground and hug him close to my body, his heart knocking against mine.

'Tell me when I'm doing something you don't like, ok?'

He starts to hit me, trying to break free from the embrace.

'Too tight, Yaya.'

'Sorry, darling. Will we do our spinnies?'

He nods, and I put him on the ground for a moment before lifting him underneath his arms and twirling him round and round.

'Higher, Yaya, faster...'

The air is whistling in our ears, the dog running in circles around us.

'Herbie loves this too, Yaya.'

I spin and spin, determined to give him the ride of his life, until my legs give out beneath me and I fall to the wet, puddling sand, my little boy collapsing on top of my chest, the two of us panting and laughing, Herbie licking us all over.

'Best Yaya in the whole world.'

The only Yaya in the whole world, a name he concocted in response to me calling myself Sonya at times, then other times Mama, and his little head got confused. I close my eyes and let the world tilt, my whole body spinning like it's on a psychotic fairground ride that loses control of itself, its operators looking grimly on as the machine cranks its speed up, over and over. I think I remember this same sensation around my own mother: of speed and spinning.

Tommy snuggles deeper into my tummy. The only thing that is mooring me to the here and now is the warm, beating body of my son. When I open my eyes I find him staring at me with a concentration as intense as a lover's. Not that anyone has looked at me in that way in a while, but I recognise that gaze that contains all the aspects of love as I inspire it: confusion, possessiveness, protectiveness, and something else, cloudy and worrying.

I point to a spot in the sky. 'That's where Mr Sunshine is hiding today. He must be sleeping after yesterday.'

Tommy looks to where my finger is pointing and transfers his intensity to the bright place in the clouds where the sun is obscured.

'Maybe we could brush away the cobwebs and let Mr Sunshine wakey up?'

'What a good idea,' I say, standing, brushing the wet sand off my clothes. 'Let's get our magic brooms and sweep away those pesky clouds.'

The two of us mime swiping at the air, giant sweeping brushes in hand. Herbie barks at the sky.

'It's not working, Yaya,' Tommy says after some minutes. 'Mr Sunshine doesn't want to come out today.'

'I think you may be right, Tommy. He overdid it yesterday.'

'Oh well.' He drops his imaginary broom, kicks it, picks Herbie's wet lead off the sand. 'Come on, let's go. Yaya, can we get some fishies and food for Hewbie? He says he's hungry too.'

'Yes, of course, let's all go to the supermarket and get some of our favourite treats.' As I say this, the thought of Tesco with its fluorescent lights flickering overhead, the long aisles stacked with all kinds of dead animal, makes my eyesight blur and my breath come short and sharp. A fluttering starts high in my chest and I rest my hand on it, trying to make the winged creatures settle. I can do this, it is necessary, it is normal, I must do this. I'm grateful for the rain that has decided just at this moment to fall on us: it dampens the wings, weighs them down. My boy raises his face to the sky and licks the drops as they fall. 'Will there be a storm, Yaya?' He loves storms, like me, loves the thrill of thunder, his tiny body rocking to the bass notes, his eyes fixing on the flashes of lightning. I think of the early-summer storm of three months ago when the two of us flew out the front door to the green and danced barefoot, bodies swaying, chasing the flashes, willing the lightning to come find us. Herbie stayed by the back door, whining.

'Last one to the car is a pooper,' I say, running in my bare feet, flip-flops in hand.

'Pooper scooper...' he sings, laughing.

In the car we play the game of 'colours'. Any colour we see we have to describe in terms of something else. Tommy started this one himself accidentally – when I asked him to name all the colours he could see inside and outside the car, he started by saying: the colour of snot and grasshoppers, yuck, the colour of the sea on a sunshiny day, the colour of the sky on a cloudy day, the colour of Herbie's eyes, the colour of rain, the colour of Yaya's hair, the colour of Yaya's happy. What he is actually seeing as he says this, I can't imagine. 'What is it, Tommy? What do you see? Is it that seagull?' 'The colour of ice cream,' he says.

We pull into the Tesco car park, which is teeming with shiny, glossy four-by-fours and Volvos, most with registration plates no more than five years old. I count, obsessively: none are as old as mine, pushing fifteen years and way past its NCT date. Heat rises in me as I drive to a faraway corner, hidden, camouflaged by bushes, so no one else can see the moss that has incubated in the windows, the rust that is ingrained in the scratches. Try not to think of the vintage Spider my Italian fling, Roberto, the rising film director, bought me for my twenty-fifth birthday. 'A thing of beauty for a great beauty,' he said, framing me with his hands. What would he make of me now? Harsh, soundless laughter rises.

I park, then turn to my two bedraggled boys in the back seat and tussle with myself for a moment. Herbie pines terribly if he's left alone and whines like a banshee, drawing attention to the cruel woman who'd abandon her dog in a crummy car, and Tommy becomes overstimulated inside any place where there is food, pulling anything orange off the shelf. I look around and see we're pretty much out of sight here. 'I'll only be a sec,' I say as I jump and run, incanting: fish fingers, bread, toilet roll, dog food, beans, over and over compulsively, the way I used to learn my lines. I can hear Tommy's hands banging against the window, or maybe that's just my imagination, I'm not going to turn around to check. This is a mission that's been embarked upon, and if there's anything in myself I can count on, it's that I never give up on something once it's in motion, even when it's blatantly bad for me, even when it might just be laying its hands on me, stroking and beating me in the same moment. I shake my head and rush through the door.

My pulse is loud in my throat, my eyesight dims and blurs as the lights get brighter overhead, the noise of the muzak fills my head, people bump into me, without even an 'excuse me' or 'sorry'. Children are screaming – why don't they teach the little brats some manners? And trolleys, bright shiny overloaded trolleys, greedy glutted trolleys, bulging fat guts bumping into me, the tinny beats building into a scream. If I can only manage the fish fingers, Herbie can eat them too. Find the freezer aisle, fuck it's cold, grab Tesco's own brand, five packets, feel fingers scraping my hair back, a tug at the roots. Don't have to go far – a Chardonnay is on special: Le Versant, a lively French number, fresh and aromatic with notes of honey and flowers. Sweet nectar. Some have no security tags. I manage to get to the self-checkout, run the fish fingers and one of the bottles in front of the sensor, just in case.

The car windows are steamed up when I get back, Herbie letting out long indignant wails, Tommy crying soundlessly. 'Ok, darlings? Ok… I'm back. Now, let's go home and eat our fishies.' I drop into the driving seat, twist around to pat Tommy absently on the head, the dog panting quietly. It amazes me the calming effect I have on that creature – even when I'm hyperventilating myself, my presence seems to clear the dog of any stress. Never known such unconditional adoration, and I have to admit, he's the only stabilising influence in my life right now. Tommy's moods are increasingly volatile, and his needs are far greater than the dog's. 'Stop that right now, Sonya. Just stop it. Grow up.'

'Who are you talking to, Yaya?'

'My guardian angel.'

'Is she called Yaya too?'

'Yup. She's made in my likeness. Isn't that a scary thought?'

He says nothing for a while, just presses his nose against the window, then rubs his nose with his sleeve. I don't correct him.

'She must be beeootiful like you. Does my guarding angel look like me?'

'He or she can look like anyone you wish.'

'My dada,' he says, sticking his thumb back in his mouth and staring out the window intently. His face has closed down.

'A big tall handsome angel, like your dada. What a good idea. I might borrow him sometime.'

He half-bites down on his thumb, which looks raw and red, a welt at the bend in the knuckle. Enough talk of the deceased hero of a father. Tommy will never know that Howard didn't want him, was true to his word, abandoned him in my womb. News of my pregnancy was met with: 'You're making a terrible mistake, Sonya, you're not mother material… and your career, what will happen to your career?' An aspiring actor, Howard had enough ambition for both of us, and no intention of letting an unplanned pregnancy get in the way. I start to sing, 'Old MacDonald had a farm and on that farm he had some monkeys, eee, aye, eee, aye, oh, and on that farm he had some tigers…' Tommy pretends he's not listening but when I make really bad monkey sounds he starts to chuckle in spite of himself, and when I make a monkey-lion-gibber-roar he bursts into uncontrolled laughter, aping me, 'OohoohoohooheeeahahahROAR!'

The rain gathers in intensity and falls heavily on the car, the wipers screeching back and forth, barely creating any clearing in my view. The car swerves and slides on the wet roads – I'm pretty sure the tyres are bald or flat or both – but the impetus to get home to my bedtime routine is pushing me on at great speed. 'Wheee, Yaya, wheee…' Tommy shouts from the back, his eyes sparkling, seeking out the danger. He can sense it, Herbie too, I can tell from the way his ears are pinned back. 'Ok, boys… hang on!' I flick my eyes to the rear-view mirror to make sure that Tommy's seatbelt is fastened, and when I see it is I put my foot to the floor. The car screeches, Herbie yelps, a new-puppy-sounding cry, and Tommy starts clapping madly. 'Faster, Yaya, faster!'

Speed helps, I've always known this, in whatever form it comes: running used to do it, sprinting, then amphetamines, anything that sped me up helped me outrun the voices. The kick of performing did it – let me step outside of myself, my only awareness the pulsing of blood in my throat, wrists, veins popping – and dancing, swimming, fucking, oblivion. Roberto taught me the feeling of speed behind a wheel, usually some kind of Ferrari. Granted, this old jalopy can't exactly break speed barriers, but it helps – the car shaking, loose parts rattling, the engine roaring – it creates an illusion of winning, of outsmarting the shadows, outrunning the curses. Anything that lifts me out of myself, even for a sweet blessed moment, even the blaring of the horn in the opposite lane, the car swerving to avoid me. My breath is caught high in my chest, and I feel turned on, like when Roberto would take me in a public toilet. I catch a glimpse of my son in the mirror, jumping up and down in his seat, rocking against the belt, testing its limits.

4

'Home sweet home,' I say as the turn to the cottages materialises as if out of a fog. I've no idea where I've been these last few minutes. Force myself to slow down, to climb back inside myself, as I drive in second gear up our road. 'Yaya!' Tommy shouts. 'You're driving like a smelly ole granny! Fasterfasterfaster!' As soon as I pull on to the kerb outside our house I can sense that we're being watched. Might have to make that call to the guards after all – this is clear-cut stalking now, harassment. I fling open the front door, then lift Tommy (see what a considerate mother I am, you watching, Mrs O'Nosy?) into the living room, where I settle him on the couch, Herbie hopping up beside him. I run back and retrieve the bag with the wine and the food, then slam my front door and lock it from the inside. Damn, I'd forgotten the grill was unusable, I'll have to put the fish fingers in the oven. Would that work? 'MiWadi, Tommy?' I shout, looking around for the orange squash. The TV is already on, two packs of ten fish fingers are in the oven and the full glass is saluting me, with its pledge to numb and soothe. Ice, clink, cheers. Herbie pads into the kitchen, panting. 'Ok, Woofter, ok, don't give me that look. I know you're hungry. Just a few minutes more.'

'He's thirsty, Yaya. Like you,' Tommy says from the couch. How can he hear with the noise from the TV so loud? I don't like the tone of his voice. How can a four-year-old be supercilious, act like he knows more than I do? I run water into Herbie's bowl and no sooner than it touches the floor the dog is lapping, gulping. When was the last time I put water down for him? It was one of the things the people in the pound said: fresh water twice a day. A large dog like him needs plenty of rehydration. 'Sorry, old boy,' I say as his big tongue swallows the contents of the bowl, and then he waits patiently for more. I fill and refill the bowl four times, the same number of times I quench my own thirst.

'Yaya? Are the fishies burning again?' Jesus, that tone again, and he's right, again, smoke is seeping from the mouth of the oven. *Fuck, fuck, fuck, fuck, fuck, fuck…* My boy parrots me: *Fuckety-fuck*, he sings. I scrape the carbon off the top and remove all the orange coating, the very thing, the only thing, that entices Tommy to eat them in the first place. Place them bottom-side up in a mound on a plate and present them with a flourish to my son.

The three of us sit side by side on the couch, some humongous guy singing on *Britain's Got Talent*, everyone up on their feet and cheering, like at a gladiators' battle or a public hanging. I know only too well the serpents that seduce one moment and bite the next. How did I – a nobody, from nowhere (suburban Dublin nowhere), with no experience, no connections – ever get accepted into RADA? I look back at my decision to audition and I marvel. *Ms Nobody determined to be Ms Somebody!* That capacity for self-delusion, it served me sometimes.

I manage to eat one of the fish fingers, while Herbie polishes off eleven and Tommy seven. We all cuddle into each other before the curtain falls on this particular scene: the audience is giving me a standing ovation, I'm bowing from my waist, and tears are flowing all round. 'Electric', they gush, 'Simply stunning', 'Touched by greatness', 'A miraculous performance by an Irish unknown set to take the London scene by storm', 'A whirlwind of emotion', 'Beautiful and terrifying in equal measure', 'Vulnerable yet ferocious'… The reviews keep coming; it's possible I might drown in the sudden flood of attention: words in print and out, hands clapping, people standing, feet stamping, those tears (crocodile or genuine?), thousands of new friends on Twitter, Facebook, Instagram (stupid addictive spaces, stupid fawning people), autographs, chat shows – and the standing in the spotlight, drinking it all in, pissed, high, out of my skin. My appearance as Hedda in a revised version by a trendy new playwright is *the* performance of the decade: sex-starved, voracious, vulnerable, powerful, trapped, free.

I'm living in a hall of mirrors, my image distorted and bounced back at me: beautiful, grotesque, famous, grotesque, brilliant, grotesque. I'm a sad, needy clown.

'Yaya? Yaya?' Tommy's voice tugs at the edge of my consciousness as I rock, clutching my stomach, sweat pouring out of me. He's blowing on my face and Herbie's big tongue is licking me. Five years ago now. How fast I slid down the snake's back and how perilous that climb on the ladder was in the first place. The sensation of being judged, good or bad, strangled me. That, and the fact that I always knew one day I'd be found out.

Tommy is pinching the skin on the back of my hand, twisting it. 'Yaya, wake up, wake up, stop talking to yourself.' I jolt fully awake and see my son's face, wet and hot. Herbie is panting heavily, his filthy breath hawing on me. Push myself to sitting and take in the scene around me: the cold congealed final fish finger, the carpet strewn with clothes and wrapping and crumbs and muck. 'A rat would have a party in here.' I can see my father's face, his nostrils flared, his body hard and brittle as if it could hardly contain all the disappointment I have heaped on him, as if it might break with the shame. His only daughter, first treading the boards, exposing her madness to the world, then hiding out, a single mother, a common layabout on benefits. There was no pride for my father in my unexpected talent on the stage. He didn't want that path for me, and he certainly didn't want this one.

These moments of lucidity are the worst, when the fog has cleared and cold reality lays claim to me, nipping at my heels, making me need to run again, and fast. Can't sit with this laying-bare of my failings, and again I find myself in the kitchen opening another bottle, Tommy looking in at me from the living room. 'Are you still thirsty, Yaya?' *This is unquenchable, sweetheart.* I'm sorry I'm sorry I'm sorry. I can't do it any other way. I drive the bottle opener too deep into the cork so it crumbles and splinters. Next time I'll make sure they're screw-tops. Next time... There won't be a next time. I manage, I swallow, I soothe, I sleep, my boys climbing on top of me.

Sunlight pours through the window and stabs me with its edges. I draw Tommy to me, cuddling his warm, sleepy body.

'Mr Sunshine has slept enough, Yaya, he's come out to play.'

Little fingers drum on my head, pa-rum-pum-pum-pum.

'Shh, little man, come here and let's sleep a little longer.' I hold his hands, kiss his fingers. Little torturers.

'Up, Yaya, up.'

Tommy pulls the duvet off the three of us and runs around the bedroom chasing and cupping the light with his hands. I don't remember going from the couch to the bed. Pity I can't block out other unwanted memories. 'Tommy, pull the blind down, there's a good boy,' I manage, my voice catching and breaking on every syllable. 'Can you get water?' He nods, goes into the kitchen, pours a glass, brings it back and holds it to my mouth, then to Herbie's. 'Unhygienic...' I try, but it's too much effort. Tommy puts a towel over my eyes and strokes my hair until I go under again.

'Tommy?' The TV is on; I can hear shouting and booing, probably one of those daytime therapy circuses that Tommy loves. *Jeremy Kyle* is his favourite. *He's kind, Yaya. He wants to make the peoples stop screaming.* We'd make great fodder, top-rating viewing. I crave my son's snug little body and the heft of Herbie, so I call out to the dog, who doesn't come. The door is closed to the living room, which I've told them is strictly forbidden. We have nothing to hide from each other, not even number-twosies, which Tommy finds brilliantly funny. Closed doors make me panic, so I heave myself to the side of the bed, head spinning, sick rising, place my feet on the carpet and haul myself to standing, open the connecting door and find Tommy curled up in Herbie's belly on the couch, the two of them locked in a circle of love, the dog snoring, the little boy's arms draped around his neck. The picture is of such tenderness that my breath catches and I have to sit, my vision blurred. When did I become such a crier? Everything these days brings on the water-works, everything beautiful and everything cruel, and this scene seems to contain it all.

My stomach is raw and distended. Run my hands across my belly and imagine an alien life form in there, eating me from the inside out. Some otherworldly force has made its headquarters inside me and is issuing instructions I'm powerless to resist. I look above the mantelpiece at my reflection in the mirror and see a bloated face, red, mascara-streaked (when did I bother to apply the last slick from my dried-out wand?), blackened lines running in rivulets down my cheeks, evidence of my tears inked in black. My eyes move to the form of my little boy, his trousers smeared with ice cream, his T-shirt rumpled and grimy at the neck, odd socks, one of them mine, his tiny foot swimming in all that space. I sit at the edge of the couch. Herbie's eyes open and his big tongue reaches out to lick my hand. 'What are we going to do, Woofter?' His head tilts to the side, his eyes huge and shining. I imagine myself reflected in them, in a much more favourable light than the mirror's cold glass. In his eyes I am goodness incarnate, his life prior to coming to me one of neglect and wilful cruelty. Oh, Herbie, old boy, I don't know if I'm up to the job. I can still see the scars underneath his thick coat, the round cigarette burns on his neck, hidden by his collar. What kind of a person, what kind of a world—?

'You need to learn to control yourself,' my father used to say after my mother died, when I'd taken to slamming doors just to get some kind of a reaction, a habit that was resurrected with great gusto in my teenage years, after Lara came to live with us. 'I hate…' my favourite starting point for any sentence, followed by 'I love…' 'There is somewhere in between, Sonya. You just need to learn to calm yourself down, be less extreme.'

Tommy turns himself in his sleep and I hear him muttering gibberish interspersed with some intelligible words: Herbie, Yaya, Herbie, Yaya, on a loop. He's holding his stomach in his sleep and

I wonder if his is sore too. I reach out a hand to lay on it and feel a bloating, bend to kiss him lightly on his belly button and go into the bathroom, where I step into a scalding shower, full of resolve. I can do this. I rub Clarins body lotion on my skin, a present from Howard four Christmases ago, just before he left for good, and step into a long-sleeved below-the-knee dress that's only been worn once, a cardigan that's fraying at the seams and pumps that are seven years old but have held their shape. Relics from a former life: an outfit for an audition for the 'demure' part. I towel-dry my hair, smear some cold cream on my face and neck and curl my eyelashes with a metal contraption I'd forgotten I had. It doesn't take much. I wink at myself in the mirror, run my hands over my hips.

'Beeootiful,' Tommy announces brightly at the door.

'Shall we go out to lunch, sweetiekins? Just you and me?'

'And Hewbie?'

'Ok. We'll have to sit outside somewhere but that's ok 'cause Mr Sunshine is back. Now, let's get you into the shower.'

He backs away from me, as if he's terrified at the thought. Funny little thing, knowing how much he loves speed, and thunder and lightning, and jumping in the sea, even with high waves, and hanging upside down and spinning round and round. 'Come on, will we bring Herbie in too?' Tommy nods and holds on to Herbie's collar, his eyes screwed shut, as the water cascades on both their bodies, Herbie stoically shaking, Tommy wriggling and sticking his tongue out to catch the spray. 'There now, it's not so bad, is it, lovie?' I really should do this more often, get him used to it.

Once they're dried and Tommy is dressed, I head into the kitchen and pour cornflakes for us all, soaking them in soya milk. I empty the dregs from the third bottle of white down the drain. The two remaining full bottles stand defiantly, whispering threats and dares and assurances. Fuck you. I put them in a black sack, tying it firmly before dumping it outside. *Fuck you.* Tommy claps. 'You can have MiWadi owange, like me, Yaya. It doesn't smell and won't make you go all flop or your voice go gooey.' I go to him and tickle him, rubbing my nose to his. 'Eskimo kiss?' He rubs my nose back. 'Let's go to the park before we have lunch?' I say, although it's already three o'clock and way past lunchtime.

He jumps up and down. 'Can we feed the duckies?'

'We'll have to get some bread from Spar.'

'Okey-dokey, super-duper,' he says, and goes to get the lead that's hanging on a hook under the stairs. How did I produce such a brilliant boy? Herbie throws his head back and barks in delight.

Mrs O'Malley is outside, watering her pink and red old-lady chrysanthemums, or rather loitering, hoping for a view of us. 'Hello, all,' she sings. 'And how are we today?' I wave, put my head down and attempt to walk by, but Tommy runs over and throws his arms around her considerable bulk, his face burrowing into the fat above her knees. Must teach him boundaries, let him know it's not ok to go hugging virtual strangers. 'Hi, little man. And where are you off to?' Herbie is tugging at my arm, his whole body shaking with excitement. I always thought that dog had such an instinctive understanding of people; he'd usually never go anywhere near anyone except Tommy and me. Get your own goddam dog and son – my head is beginning to fill with that angry swarm, dark and maddening. Mrs O'Malley lumbers towards me, one hand grabbing Tommy's.

'Sonya, have you given some thought to what I said yesterday?'

Shake my head to drive out the insistent hum and buzz. 'We're just on our way to the park and then for lunch. Tommy?' Mrs O'Malley checks her watch. Stupid, Sonya, careful. 'A late lunch/early supper, that is…' The old meddler whispers something in Tommy's ear and hands him a biscuit, home-made no doubt, from the pocket of her apron, one for Herbie too. They both swallow without even chewing, like savages. Where are their manners?

'Let's all have dinner together later. We can talk then, Sonya.'

Interference, like static, builds in the air in front of my eyes and I swat it away.

'Yaya, there's nothing there.'

'I know that, silly, I was just feeling a little hot. Now, come on, let's go feed those hungry quack-quacks.'

Tommy hugs Mrs O'Malley again before saying, 'Bye-bye, thank woo.'

'Seven o'clock, Sonya. I'll have some dinner for the boys.'

Mrs O'Malley morphs into a giantess with a looming shadow that covers me in shade and gloom. I fight the good fight and stop myself from throwing curses her way. Pull my shoulders back, plant my feet squarely on the ground and stand tall: all regal and upright. 'Thank you. We'll be delighted to come later, won't we, boys?' Tommy nods, Herbie wagging that treacherous tail as I grab them both, one by the collar, the other by the hand, before taking my leave. *Don't look back, don't look back, don't look back.* Once we're out of earshot, words fly out of me: 'Don't ever go near that woman again. She's trying to take you away from me and keep you in her house and fatten you up like the witch in Hansel and Gretel.' My little boy's face crumples. Where did I get such capacity for cruelty, for puncturing happiness? My father's voice: 'No daughter of mine is going to be parading her wares in front of any Tom, Dick or Harry…' And this, straight after I received the letter of acceptance from one of the most prestigious drama schools in London.

In the Spar, on automatic, I stuff a batch of white bread under my arm, paying only for the luminous-orange ice pop Tommy presents me with on the way out. No one even asks about the other, presuming a woman of my bearing and stature and, yes, breeding wouldn't bother with anything as low as snatching bread. Anyway, it's for the ducks, no harm involving the shop in my philanthropic activities.

The sun is a soft lemon shade of yellow today, or 'mellow wellow', as Tommy says, licking his orange ice pop as we walk around the duck pond. I lift my face to receive its gentle caresses and feel myself settle back down inside. That encounter with Mrs O'Malley was distressing, and stealing, though I'm such a pro, always gets my heart racing as if it might fly out of my mouth. I find a bench and sink down into it, pulling my dress above my knee to expose my long limbs and slim ankles, an attribute that only those in the theatre world gave a damn about: 'Such dainty ankles and wrists, such a "drawing room" physique.' Indeed. I stretch my legs and point my toes and let myself remember the feeling of being adored.

'Stop them, Yaya. Stop them. They're hurting her.' Tommy is shouting. How he instinctively knows it's a she I don't know, but the two of us grab sticks and a ball and anything we can find and lob it at the gang attack. Five drakes are going at one duck, dragging her under, banging her head against the concrete rim of the pond. I pick up a big stone, throw it, whack one of them, but they're only momentarily distracted, and then go at their victim even harder.

A man leaning on a walking stick speaks very loudly: 'What an example to teach your young boy.'

I throw with more fury. 'I'm teaching him it's not ok for a female to be raped.'

The man shakes his stick at me. 'Lunatic. You're going to hurt one of them.'

'That's the intention, old man.' Can hear the mania in my voice, see my boy all riled up, the colour high in his cheeks, his focus intense. Herbie is running up and down along the side of the pond making a wailing sound like keening.

Tommy trips over his clown-like feet. I put the wrong shoes on the wrong feet, of course I did, and now my boy is hobbled. A big swan glides to the edge of the pond and hisses. I see white.

5

'Is Mary's house made of sweeties, Yaya?'

'I don't think so, darling. *Mrs O'Malley's* house looks like bricks and mortar to me.' When did he start calling her Mary?

Tommy has his nose pressed to the window, staring at the house opposite. I find myself in the yard rummaging through the black sacks and picking out the two full bottles. Funny how I didn't pour their contents down the sink; funny how the bottles were carefully placed to avoid any breakage; funny how I know there's nothing remotely fucking funny about this. No conscious control, none, beyond a feeling that I should stop, but I'm not able I'm not able I'm not able. The corkscrew is in my hand, it's in the bottle, it's twisting and turning. The neck is between my lips and I'm sucking on it, like a greedy baby at her mother's teat. It takes the full one this time to feel anything other than sad ole lonely ole pathetic ole me. Wavy lines float in front of my eyes, followed by hollowed black spots. Dizzy, and giddy. Now I am a Tennessee Williams character – Amanda, say, in *The Glass Menagerie*. Sashay my way into the living room, draw the curtains tight, press play on my resident blues album, *The Essential Billie Holiday*, and lift my boy high in the air, swinging him. High, higher, highest. One, two, three, wheee. Herbie is running around us wildly in circles. Tommy is giggling, then full-on laughing, then chortling, or is that choking? I stop and draw him closer. 'Ok, little man? Everything's going to be ok.' Close my eyes and continue swaying, my boy now a lover in my arms, his body pressed against mine. Feel wanted, needed, and all is well with the world. I sing-croon into Tommy's ear: 'Your eyes of blue, your kisses too / I never knew what they could do / I can't believe that you're in love with me…'

Tommy is pushing against me with his hands, and when I release him his fists pummel my shoulders. 'Not ok, Yaya. Don't like…' Oh, what a little worrier. I kiss him, all over. 'Ok, Poohead?' – expecting peals of laughter to follow this term of endearment. 'Down, Yaya, down.' A flash of anger erupts inside me. No one likes to feel rejected, particularly by one of your own, and after all I've given up for him. Ungrateful little so-and-so, but oh, how I love him so! Hug him tighter, sing more loudly into his ear, feel his taut body go limp and a surge of electricity flows through me. This is the only place in the whole world where I now hold any power, where my actions have any agency. Finally I have stepped into the role of the director or, even better, the writer, and these characters are mine to do with as I want. Right now I feel the urge to suck Tommy right back into me, to merge with this boy whose head is pressed against my chest. And Herbie? What could I do there? Test myself. Kick him, throw him out into the dark, light a candle and hold it to his fur, the smell of it singeing and then burning, catching light, flames leaping and licking through to his skin. Creeping shadows gather themselves into a solid mass and cover me in darkness. My hand is on the back of Tommy's head, which is rocking beneath my palm, as I continue to push his face against my chest. 'Shh, darling, shhh.' Herbie is whining now in earnest, which prompts my leg to shoot out and make contact with his ribs. He freezes, huddles, makes himself as tiny as a big dog can be and starts to shake.

My heart clutches. My heart. I have one. I can hear it in my ears. A creeping, tingling feeling of disgust crawls over me. What am I? What have I done? Herbie, darling, I'm sorry, is this what used to happen? I release my boy, his face red and creased, and watch as he crawls to Herbie and rests his head on the dog's flanks. 'Ok, Herbie, ok, you no worry, you me, me you, ok, ok, ok…' he whispers to his friend, not looking at me.

I walk away, through the kitchen and into the yard. The air smells of summer rain. I lift my face to the cloud-scudded sky, fall to my knees. What I could have done back there. Shake my head to try to dislodge the tumbling thoughts. Feel like I'm drowning, water rushing in. Try to hold my breath, rock on my knees incanting, help, help, help, please help, not knowing who I'm beseeching, but someone, something, some force for good, something bigger than me, wiser, kinder. Mother? Father? Bigger than that, more benign, less prone to causing hurt.

In that moment back there she got me, that lethal bitch, and I didn't even see her lurking.

I stand, legs unsteady, smooth down my skirt and rub away any trace of tears with my knuckles. I have to fight a desire to knock myself out, my fists clenched, containers for all my rage.

Back in the living room my boys are still crouched low, still talking to each other in their own gobbledegook language. The clock says seven and we never had lunch, but dinner is on our neighbour's table. *Normalise: steady, Sonya, steady.* Tommy eyes me from his position of safety. I feel sure that if I took a step too close, Herbie would spring and attack me, protecting his rightful owner. 'Herbie, old boy, I'm sorry. Mummy's sorry. I don't know what came over me.' I keep my voice low and soft, being careful not to spook him. How I wish I had a treat to tempt him back to my side. I reach out my hand to my son.

'Sorry, darling, sorry.'

Tommy stays where he is, still staring, as if he can see right inside me.

'I was gone there, Mr T, and now I'm back. No need to be scared. Ok?'

He remains stock-still, sniffing the air around him.

'It's really me, Tommy. It's me!'

He bends to kiss Herbie on his head. 'Yaya gone, Hewbie, gone away, now she back. Bad fairy gone.'

What the hell did he see?

'Bad fairy in the bad bottle, Yaya.'

'Oh, Tommy, I think you're confusing a fairy for a genie in the bottle. Remember *Aladdin*?'

'No, Yaya, not genie, badblackmean fairy and she makes you do mean things.'

What has he just witnessed – a kind of possession? Has he seen this kind of a blackout before? I shake my head, my whole body, to rid it of the bad black meanness.

'Nothing there, Yaya.'

'No, you're right, my clever baby. It has all flown away.'

He moves towards me, Herbie making an unsure growling sound. 'Ok, Hewbie, all ok now.'

I need to pull this back somehow, normalise, distract somehow, make them both forget, somehow. 'Tommy, would you and Herbie like to go to Mary's for scrummy dinner?' As I say this I know I'll have a job persuading him that our neighbour has not stepped out of the pages of a sinister tale, and there's no way either of us could eat a beef bolognese. My mind starts its familiar looping: images of creatures being transported in concentration-camp trucks to slaughterhouses where they're made to watch each other die. I can smell their fear, never mind eat it. Feel cruelly sober now, shocked into a moment of crystallised awareness so acute that I can see everything, all of it, reaching into eternity. Bleak and terrifying, and a future that's so very, very fragile.

I study my dog and my son, swallowing hard, a fist punching its way deep inside me. Should I call my father? Immediately I steel myself against that particular onslaught. No one else need enter the arena right now, not until I have regained some sort of balance. I need to eat; blood sugar levels are low. Diagnosed with hypoglycaemia by a doctor back in drama school, I used to go without food for as long as possible, allowing the world to take on its own peculiar lustre. Sometimes there were blackouts, and this woozy sensation was usually a warning, accompanied by chaotic moods, which were great fodder for the characters I was playing. Perhaps that was just a character back there, and I'm in a Pirandello play, cast as the despotic director.

'No way, Yaya.' Tommy is shaking his head manically. 'No way going to Witchy Mary's for dinner.' I place my hands lightly on each temple and hold him steady, butterfly-kiss him on the cheek with my eyelashes. His body softens, a suggestion of trust coming back into his eyes. 'Ok so, let's go get some pizza.' He covers Herbie's head with kisses. 'You love pizza too, Hewbie. Cheesy yum.' The dog licks his face all over, unhygienic but sweet and lovely. My eyes well.

I don't have the energy for stealing right now; I hope I have the cash. I open drawers and check pockets for any loose change and find a fifty-euro note in the jeans I wore all week. No recollection of it being there or where it could have come from, every penny from the dole last week accounted for. Perhaps the Man Above was listening after all! As we leave the house I notice Mrs O'Malley's door is open. I whisper to Tommy, 'Let's bolt for it.' We run, hand in hand, Mrs O'Malley's voice trailing me, a cold wind blowing at my neck: 'Sonya. We need to talk.' Interfering old bag.

Once we clear the corner, we slow down and Tommy turns his face towards mine. I puff up my cheeks in a parody of pudgy Mary. Tommy does the same and starts to waddle in a pretty accurate imitation, then mimes eating his arm, his fingers. 'Scwumptious yumptious… Deelicious!' How could I ever want more than this: this boy, who is brilliant and funny and all my own making? He is my best creation yet, the only thing I've ever produced to be truly proud of. Surges of heat flow through me, energy pulses like mini-shocks, as I hoist him on to my shoulders and start running again, Herbie keeping exact time, six paces to my every step, his four squat legs working hard to propel his bulk, his tongue lolling. My son's squeaky-pitched screams of excitement peal in my ear. 'Faster, Yaya, faster, giddy-up-hup-hup!'

'We'll have three large vegetarian pizzas, please.' I can hear my voice ringing loud and high in the packed waiting area of the local pizzeria. I lift Tommy off my shoulders and put him on the floor. There's no sign of Marco, only that surly daughter of his, who looks as if she'd rather be anywhere other than here. I see my younger self and have to suck down an urge to slap her. The girl ignores me, busying herself at the till. My voice goes an octave higher: 'I said three large vegetarian pizzas.' Tommy is tugging at my sleeve. 'Say "please", Yaya.' How dare he chastise me like this in public? Make a show of me? My hand reaches out to cuff him around the ear. The room falls silent, heat rises in my cheeks, the palm of my hand is trembling and hot. A man's voice: 'No need for that.' My tongue feels too big for my mouth. A dyed-blonde girl checks her phone obsessively, swiping the screen with her thumb, an older woman with a high starched collar looks down at the floor, two others look out the window, but the man who just spoke stares straight at me, quizzing every inch of me. *Steady, steady.* I flick my hair out of my eyes, square my shoulders, suck in my tummy. The daughter says loudly, 'Two large pepperonis', and hands the bag to the man, who is slight and wearing shorts and socks pulled up, giving him the appearance of an overgrown schoolboy. He hands the money to the girl and says to me, 'Do you have a licence to own that dog?'

'As it so happens, I do. Adopted.'

'What about the poor child? Do you have a licence there?'

I walked right into that one. Tommy reaches his small hand towards me and I take it, encircling it in my own. He looks at me with his serious face, his ancient barn-owl expression, and shakes his head at me. 'It's ok, Yaya.' The man bends over and speaks in Tommy's face: 'If your mother does anything like that again you tell your teacher, yes?' Tommy nods, deflecting attention away. The man leaves, looking back over his shoulder, his overdeveloped sense of responsibility leaving him struggling with all sorts of stuff that's not his to carry. How I intuit this is beyond me, but it always served me well as an actress, that flash of insight into other people's psyches. How much easier it is to inhabit someone else.

'I'm going to have to ask you to leave,' the girl says.

How old is she to adopt that tone with me? What does she know about rearing children? It wasn't so long ago that it was perfectly acceptable to give your offspring a wee smack. I know, I was at the receiving end of many, and I know: too the humiliation, how it doesn't achieve anything. Even still, my palm is tingling at the thought of making contact with the little madam's cheek, knocking that smug expression from her. But my boys need to eat, so I open my mouth to speak in what I think is a reasonable manner: 'I'm sorry about that. Just had a stressful day. Your dad knows me, I'm a regular.'

'I know you too.'

'So you know this is a one-off and I'm a repeat customer.'

'You owe thirty euros.'

The daughter hands a box of steaming contents to the woman wearing the perfectly ironed, crisp shirt, whose eyes have not left the ground until this point. She says thank you and leaves.

'Seriously? I'll tell your father about this.'

'Dad is the one who told me not to serve you unless you pay your debt.'

I place my hand in my pocket and get the fifty euros, waving it triumphantly in the girl's face.

'That's not enough.'

'Oh, for God's sake.' One of the two men that were staring out the window, pretending not to notice anything, suddenly breaks his charade. 'Serve the poor woman and her kid, and I'll pay any shortfall.'

I think I might be about to cry, so I twist the skin on the back of my hand and force my mouth into a bright smile that accentuates my one dimple. 'No need, no need at all.'

The man doesn't look at me. 'Just feed the little fella, will you?'

Heat rushes through me and my skin becomes red and blotchy.

'How much does she owe?' the man says to the girl.

'I don't want your charity—' My helium-high voice escapes me.

'It's not for you,' the man says.

Tommy is petting Herbie on the same spot on his head over and over, so it looks as if he might rub away the hair. I take Tommy's hand in mine and bend to kiss his fingers. 'Ok, thank you,' I say.

'You're welcome,' the man says in a gentler tone. 'Here.' He hands me a business card with his name and number: 'David Smythe, McManus Smythe solicitors'. This has to be the most perplexing mating strategy I've ever encountered. 'I've been there too.' The man is speaking low. 'It's not fair on him.' He gestures to Tommy. 'There's a meeting later.'

Ah so, what is it about me that makes it so obvious? And now it isn't just old ladies that are noticing. Uncle Dom, my father's younger brother, floats unbidden into my mind. He found sobriety and Jesus in the same instance. I preferred him before, when he went around with red-rimmed wet eyes, and lamented the world as being in a permanent 'state of chassis'. I liked his taste for the melancholy; he seemed to walk straight out of the pages of an O'Casey/Chekhov hybrid: a frustrated, apparently brilliant man thwarted by the world and its machinations. I was his 'little dolly' before he fell in love with Jesus, his special little girl, and he used to love to brush my hair and sing to me. There was nothing in it, not in the way my father later interpreted, but his banishment from our house was part of him getting sober. Jesus cards arrived, addressed to us all. My father had always welcomed God in all his guises into the house, but Dom never entered our door again. I missed him, like I missed my mother's sister Amy, a blowsy 'floozie' (according to

Lara). Following a spectacular row with Lara the Christmas Eve when I was thirteen, Amy left, or was thrown out, I can't remember exactly, but I never heard from her again. Lara orchestrated this: our insular life, where she held all the control.

The man has turned his back on me and is staring out the streaked window at the traffic hurtling past. A silence has descended in the shop and the noises from outside are amplified. The daughter's voice rises over the rush and roar of the cars and speaks to the man's back: 'That will be an extra eight euro fifty.' He hands her a tenner and says, 'Keep the change,' and walks out of the shop. The girl shouts after him, 'Your pizzas are nearly ready.' He's gone.

I turn the card over in my hand and study it: David Smythe. A sturdy name. In his wake he has left an impression of orderliness and togetherness, though I can't recall a single fact about his appearance. Hair colour? Eyes? Clothes? Nothing, except polished brogues and his long fingers. And cheekbones, taut skin pulled upwards. A reverberation. A voice that knows things. And a feeling of solidity, being near to him.

The girl is holding out a bag for me. 'That'll be the fifty,' she says. I hand over the note and leave, my legs heavy. 'It's a lovely evening, T, shall we have a picnic on the green?' Tommy is trailing his trainers along the ground, scuffing them. 'Pizza on the grass?' he asks Herbie, who is still subdued and tense. Whoever said dogs have no memories? I could bet every second of our time together is inscribed in that fella's brain, and this latest incident made no sense at all of what went before. Maybe all humans are just assholes, not to be trusted. Maybe you're right, Herbie.

The air is sweet and soft, carrying all the scents of the aftermath of summer drizzle. My senses are heightened as I inhale the smell of the grass, the damp earth, the mossy tree trunks looking like gnarled elephant skin. As soon as we reach the green I take off my cardigan and spread it on the ground for my boys to sit on. I pull off a slice of pizza for Tommy, who gives the first one to Herbie, then takes his, sinks his teeth in, his eyes closing, a parody of a grown-up experiencing a moment of bliss. One bite is enough for me, unable to deny the origins of the cheese. Tommy opens his eyes, looks at me, studies me.

'Yaya, the black birdies will come if you don't eat.'

Jesus, when did I tell him about the black birds of worry? I remember being told something similar. By whom? My mother? Lara? Unlikely that it was Lara, who never told me anything, except when she wanted me to know about my father's disapproval.

'Yaya, you must eat!'

I tousle Tommy's hair and say, 'I will later – promise, darling – you're not to worry now. You enjoy your pizza.'

My stomach feels full and bloated, though it must be empty, and I'm scared I might swallow my tongue, which seems to take up all the space in my mouth. I lie back on the patch of scrub and stare at the slouchy night sky above, so low it looks as if it might fall down on our heads and cover us in a cloak of cloud. I allow myself to absorb the moment: the sound of my boys munching, the heaviness in my limbs and the realisation that something has caught up with me. My eyelids droop, exhausted by the job of framing eyes such as mine: *Woe is me, to have seen what I have seen, see what I see...* The crowd is hushed, awed into silence. Ophelia's way out was always an attractive proposition, a poetic end to a life of tragedy. As a mother, my own sense of the tragic, the personal absorption in that realm, has been punctured. I have someone else to think of and this doesn't fit with my former view of myself. I would never have been cast as the role of the mother. A famous casting director told me this. I didn't embody those particular attributes: I was 'too angular and febrile'. I think this was meant as a compliment.

The warm body of Tommy climbs on top of me, lying heart to heart, an arrhythmic duo. I cuddle him to me, not too hard, not too much, not too needy, careful not to spook him. His body remains soft as it falls into sleep. I watch his eyelashes flutter as I gently caress his flushed cheeks. My body floods with a painful love. *Take him and cut him out in little stars, and he will make the face of heaven so fine that all the world will be in love with night and pay no worship to the garish sun.* Juliet's words float on the air. I bury my nose in Tommy's hair, which really is as fine as silk. Herbie is lying close, but not too close, his eyes trained on his real master, as if protecting him. 'Sorry, Herbie, old boy.' His tail thumps, an emblem of forgiveness. No wonder we use dogs in our lives the way we do. They make us feel better about ourselves than we ever deserve to.

6

All residual light has drained from the sky, and the damp is soaking through my cardigan, crawling its way inside my bones. I whisper in Tommy's ear: 'Come on, T, time to go home.' It's way past Mrs O'Malley's bedtime, nothing to fear there, and yet the thought of going back to that house, where the reverberations of my actions of only a few hours ago still linger, makes my heart beat wildly. Tommy stirs. 'Rat-a-tat-tat,' he says, lifting himself off me.

We slink along the road, the three of us crouching in the shadow of the wall, Herbie still smaller than he should be. Tommy's hand is holding tightly on to mine. 'Ouchy tummy,' he says. I bend down to kiss it. 'All better soon.' I know that feeling of not eating, then eating too much and too fast and the pains that follow. The two of them, Tommy and Herbie, polished off the three pizzas, and I can only imagine what kind of shape the dog's intestines must be in: all twisted from stress and too much bread and cheese. My own must be pickled, in a permanent state of acid reflux, and yet I'll have to add more to the mix tonight. It won't be possible to get through the night otherwise; the shakes have already started. This time there are no dissenting voices, just a realisation that my hangover is too intense and the cravings too insistent. I finger the card with David Smythe's number on it. Tomorrow – there's always tomorrow.

As our house comes into view I see a car parked directly outside, blocking my access. *Some people…* A familiar spike of fury pushes its way through me, keys at the ready. Just as I'm about to sink the serrated edge into the metal, I realise this is not a stranger's car. I place the keys back into my pocket and breathe deeply.

A man steps out. 'Hello, young man.'

Tommy looks at me, troubled. We never have visitors.

'Hello, Sonya,' the man says.

'It's late.'

He doesn't move. 'I think it would be better if we stepped inside?' His voice is caught way back in his throat. He looks around to check no one is listening. Still worried about the neighbours; I know better than to give voice to this provocation. 'Do you know how late it is, Sonya? Way past the boy's bedtime.'

What does he know about Tommy's bedtime, seeing as he hasn't been anywhere near us for almost two years?

'Where have you been?' I manage.

'You told me not to come.'

You should know me better than that. If not you, then who? My thoughts swirl about, not being spoken aloud, and I have to lean against the wall, dizzy from the effort of containing them.

'Are you ok, Sonya?'

'Fine.' I try and fail to crank up my megawatt smile.

'Are you going to invite me in?'

'Now isn't a good time. Tommy needs to get to bed.'

He nods, but still he doesn't move. 'I need to speak to you, Sonya.'

These words sound like a portent and raise the spiky issue of when I might get to my nightly fix. My hands are actively shaking;

it's been some hours now and my mind is overtaken with an image of my silky liquid soother. My beautiful respite.

'Strange-looking animal.'

Herbie growls in response.

'He doesn't like that,' I say, managing a half-smile that expresses itself more like a smirk.

'I'm coming in, Sonya. I didn't drive over here for nothing.'

As if driving ten kilometres or so to see his only daughter is such a sacrifice. He surely didn't let Lara know he was coming. Lara would have been instrumental in keeping him away from me, to protect him from me after the last time. Shame constricts my airways as shards of memories lodge themselves in my throat: me losing it, screaming, hitting out in impotent rage. But Tommy? I can't square any of it with the abandonment of his only grand-child. My body reacts, coils in on itself and hardens. Go away, I will him silently, go away, go away. And in this moment I mean it, although in the next I could just as easily be choked by the sight of his back again. We've always played this push-me-pull-you game. It might have been easier if he had passed away, I often think, then my grief would be justified and finite and 'normal'. As it is, I mourn his loss just as forcefully when he's standing right in front of me.

'Now isn't a good time.' I try to keep my voice reasonable, adult. 'Come on, Tommy, time for bed.'

Footsteps follow us up the path.

'Yaya, that man is coming.'

'That man is your grandad,' I snap. 'Say, "Night-night, Grandad."'

We're at the door now and I'm trying to tug Herbie in by the collar – he's rigid and the hair on his back is doing that punk thing – when I feel my father's arm knock the keys from my hand. He brushes past us into the hall. The moment is so unexpected and strangely violent that I'm stunned into silence. Herbie fills it with his growling.

My father turns to me, helpless. 'Sorry, but it seemed the only way to get an invite…' He trails off, his attempt at a joke failing to raise any smiles.

Herbie moves closer, sniffing, circling.

'Will you put that mutt out?'

'The mutt's name is Herbie, you met him when he was a puppy, and he's an indoor dog.'

Tommy has put his thumb in his mouth and is sucking vehemently. 'Ok, Mr T, less of that, now. That thumb is red-raw and your teeth will be bucked. Do you want me to cover it in mustard?' As these words rise up out of me I can sense my father's eyes boring into the two of us, then moving to take in the whole glorious mess as it unfolds from the hall into the living room.

'Jesus, Sonya, the state of the place. A rat would have a party in here.'

Always the rat metaphor, never cute little pigs in pigsties, rather rats as fat as cats, gorging on people's filth. What a shame Mrs O'Malley didn't think to clean beyond the kitchen.

'I can't exactly afford a cleaner.'

He looks at me with something like disgust mingled with pity. 'A hoover once in a while. Spritz of polish.'

And I thought he was scared of me, and that's why he stayed away. The guilt I carried. And I thought I was missing him. He moves on into the kitchen, positions himself with his back to the sink. We all follow.

'Young man, how would you like to come for a little holiday?'

'What are you talking about?' I ask.

'I think it would be good for the boy to get away from all this for a while, just until you sort yourself out.'

'Just like that? Two years of no contact, then you turn up uninvited and threaten me?'

'Hewbie?' Tommy asks.

'Don't worry, Mr T, you're not going anywhere. Don't mind this wicked old man. Maybe he wants to fatten you up too.'

'Sonya, stop filling the boy's head with nonsense.'

The affront of this leaves me breathless. 'I'd seriously like you to leave.'

'What about the boy?'

'Tommy – his name is Tommy.'

'I know that,' he says, sounding exhausted at the futility of our conversation. 'He's still young enough...'

These words raise the winged creatures from their slumber, and there's only one thing for it, only one way to settle them: drown them.

'I'm here now, Sonya. I'm here now. Cup of tea?'

'Not a tea drinker, *Dad*,' I say, trying on the word, which sits in my mouth like a lump of raw liver.

'You could develop a taste, if you practised hard enough.'

I shrug that one off and go to the fridge and brazenly pour a glass of vino blanco, its whispers loud in my ear, blocking out any noise in my head or anything my father might say.

'Sonya?'

I swallow a mouthful.

'Please, not in front of the lad.'

A laugh erupts out of me and I put my hand to my mouth to try to stem more. Bubbles of laughter are forcing their way from my stomach up to my throat, which is sore from the effort of pushing them down. The wine is helping. Swallow, breathe, swallow, breathe. Water, surrounding me, holding me. My father moves to the kettle, switches it on, and waits. It boils while Herbie, Tommy and I stand to attention in a line, eyes flicking from one to another, to the strange man in our kitchen, where our bowls of soggy cornflakes still sit on the table. He carefully opens cupboard doors, as if scared of what might jump out at him. He locates the tea bags and puts them in two mugs that he sterilises first with the boiling water. I'm surprised he's not sniffing the air.

'Come on, young man, let's put you to bed. Your mummy and I need to talk, adult chat, ok?'

Tommy looks at me and I wink surreptitiously. 'Anything that needs to be said can be said in front of Tommy.'

'Oh, for God's sake, Sonya, he's only a child.'

I don't move, or speak, just swallow more wine. Tommy continues looking at me.

My father whispers, 'I don't want to upset him, Sonya. Please, put the boy into his bed and come back out and talk to me, adult to adult.'

I have to clamp one hand over the other not to throw my glass in his face.

'The guards have been alerted, Sonya.'

A cramping in my stomach so intense that I almost double over.

'Who by? The auld snitch who lives opposite?'

'Sonya, please…' He gestures at Tommy.

I can't bear the look on my boy's face. 'Ok, ok, Munchkin, let's get you into beddy-byes and I'll have an adult chat for a few minutes, ok? Then I'll come join you and we'll all go to the Land of Nod together, ok?'

Tommy tucks his hand under Herbie's collar. 'Come on, Hewbie!'

My father looks at me in disbelief as I take Tommy by the hand, the dog following, and close the door behind us.

'Who that man, Yaya?'

I decide now is not the time for explanations of abandoning fathers.

'It's ok, sweetie, he won't be here long, I promise. Now, let's get you into your PJs and you climb on into bed with Herbie there. We'll brush your teeth when the man's gone, ok?'

'Ok.' He climbs out of his clothes, puts his hands in the air as I slip his pyjama top on. He steps into his bottoms himself.

'What a big boy you are, Tommy!' I kiss his forehead.

'Yaya?'

'Yes, darling?'

'Don't let the bad fairy fly inside tonight, please, Yaya.'

'I won't, darling, I promise.'

'No more bottle.'

I smile at him, reassuringly, but with the night that's in it that is an impossible promise and I won't lie to my boy. I'll be careful, I'll be moderate, I know when to stop.

'Now, I better go out and talk to the man, and I'll be straight back in, ok?'

'Stwaight back, Yaya?'

'Yes, baby, straight back. Love you more than the whole world.'

'Love you bigger than all the planets,' he says as he stretches his arms to their widest span. I blow him a kiss; he catches it and makes a big show of eating it.

'Yum, yum, yum.'

'Yumptious, scrumptious, yum, bum,' I say, which makes him giggle. 'I want you to think of the best bedtime story ever, ok?

Tell Herbie all about the adventures you're going to have in Nod tonight… Herbie, mind Tommy till I'm back, ok?'

'Let's go to the land of the sleeping giants, Hewbie, and wake them 'cause they want to help the scared little peoples.'

'Great one, Tommy! See you two in a flash!' I twirl my hand like it's holding a wand.

He zaps me back. I walk to the door, close it gently behind me.

My father is still standing with his back to the sink, tensed.

'Sonya, will you please join me in some tea?'

I ignore him as I pour more wine into my glass. Need to knock the edges, though not the lights, off. Just the right dose: I'll be careful, I'll count.

Tommy shouts, 'Yaya, will you come kiss me goodnight?' I'm not capable of going back in there right now, not while my father's here, knowing that any display of emotion would be taken as proof of my intemperance, my instability. 'In a minute, ok?' I sing-shout into the bedroom. I can feel my father's eyes on me.

'What? What are you looking at? Two years of no contact, not even your grandson's birthday.'

'You stand to lose Tommy if you don't get this under control.'

'You stand to lose me for real, for ever this time. I'd divorce you if I could.'

'Mrs O'Malley has notified the guards.'

'Seriously? Do you not think she might just be a crackpot? It's disturbing, the level of interest she displays in my life.'

My father switches the kettle back on and as he's waiting for it to boil he opens the fridge. 'Jesus.'

'Did I give you permission to go rummaging in my cupboards, my fridge?'

'There's nothing there.'

'As I say, a bit of a cash-flow problem.'

'Can you hear yourself, Sonya?' He stares pointedly at the wine bottle. 'How much do they cost?'

'None of your business.' Thirteen years old, hormones devouring my reason.

'Your voice… It's not even yours.'

The kettle boils, the steam rising towards the damp, mildewed ceiling. I watch the vapour dissolve into the cracks. I notice a large one, running the whole width of the room. Maybe the ceiling will fall on our heads and the whole matter will be settled. He pours the scalding water on the tea bag, tops it up with a dash of cold and sips warily, like he's doing penance by the very act of swallowing anything from this rat's lair. I open the back door and lean against it, inhaling the night air, which contains traces of barbecue smoke from gardens on either side, and a damp-earth smell mixed with something decaying, rotten. It's been weeks since I put the bins out.

'Sonya, you're simply not coping.'

'And where have you been? Maybe if I'd had just a little support I'd be coping better than I am.'

'Sonya, you have a problem with alcohol.'

How dare he waltz, jive, shimmy, slink – no, shove – his way in here after all this time, with his disdain and his arrogance, telling me what I am, who I am, what kind of a mother I am. My love for Tommy is bigger than anything I've ever felt before, bigger than any love he ever showed me.

'It's in the family, Sonya.' He looks like he's struggling to say something.

'What? Who in the family?'

He weighs up his words before saying, 'You know it almost destroyed your uncle? I'm scared the same thing is happening to you.' He sits from the effort of having this confrontation. This is not his habitual way; he'd usually manage a situation by pretending it wasn't happening, until something thunderous did happen, like with his brother, like now, with the guards threatened. There's something he's not telling me.

'You're a terrible coward,' I say, my voice smudged at the edges.

I want to go to him and snuggle against him, bury my head against his chest as I used to before Lara came into our lives, his heartbeat reverberating in my ear, but I'm scared I'll break if I make a move in his direction. Although my vision is soft, blurred by the booze, I'm surprised to see him slumped at the table, a man defeated. Finally, finally, I have him beaten. And what wells up inside me is an unbearable sadness: mine and his. We remain silent as tears build inside me, until my whole body is shaking, racked by the effort of pushing them down. Is this even real?

'Stop that now, Sonya, think of the boy.'

There he goes again with his directives: wrong, wrong, all wrong. When do I ever not think of my boy? I roughly rub the tears away.

'Sonya, we have to talk…' He tells me that Mrs O'Malley is an old family friend, and despite appearances he didn't completely abandon me; he asked my neighbour to keep an eye and to keep him updated.

'You asked that old bat to spy on me?'

'Mrs O'Malley said you were becoming increasingly erratic, leaving doors and windows open; she said you almost set the house on fire.'

'Oh, for God's sake. You weren't exactly a stranger to burning food either.'

'That was only in the time immediately following your mother's death,' he says quietly. 'Look, Sonya, Mrs O'Malley's worried, and I'm worried. The boy is obviously not in good hands.'

'And do you think you were a good set of hands?'

He looks down at his large, cumbersome fingers encircling the fake-china hardware-store cup, ornate and fussy, with blue calligraphy: willows, or catkins, a pagoda, blossoms, boats and gargoyles chasing each other across the enamel surface in never-ending circles.

'Did you pay her?'

He ignores this last question, suggesting that perhaps he did.

'You should have come to see us,' I whisper.

'Have you forgotten you told me to never, ever contact you again?'

'And you couldn't even send your grandson a Christmas card?'

'Sonya, there's selective memory at play here. I did send cards, which were returned unopened.'

It's true that I kind of edited that part out. It almost felt too painful to get those scraps when he wouldn't show up in any real sense.

'And I suppose there's "dramatics" going on too?' I say.

He's rubbing his temples in exactly the same circular motion that I do. He closes his eyes and breathes deeply, the exhalation sounding like a long sigh. Now words will pour out of my mouth, words I'll later regret if I don't get a handle on myself. I can see the mist, feel the heat rising, and my mouth is burning from holding in all the invectives I need to spew. I too breathe in deeply and exhale slowly on a whistle. For the next few moments the only sound is of us both breathing in an exaggerated fashion. *Impulse control.* I can hear my father's voice ringing in my ear. I was four, or maybe five, too old to be having a toddler tantrum – or in his words a 'hissy fit' – in the aisle of an overheated, overly lit supermarket. I have a flash of me lying on my stomach pounding the tiles with my fists, grazing my knees and my stomach in the process. He walked away, pretending not to know me. I wonder where my mother was. I don't recall her ever shopping or cooking or reading me bedtime stories. An absence, even before she passed away.

'Yes, I paid her, Sonya – Mrs O'Malley. She said she'd look out for the boy.'

I bite down on my fat, slippery tongue now that my father is being honest. There's a tone to his voice I haven't heard before, stripped of its usual self-regard.

'You were doing ok, as far as she could tell, up until a few months ago, when your drinking escalated to the point that you nearly burned the house down the other night. Think about it, Sonya. What could have happened.'

'Christ, it was only a few burnt fish fingers.'

My father turns his back on me, staring at our reflections in the window and the darkness beyond, his fingers feeling for a spot on the back of his neck that is red and raised. He speaks without turning around.

'Did something happen a few months back? Something to tip you over?'

Did something 'happen'? I don't think so. My 'tipping point' was just an inevitable destination on the journey I had embarked on. My flirtation had turned into a full-blown affair. There wasn't an 'aha' moment; the relationship was going along nicely, smoothly – a buffer – and then I woke up to find my every thought consumed. This is my story with alcohol, as with all the men in my life up to now.

Who am I if I'm not acting or fucking?

He turns to face me. 'Is there something funny, Sonya?'

My mouth must be doing its twisted thing. 'I can't believe you paid that auld bitch to "keep an eye".'

'What are we going to do?'

I surprise myself by saying, 'I'll have some tea, for starters.'

My father looks relieved, busies himself with the task at hand, concentration intense.

'Thank you.' I sip the bitter liquid, tongue scalded, my penance.

7

The two of us sit in silence, my father's shoulders and fingers hunched in a way I've never seen before. I want to unbend his fingers, straighten his back. I tentatively swallow the peat-brown liquid, now tepid but still uncomforting, and crave the smack that sits patiently waiting for me in the fridge. Am I fooling myself? Do I ever really 'taste' it at all? It's the sensation I'm chasing: the emptying and stilling and the nothingness of it. Blankety-blank. *Fuck, Dad, I missed you.* Bite down hard on the inside of my cheek.

'I'd like to take the boy.'

'I'll go to AA.'

'You need more than that, Sonya, at this stage. A stint.'

'I'm not leaving my boys.'

'Just for a while. You'll be a better mother the other side.'

The other side.

'He should be in preschool by now. Why isn't he?'

I think of my GP's concern the last time I visited with Tommy, when he had a high fever. The doctor seemed much more concerned about plans for Tommy's schooling than his sore throat.

'He doesn't want to go. I asked him.'

My father stares at me, scratching that spot on the back of his neck.

'Who's the adult here, Sonya?'

I turn my back so he doesn't see the heat in my face.

'Sometimes we all have to do things we don't want to. It's important Tommy knows that.'

I open the cupboard where I keep my Cif lemon cleaning fluid; there's a Brillo pad there too. I spritz and scrub every surface, obsessed with every streak on the wall I haven't noticed before. Mrs O'Malley's cleaning spree was far from thorough. The sweeping brush is in my hands and I'm swiping at a cobweb in the far corner of the kitchen. The poor spiders. What will become of them now? My eyes fill. A flash of Tommy's face illuminated by flames, his eyes reflecting the flickering fire. What might have happened plays out for a moment... My boy engulfed in fiery heat. My boy suffocated. My dog abused.

'Sonya, it has to be this way. Mrs O'Malley won't let this continue... Nor will I... You'd be doing the right thing.'

Has he ever said those words to me before? It was Lara who stoked his disapproval, his distaste, his visceral dislike of me. I'll never understand the wedge that woman felt the need to drive between us. The thought of Tommy around her almost strangles me. A coughing fit grabs me by the throat. My father gets up and pats me on the back. 'There, there, Sonya, there, there,' as if he's trying to soothe a colicky baby.

'I'm going in to Tommy, need to check up on him.'

'Is that wise? He's probably asleep.'

I go into the bedroom, close the door softly behind me and find the two of them curled into each other, snoring soundly. I sit at the edge of the bed, reach out a hand to smooth Tommy's worried forehead. His worried forehead, and he's not yet five. His little head full of bad fairies and black birds of worry and his tummy that's often sore, his filthy home, and his mother who's a lush, a self-ish, selfish, selfish lush. How many more times am I going to say 'tomorrow'? How many more times am I going to say 'sorry'? And the house almost going on fire is not the worst of it; the worst of it happened earlier today with no witnesses, and I was capable of that. A woman capable of that is capable of anything. *Monster Mother* – I can see the blaring headlines. Everything in the room comes into sharp focus, my vision as if filtered through crystal, and I can see a future where my bitch imp has me in her grasp. I whisper to them both, 'You are not safe with me as I am.'

I stand, go to the window and lean my forehead against it. I open the wardrobe, get my wheelie bag and start to throw things in haphazardly.

Tommy opens one eye. I stop what I'm doing.

'How's Nod, darling? Have you found the land of the kind giants yet?'

He smiles, still half asleep.

'Remember, you have a special guardian angel looking out for you. Always.'

He turns over, cuddles into Herbie.

'See you later, alligator,' I whisper.

'Not for a while, cwocodile,' he whispers back, in his sleep.

I walk back into the kitchen with my bag, just in case, though I'm not even sure if I packed any underwear.

'How long?'

'Three months.'

'What? That's way too long. Tommy would never survive that long without me.'

'My concern is whether he'll survive with you.'

A feeling lands in me I've never felt before.

'I'm sorry, Sonya. I know this is a shock, I know you'd like to hear me say, "Let's try to make this work with AA," but he's too little, it's too dangerous. You can't beat this disease on your own.'

He sits, slumps, looks exhausted.

'Can't you come back in a few days? I need to get Tommy used to the idea.' I almost say 'and Herbie', but don't want my father more alarmed than he already is.

'There's a place for you tomorrow, Sonya. If you'll agree to go. You have to agree to go, willingly.'

'Not tomorrow, Dad.'

'These places don't come round very often, Sonya. Please, think about it. For Tommy. The sooner you tackle this thing, the sooner you'll all be back together again.'

I sit at the opposite end of the table.

'Where will Tommy go?'

'With me.'

'And Lara?'

'She'll just have to understand.'

'So you haven't told her?'

He looks miserable. This could be a huge problem for him. He looks down at the table, swipes a crumb off it, gets up, goes to the sink, gets a cloth, runs the water, returns to the table and wipes.

'Dad, seriously, think this through. Lara probably won't allow it.'

He holds the cloth up, studies it like it's something he's never seen before.

'There is no other way, Sonya. Mrs O'Malley has said that she'd call the guards tomorrow, and if they do nothing, the social workers. She's not kidding.'

'Stupid bitch.'

He looks directly at me. 'No, Sonya, she's thinking of Tommy.'

A silence falls. I break it with a whisper: 'And Herbie?'

'The dog? We'll have to find him a temporary place. Boarding kennels or something.'

The thought of Herbie curled up in a dark kennel, in strangers' hands, strangers who wouldn't care for him the way I do – until today. I have to remind myself: until today.

'Tommy wouldn't survive without him.'

'That's unnatural, Sonya. That level of bonding with an animal.'

My animal hackles rise, in sympathy with Herbie.

'I won't do it unless I know they can be together.'

'I'll see what I can do.'

At least he hasn't followed this up with a 'Don't be ridiculous, Sonya', which used to sting more than any amount of slapping.

'Tommy can visit after the first two weeks.'

Resistance hits now, a hard wall. Two weeks without seeing Tommy. No way, no fucking way.

'I can't do it, Dad. I can't leave them.'

'If you don't do it this way it'll be much more traumatic for you all.'

'What will Lara say if you arrive home with a dog?'

'I'll see if Mrs O'Malley will take the dog. She sounds fond of the thing.'

That scenario sets up such conflict that I can't sort through the jumble of images that accompany it. At least Herbie knows her, and seems to like her, but he'd be looking every day at his empty house

opposite, and no one could explain to him that it's only temporary *and* Mrs O'Malley would probably make him sleep on the
back porch on his own *and* he'd pine *and* she wouldn't like his loud
whining *and* she's too fat to walk him *and* she'd give him way too
many treats *and* I can't bear the thought that he might like her *and*
my son will break in two without his big shaggy beating comfort
blanket. *And.*

'Maybe she'd take them both?' The words escape me before I've
had time to process them. My father looks relieved, instantly, as if
this is something he hadn't even thought of. He could do the right
thing by sidestepping the issue and Lara won't need to be involved.

'You could pay her' slips out of my mouth. I quickly zip my lips,
like my father taught me to when I was being particularly rowdy.
He'd mime closing a zipper over my mouth and the action of it
would have me feeling stitched up for the day.

'I could,' he murmurs. 'Of course I could. I would keep a close
eye.'

I wish I hadn't planted that image of our neighbour as a witch in
Tommy's impressionable mind. I want to see him like he was yesterday morning in Mrs O'Malley's kitchen, with his book, his dog and,
hell, his milk. His little contented face. He could even eat animals,
if he were lied to.

In the morning, at first light, my father walks over the road to Mrs
O'Malley, who's awake, on high alert, having been forewarned of
this intervention. I go to the fridge, finish what's left of the bottle,
slip another two from my emergency stash under the sink into my
suitcase. Mrs O'Malley bustles in like she owns the place, nods at

me, then speaks directly to my father: 'Don't worry, Mr Moriarty, I'll look after them well.'

I battle an urge to scream, to slap the woman, to throw my arms around her and say thank you, thank you, be good to them, love them, but not too much, all my thoughts tossed and rushing, each one contradicting the last.

'I'll come straight back, Mary, after I've dropped Sonya off. We can discuss further arrangements then.'

Am I imagining it or do I see euro signs flash in front of the hag's face? A swarm of them. Is this the only reason she's here? How much has she taken from my father over the years to spy on me and my son? Even as all these thoughts barrage me, I know this is the best option for now. They are both familiar with her. Why did I plant that terrifying tale in Tommy's mind? Could I get my father to talk him down from that one – like he used to with me, when I was having night terrors about cancer eating away at him from the inside, or me, or the rest of the world? You couldn't see it in my mother, yet it claimed her, all of her. I remember his soft, soothing voice in the middle of the night, telling me it was all just a dream, nothing to be afraid of, just an overactive imagination. And those Pierrot dolls staring down at me in the darkness, eyes flashing, gearing up.

He could tell Tommy that I was just pretending, playing, making up stories. Not lying, not that.

'I'm just going to look in on them.'

'Sonya…'

'I promised him.'

The one thing I remember from the time immediately following my mother's death are the lies, or rather the omissions, the silences the adults held when I was around, which only fuelled my already

65

growing free-floating anxiety. It was a girl in school who said the dreaded C-word, which her mammy had told her had done for my mammy.

I stall, not trusting my instincts, but my feet take me to the door of the bedroom, and I push it ajar. My two boys are cuddled into each other, fast asleep. The struggle not to tell my father and my neighbour to fuck right off and leave us here. I look back at them both: the set of Father's jaw, a twitch in his right cheek, Mrs O'Malley's face a mask of resolution. Neither of them is going to back down now. Next step would be the guards, the social workers, which (my father is right) would be a whole other level of trauma for Tommy. A tearing in my centre. I look towards the ceiling, and beyond. I blow Tommy and Herbie ten kisses each and a silent blessing, even though I don't know who the hell I'm calling on. I would sprinkle them in holy water right now if I could. I would rip my heart out and leave it under the quilt with them, if I could.

I turn to Mrs O'Malley. 'Thank you.' I think I mean it.

The woman looks sad and, for a moment, real.

'I will take very good care of them, Sonya. With your father's help, of course.'

'Sonya, I need you to call the centre, say that you're coming in. The final decision has to be yours.'

He holds his phone out. They have me cornered and, like a wild animal caught in a trap, I'm flailing, losing my reason. I want to bite, snarl, get the fuck out of this bind.

'Mrs O'Malley, how about you give us a few more days? I'll get Tommy used to the idea. I'll go to AA, I promise.'

Mrs O'Malley looks down at her feet. 'Sonya, I'm afraid I couldn't let that happen. I've seen too much in the last few days to let that happen.'

I want to punch her in the face, drop to my knees, cling to her ankles, plead with her: hit me, hug me, tell me I'm not so bad, tell me you trust me, tell me it doesn't have to be this way.

'Please, Sonya, can you make the call before Tommy awakes?'

I take the phone from his hand. I look at them both defiantly. I will show you: this is what a responsible mother looks like. I am never, ever, ever going to get drunk around a child again.

8

We drive for almost two hours with not a word passed between us. Classic FM provides the soundtrack: a mournful medley of Saint-Saëns and Bach. A pretty obvious underscore, straining and melancholic. A close-up of my father's face, closed, giving nothing away. We arrive at big, scruffy black gates; a guy in a security hut waves us in. On either side of the driveway are dense, artificial-looking trees, poplars or something – how I hate their formality, their *constraint*. I think of that game we used to play: Mr Gnarly, Ms Sappy, Mr Knobbly, Ms Dewy, Mrs Weepy, Ms Mossy... The ancient birch in our garden, Mr Silver Fox, was my favourite; his leaves used to quiver with excitement as I'd pour all my secrets into him. I look sidelong at my father, his mouth tight, and find it impossible to see the man who would play such games.

'Well, here we are.'

The building in front of us is large and grey, institutional. An oversized statue of the Virgin Mary in a grotto looms in the neat, ordered gardens.

'You've got to be kidding me. I didn't think these places still exist.'

'This centre has an excellent reputation.'

And Lara wouldn't have let him spend all that money on a private rehab for me.

'What on earth do nuns know about the wanton wiles of the flesh?' I throw at him.

'Discipline, structure, order...'

He's not joking. My heart speeds.

'What was I thinking? Turn around now. Tommy needs to say goodbye to me.'

I see his little face, snot-caked and hot.

Pwomise, Yaya?

'Lovely hibiscus,' my father says.

Fuck's sake. 'Dad, he's too little, he won't understand. I shouldn't have left without explaining this to him.'

'Sonya, you'll only make it worse. He'll be fine.'

'When you went silent, after Mum died, I wasn't "fine", much as you liked to convince yourself I was.'

'This isn't the same, Sonya.' He sounds so tired. 'The experts advised this would be the least traumatic way of doing it.'

Of course he consulted the 'experts'. I breathe deeply, close my eyes and dive down to the depths. For a moment the sensation cancels out the buzzing noise in my head, my body softens, and I let my mind float. A space opens up: maybe he's right, maybe it would cause more damage to go back now. Lots of children have to deal with sick parents having prolonged stays in hospitals. At least this one is coming back alive.

'Sonya, are you with me?' My father's voice hooks me back up. 'Are you with me on this?'

I let myself imagine this is my first day at boarding school, something I wished for as an only child after reading *Malory Towers* obsessively, with its depictions of midnight feasts and best-friend-ever-after pacts. I feel young and overly stimulated, like I've gorged on too many jelly beans at a birthday party where no one spoke to me. I have the shakes, something I've become pretty used to in recent months.

'Cold?' My father takes off his jacket, awkward in the small space, his elbows hitting off the roof of the car, and wraps it around my shoulders.

He gets out, opens my door, takes the bag out of the boot and leads the way. *Where have you been, Dad?* I'm being led to the sanatorium, the madhouse where they used to lock up wild women in this country not so long ago – when it was still a land of priests and patriarchy – women with hysteria, with desire, with too much of everything in their veins, women who incited and inflamed. Yup, that's me! I almost start to skip. Where is my camera?

There's a desk behind a glass frontage and a man discussing his medication for depression. This sight disrupts the female-only fantasies that were building in intensity, aggravating the winged creatures slumbering under my ribcage. The man seems embarrassed to be so exposed publicly. A woman with a clipboard walks towards us, shaking first my father's hand, then mine. 'You must be Sonya? Take a seat in the waiting room and we'll get the nurse to have a chat when she's free.' My father nods at her as if he knows who she is and moves into a room with frayed, shiny corduroy couches and a TV on mute. There's a big man enveloped in one of the couches, wearing pink pyjamas that are too small for him, his wrists poking through, his old duffel bag at his feet. He smiles, actively beams at us.

'Hope you brought your PJs? I forgot we had to wear them for the first week, so they gave me these.' He gestures to the faded, shrunk pink pyjamas. 'They wouldn't let me wear my tracksuit.'

Laughter shoots out of my mouth, airborne.

'Sonya,' my father says.

'Sorry,' I manage, before another wave of hysteria moves through me.

The man smiles. 'Look at my big belly in these little dinky things.' He pats his stomach, winks at me. 'First time, darlin'?'

My father answers for me. 'Is this place mixed? I thought it was segregated.'

'Separate sleeping quarters. Otherwise mixed. This disease isn't particularly fussy who it chooses. And I should know; this is my third visit.'

My father reflexively wipes the seat with his starched white handkerchief before sitting. I sense his mood shifting, see his judgement hanging in the air. Third visit: how could anyone be so weak-willed? A familiar surge of rebellion moves through me. Fuck him, with his patronising distancing ways. How have I let him back in like this? A familiar giddy breathlessness.

'Sonya Moriarty?'

I get up, called to action, although I'm not sure whether I'll follow directions.

My father stands, air-kisses me, cheek to cheek, eyes unfocused.

'I'm proud of you, Sonya.'

That hurts. There have been so many times in my life when he could genuinely have been proud of me.

He walks away down the hall, holding himself carefully as if bits of him might break off.

The sight of his back sets up an ancient terror in me. I go off-script. *No no no no no no no.* I shout after him: 'Dad?'

He doesn't turn around.

'Dad? This is a terrible idea. You know it is… Come back, Dad. Take me home. For Tommy…'

He has pushed through the front door. A hand on my arm, restraining me.

'Time for your medical, Sonya.'

9

The 'medical', it turns out, is just a weigh-in, a blood pressure test and a chat with a nurse about my 'habits'. No blood tests or urine samples, just a series of questions, rat-a-tat-tat. My instinct is to minimise, to convince this woman of my intelligence, my ability to manage myself, my father's overly protective stance in all this. I wear my serious face, tell her I have been sober the last few days, that it really wasn't that difficult. I don't think I'm slurring; to my ear I am cut crystal, perhaps overly articulated.

'Is there any way I could shorten my stint in here, Nurse? I have a little boy at home who needs me.'

'It's a twelve-week programme of abstinence. Designed that way, for a reason.'

'Yes, I understand that, but I'm really not that bad.' Ms Perfect Diction. 'Is there a bathroom nearby?'

She points at a room down the corridor. 'You can leave your bag here.'

'I need it. Women's stuff.'

In the cubicle I unscrew, swallow, soothe. Down the hatch. Nice n floaty.

Nursey Nurse brings me to a room with fluorescent tube lighting running the length of the ceiling, flicker flicker hum, and four beds. I'm shown to the bed by the window, which I'm glad about as the air is stifling, not with heat but with something heavy and stale. The colour and sense of brown, a gagging smell of Dettol. I'm in Mrs O'Malley's stuffy front room with my boys, surrounded by plastic-covered furniture and tiny knick-knacks that line every surface. *Don't break them, Herbie!* Static has built up in my head and I can't hear the words the nurse is saying, something about needing to check my luggage, is that ok? I shake my head as she removes the remaining full bottle, the other almost empty one, no judgement, no surprise, no need for any outrage: mine or hers. I place my hand on my chest. What will happen to the winged creatures without my daily dose of anaesthesia? I'm scared they'll rise up and rip out of me.

Nurse holds her hand out. 'Your phone?'

'How will I make contact with my son?'

'No contact with the outside world for two weeks, except in the case of an emergency.'

I get up off the bed. 'I've changed my mind.'

'I understand this is all a bit of a shock, but bear in mind if you leave now you may not be allowed access to your young son.'

Seriously? I hand my phone over, instantly bereft. Nursey tells me that the next twenty-four hours will be the most intense. There'll be no expectation on me to do anything, bar eat and sleep and take my Librium. I don't need that shit. I'm not that bad.

'Lunch will be brought to you shortly.'

'I don't eat meat.'

'Well, that's a shame.'

Why? Why's that a shame, Nursey Nurse? Don't you know the torture we inflict on those poor innocent creatures? My mouth is full of the taste of their fear. The looping starts: bushfires burning up koalas and kangaroos, monkeys being injected with human viruses, polar bears in shopping malls for selfies, dogs being bred in cages over and over until their wombs fall out, intrusive thoughts, images, crowding.

'Just settle yourself in here, and I'll be back with a sandwich and your first dose. Best to eat something first.' Nursey Nurse's voice is a welcome interruption.

I sit on my allocated bed, fingering the synthetic cover, which sends sparks of electricity to my fingertips. My body is experiencing a turboboost of energy and speed, yet, beyond the incessant worrying of my mind and thumb and forefinger, is incapable of moving. I smell sulphur, nothing left of me but charred remains. Spontaneous combustion! Suitably dramatic and high-pitched. Pity Tommy couldn't be here to enjoy the spectacle. His anxious face looms large, gains substance and settles itself around me like a cloak. I am wearing his worry.

The rain is falling gently, little blurred waterfalls sliding down the window. I allow my focus to soften. Has anything ever seemed so lovely? Water surrounding me, holding me. A heavy kind of apathy claims me, laying me down with the weight of it. Tip, tap, tip, God's own fingertips, softly first, then building in intensity, until the rain tapping against the pane sounds like artillery fire. The sky is chucking hard pebbles against the glass. These balls of ice are worrying, a sign of punishment from above. I think I remember being clobbered the day of my mother's funeral but couldn't be sure. So much of that day was filtered through an unfocused lens, though the sensation of being stoned by the Man Above lingers. *Bold girl.*

Then: a picture of Tommy, lying on the couch, his tiny feet swimming in my socks, tummy gurgling; Herbie and himself curled into each other, talking in their own language; his little body rigid in that stranger's arms on the beach; my hand reaching out to smack him; my overwhelming need for him; him pushing me away and the dangerous pain of that; his eyes, sparkling, reflecting the fire from the burning grill pan. *Beeootiful, Yaya. Hot and slinky like the sun.* What if I hadn't woken up? A sea of flames engulfing him.

The next few days pass in a blur of white-bread cheese sandwiches, black tea, ginger-snap biscuits, orange squash – which every time I swallow a mouthful makes me think of Tommy and I feel like I might openly sob, but I never do, just quiet leaking tears, which no one passes comment on. Bodies come and go, different shades of snores, waking and sleeping merge into one. At first I don't swallow the pills, at first I tell myself I'm in control of this, I'm not so bad, I haven't even been drinking for that long, have I? I wasn't even drinking that heavily anyway, was I? But: the sweats are bad, the spasms weird, the sensation of spinning sickening, the dreams (hallucinations?) too vivid, too intense, even for me; a woman smiling down on me, smelling of rose water, her voice sweet yet sharp, not safe, everything speedy. The cracks on the ceiling over my head are a portal to another world. Little winged creatures, fairy-like but buzzing like bluebottles, fly from these cracks and Tommy is trying to swat them away before they land on me, before they make their home inside me. Sound of Tommy crying, Herbie barking, all the dogs in the world howling, animals burning up, our greed, our greed, our greed. The sheets crackle and irritate my hot skin. Everything irritates: Nursey Nurse's grating voice, various attempts at striking up a conversation, which I ignore, plastic undersheets, the stinging smack of antiseptic, the suffocating weight of the colour brown on carpets and curtains, the buzz hum flicker of the lights, the kindly nun with her apple cheeks and the swish-swish of her habit on the ground. A palm on my clammy forehead, a prayer uttered, or maybe I'm making that up. Pretty soon – how soon I don't know, not a conscious decision on my part – the pills go down, softening the edges of my impatience, my sorrow, my crackling irritation, my anger, my impotent ravening anger, which feels like it might devour me whole. Sometimes I wake myself up, shouting – is that really me, that raving woman? Must be, as I hear the name Tommy, over and over. TOMMY. And no one answers. The woman on the beach and Mrs O'Malley blend into one terrifying hag, all my fears for him realised as he's spirited away to another dimension. SNAP. My imp appears, clad in her gaudiest gear; she looks at me in blatant disappointment, like I'm pathetic, a killjoy, no spunk. She orders me to go find my son, grow some balls, but then my father appears and Mrs O'Malley, and behind them flashing blue lights and sirens.

'How are you now, Sonya?'

The rosy-cheeked nun sits at the edge of my bed. She's not wearing a habit. I don't know how to answer that.

'I'd like to talk to my son.'

'Your first phone call home is in ten days. First visiting day is the following week. Let's concentrate on getting you in good shape before then.'

At this precise moment I'd do anything this woman says. I am cracked wide open, teary and soft.

'Right, time for a shower.'

I must really stink.

'We'll be moving you out of detox today and starting you on your road to recovery.'

'Can't I go back to Tommy, attend AA from home?' My voice sounds a little pathetic as I say, 'I feel fine now.'

'Sonya, this is a particularly vulnerable time for you. Don't believe anything your mind tells you, especially when it tells you you're "fine".'

How is that supposed to be helpful? As if reading my thoughts, she tells me there is a reason for a twelve-week period of supervised recovery in a controlled environment. Addiction is not just physical. New grooves need to be established, new patterns of thinking and behaving. There are many, many triggers in the outside world and the job in here is to strengthen not only resolve, but a sense of self that operates without substances. Blah blah. I tell her that my drinking is quite recent, that I used to be a successful actress, that I had a life in London that did not revolve around booze.

'Is your alcohol abuse linked to becoming a mother, Sonya?'

That feels terrible, a terribly cruel accusation.

'I really don't think I abused alcohol.'

'Do you think it abused you?'

I feel bamboozled, winded. I want that shower. The nun, who tells me her name is Sister Anne, explains that from tomorrow my days will start at 7 a.m. and that my routine will consist of work duty, prayer, meditation, group therapy, AA meetings and, if a need is ascertained, individual therapy, at a later stage.

'The devil makes work for idle hands, eh, Sister?' I try and fail to crack a joke.

10

The smell of cooking meat, possibly beef, though it's been such a long time since I've had such a thing, wafts – no, attacks, yes, attacks my senses, cutting through the haze. What else, besides animal flesh, are they going to make me swallow in here?

'You new here?' A skinny girl with a booming voice, leaking energy, enters the room that is to be my bedroom for the next eleven weeks and two days (IF I complete the stint, although I'm sure I won't need to). Apparently I spent five days in the drying-off ward, which doesn't seem possible. This room is a replica of the one I just came from: four beds, too-bright lights, too much brown, this one with a smattering of beige, though no plastic undersheets, thank fuck.

'You'd wanna get yer skates on. There'll be no food left.'

'I'm not hungry. Thanks, though.'

'You've a long night ahead. Need some sustenance. The rosary, followed by a meeting, followed by meditation. All before lights out at ten.'

'I'm not a practising Catholic, so I'll give the rosary a miss.'

She laughs through her nose. 'None of us are, but it's part of the programme. Something about finding a "channel" to the Holy Spirit that's meant to be a substitute for the real thing.' Her voice is dry, cracked and brittle, like the rest of her.

I initially thought she looked about nineteen, but on closer inspection her face is wizened, skin stretched taut, hollows under her eyes and cheekbones. 'I'm Linda.' She extends a bony, veiny hand. 'Sonya,' I say, though I really want to lie. I'm not sure I'm up to this – commingling, bonding. Is that what the Malory Towers lot were at? Tina is the only friend I ever really had – and Tina, always off her face, was never really there anyway.

The noise in the dining hall is raucous, not what I expected from a place like this. There are a lot more men than women. I try to count: possibly sixtyish in total, three quarters male. Clamp one hand over the other to stop the tremors, which may just be nerves. A twitch above my right eyebrow. I'm being watched, my legs almost buckling under me with the weight of the surveillance. *Only playing a part, this isn't real.* I inspect the congealed food sitting behind a glass casing. 'Bit late, love,' says a tiny woman with a hairnet placed precariously over the top of her ponytail. 'I can get you some pudding ahead of the others, if you like?' I push out a thank you past my thirsty tongue. My eyes wander, taking in the yellow-stained, pockmarked walls, the linoleum floor, synthetic and shiny, seemingly moving beneath my feet. I pull my gaze towards the one small window, high above my eyeline, which allows no sense of the outdoors in.

'There you go, love,' the remarkably small, blanked-out face, says. 'Rice pudding.'

I turn back towards the room – which I try to imagine is full of an appreciative audience, instead of nosy, sly glances – and see my new room-mate waving at me. Lisa or Linda or something. Her mouth's wide open and her teeth are crooked and small, and yellow, which may or may not be the light.

'How'ya?' One of the older women greets me as I approach the table, not looking for a response as she attacks the last of the gristle on her plate. I swallow down bile.

'Good you came,' Lisa or Linda says. 'Get that into you, now. Nothing till the morning.'

I spoon big lumps of the rice pudding, which tastes nothing like rice but rather some kind of lard, into my mouth, avoiding the act of speaking. I pretend I'm playing helicopters with Tommy. He'd like this: innocuous in colour and texture, and no living thing murdered in the making, or so I'd convince him. If I will it hard enough I can conjure his little warm body sitting on my knee, a shield against the world. *Lllove you, Yaya. Bigger better brighter than the wideroundy world. Rat-a-tat. Boom.* He points to his heart. My stomach bloats after a few mouthfuls and that old familiar pain settles in my guts. Could I ask for an antacid, or something to soothe the fire? That used to do it, before I discovered the liquid silk that could anaesthetise me to everything. A craving takes over my whole body, a longing that is physical and intense and sweet and powerful and painful. As if on the verge of an orgasm that will always be on the brink, never satisfied.

I regard the table of six women, all of whom must be struggling with similar stuff. This doesn't bring any relief, or feeling of solidarity, as it should. If anything, it just intensifies the already harsh critical voices. Such failures, such abject failures. Can't be as bad as any of these women, with their broken veins and yellow eyes. I should just get up and walk away from here.

Chew on the inside of my cheek, survey the room. My father's voice inside my head: 'Pathetic, weak-willed creatures.' Yes siree, Pops! I look at the gloop in my bowl, drop my spoon, close my eyes and feel the heat of a spotlight trained on me, the hushed crowds, the sound of the blood rushing in my ears, words, transporting words, the power of those words that make me, and everyone watching, believe I am someone else. I should never have stopped stepping into that imaginary realm; it was the only thing that made sense of who I am. I open my eyes: some of the women are staring at me. Can't imagine any of them being impressed by my glittering past. *Get down off your pedestal and get real.* I'm sure I can hear these thoughts broadcast on the airwaves, and they belong to the woman who had gristle in her mouth.

11

Post-dinner, we're ushered into a cold hall, which reeks of a stale gymnasium, old sweat and a squirt of polish mingling in the air. My sense of smell is heightened and I'm constantly nauseous, like when I was pregnant. Orange plastic chairs are laid out in rows, facing a podium, presided over by a looming effigy of the Virgin Mary. Tommy would love this giant statue. Feel faint from the longing to hold him. I pinch myself on the back of my hand and settle myself in the far corner. The old nun leading the round of prayer (ten Hail Marys, one Lord's Prayer) reminds me of the four decrepit sisters that taught in our school: Sister Rachel, Joan, Maria and... I can't remember the last one's name, the mean one, the one who had a knuckle ring that she'd grind into the back of your hand if caught daydreaming, which in my case was often. I haven't heard the rosary since those days when we'd be made to recite it in assembly. Haven't forgotten, though: an incantatory, mesmeric repetition of hazy words from another era. It's almost soothing, were it not so troubling. Folk around me mumble, drift, snooze, snore their way through, bobbing their heads at the appropriate moments, bodies swaying, eyes closed. Somnambulists. The words have no resonance, yet the effect of sitting in a room such as this with only one sound echoing is strangely soothing. People look vulnerable, on their knees, chanting words they probably don't even understand. They are like oversized children. A tenderness settles in my body, lifting me out of myself for one blessed moment.

After it finishes, I feel weepy and sleepy and alone and very, very young. A man moves to the top of the room, sits in a chair facing the rest of us and starts to speak. 'I'd like to share my experience, strength and hope...' What follows is anything but. He credits the 'guys' in here with saving his life – the men in these rooms, and the Man Above. Not a mention of a woman, although his body is framed by the giantess in the background. Voices loom from the backs of heads; I can't see any faces, adding to the surreal quality of it all. There's a kind of buddy-fraternity quality to the telling, war – hero stories swapped. Who has the greatest scars and, above all, who has the greatest capacity for forgiveness and gratitude and acceptance? – buzzwords the men trade in, with no irony or self-consciousness. One man in his fifties tells of shooting up with his mother when he was eleven; another, aged eight, watched his father throw himself into the canal on his fortieth birthday. His is three days away, he says, and he is terrified. The man on the podium is full of gratitude for all he's been given since coming here six weeks ago: fellowship, friendship, a kind ear, a warm bed, good food, a soft place, something he's not encountered in his last three years sleeping on the streets. There are stories of prison sentences: 'This is better than that,' one fella

jokes. There's lots of laughter, a jovial sense of a shared experience. The women don't speak, don't seem to take up any space. I
am welcomed as the newcomer and invited to speak. Wavy lines
float in front of my eyes.

Hi, ummm... I had a whiney wine habit, you know? Too many
feelings. Oh, and I almost suffocated my son. A surfeit of love, you
understand? Too much love. Too much everything, which was kind of
fine when I could play a character, you know...?

'No thanks, I'll just listen this time.' *Failed actress, failed mother.*
And my alcohol consumption sounds so pathetic compared to
these guys, who'd start their day on an empty stomach, a packet of
Rothmans and a naggin of vodka.

Immediately another voice clamours for attention and fills the
space. The meeting ends with another prayer: Serenity/Acceptance/
Courage/Change/Wisdom. Words that land, though I try to bat
them away, words that stir a part of me I did not know existed.

After, coffee is served, and Marietta biscuits waved under my
nose.

'No thanks. Coffee hurts my stomach and keeps me up all night.'

Miss No Thanks. Tommy is laughing at me, his teeny little
finger poking me in my stomach. How I long to inhale him and
pretend-gobble him up.

After tea and biscuits, we *meditate.* Breathing exercises. In, out,
in, out, like a bellows. Empty, soften, fill. I am panicked, overtired,
wired. I want to go home to my babies. I don't belong I don't belong
I don't belong.

Bedtime. Linda's snores are rocking the walls, reverberating in the headboard, through the mattress and my body. My jaw is clamped shut, grinding back and forth, reminding me of that time when I turned thirteen and had to wear a mouth shield, otherwise, as the dentist said, 'You'll worry all your teeth away' – which of course set up further worry in my overactive mind. I run my swollen tongue over my teeth and start to count, pushing against the top back, the top front, the bottom back, the bottom front. A tang of metallic fills my mouth. Brushing has been a kind of torture these last few months, so I've taken to rubbing my gums with a finger and paste. *Blessed is the fruit of thy womb Jesus...* Nod. Gas, that nod to the word 'Jesus'. I try it out, try to remember the whole prayer, but end up back on Ophelia's speech instead: ... *Blasted with ecstasy. O, woe is me, to have seen what I have seen, see what I see...* I can taste the smack of acid and cold and citrus and sweet; my whole body can taste it.

The darkness and the expectation of sleep and the inability to sleep: eyes full of sand, heart hammering, body needing to run, muscles bunched, tensed against all possible threat, the greatest of which comes from my own mind. Herbie in a cage, Tommy in a narrow bed, sparrow chest rising and falling in rapid successive half-breaths, never catching enough air.

I open the window as far as it will go, which is really only a crack. The meeting, although it stirred something like compassion in me, had the effect of being profoundly alienating. *Impostor syndrome* – something I seem to have been born with, a sensation that became particularly pronounced during my days of being lauded in London, and now here, in this place, where others seem to find their 'true selves'. Would I even know what that was if it slapped me in the face?

The thought of what I did to Herbie that night, and what I was on the verge of doing to Tommy... What? What was I trying to do? – no one spoke of impulses like that in the meeting. One man spoke of driving his car into a tree and almost killing his son, but it wasn't because he wanted to stuff his son back inside himself, possess him.

These men, their lives seemed inevitable, their destinies charted from the moment they were born to their crackhead fathers, criminal mothers, junkies, alcos, selfish, stunted, addled parents. Like me. These men were born to mothers like me.

12

Work, prayer and crafts: a kind of therapy I'd have thought belonged to another era, but then everything about this place seems out of tune, out of step. The fact of me being a vegetarian is met with: 'No one else in here eats only that stuff, love.' I stick to desserts, a sugar overload building in my system.

One hundred and ninety-two hours (I keep count, obsessively) pass in a haze of rosary, meetings, woodwork, work assignments, rosary, meetings, woodwork, work assignments – and appalling headaches that affect my vision and my balance. My fingertips are needling, the skin on the soles of my feet prickling. I'm not allowed anything for these, not even a Panadol, nothing that will interfere with the natural detoxification process of the body, now I'm out of the detox unit. Seems kind of draconian and ridiculous, this puritanical abstinence after years of pouring God knows what chemical in.

My work duty is to feed the chickens and clean the coop, which is both brilliant and horrifying. Part of my job is to collect their eggs, which doesn't seem to cause them too much consternation, and which means they are not killed for food, right? They really stink, but it's better than being around people. The clucking cartoon chickens become my sanctuary.

Woodwork class is a revelation, another sort of balm. I find I enjoy the act of whittling, paring, honing. The teacher – a middle-aged woman with a shrunken, balled jumper, which presses her body into fleshy folds (her antidote to stirring any kind of arousal in all these sex-starved men; she does it very well, I think) – stands too close, breathes her tuna-and-onion breath on me and tells me I'm *naturally talented*. I am that, alright, that was never in question. It's the other stuff that's difficult.

The rain outside continues. It hasn't stopped since the moment I arrived. The Man Above's out to drown us all.

I wasn't expecting to feel such guilt, but then I guess I didn't exactly have any expectations, not having made the choice myself to be here. I was cajoled – no, coerced, no, let's get real: threatened. Over and over in my mind – how is this the best for Tommy? How is he surviving without me?

I concoct a plan: submission, dedication to the cause, discipline. As soon as I'm allowed my first phone call I'll convince my father that it's in all our best interests for me to go home early and continue my recovery there. Mrs O'Malley is probably overwhelmed with the responsibility of a toddler and a dog. How much better for Tommy to have his mother around. *Yes yes yes*. Two weeks of this is all I can manage. Father wouldn't last a night in here: all this *emotion*, all these people, with their smells, their vulnerability, their damage, their desire for connection, their stories, their pain, their sharing, their dissembling, their laughing, their crying, their dumping, their need, their need, their need.

My breathing is shallow and sharp and concentrating on it in meditation just makes it worse. I don't share in the meetings. Everyone else seems to find a connection, but this place makes me lonelier than I have ever been. Or perhaps I am facing that loneliness for the first time. It's strange to think I really might have been addicted. My body tells me I was; my mind tells me I was not, I am not, I am not the same as the people in here. I just drank too much because I missed my former life of excitement and colour and attention. No one could possibly understand that high. And the ferocious comedown in its absence.

But exactly *when* did I start drinking 'too much'? A few drinks after I'd come off stage, certainly. Only normal, everyone did that. The time of my pregnancy? Did I? I was so conflicted, never sure I had made the right decision, so alone in that decision, which seemed so out of character, so like I was out to prove a point to Howard, to the world. I am capable of motherhood and I will be brilliant and beautiful. Romantic notions, always.

Is your alcohol abuse linked to becoming a mother, Sonya? Answers, justifications, denials rush in. Of course not of course not of course not.

13

The day finally comes. Fourteen days in and it's time for my first phone call home. The craving for my boys has taken over any other, the worst of the effects of the chemical addiction having left my body, the tremors over, except for today. With shaking hands – the most severe since day one – I try calling my father's mobile straight after jelly-for-dinner, and it rings out and out, the unanswered dialling tone sounding like a kind of keening. The winged creatures start to push their way into my throat. 'Fucking answer, please answer.' A line of people stand waiting for their turn. 'Not there, love,' the man directly behind me says. I slam the phone into its cradle and wonder if my father is avoiding me and what I will do if he never answers.

The following day my anxiety is so high I almost rouse her, my high-kicking sidekick. She hasn't come anywhere near me in this place, disgusted, I think, by its dullness, its routine, its grey *sobriety*. Perversely, I miss her.

Visiting hours are two to five, and family members and loved ones can come at any stage between these times. If it's a minute past five they won't be let in. He may be a cold bastard but he wouldn't do that to us; he only enforced this situation for our good. I tell myself this even as the hours slip by, trying to push away the knowledge that he abandoned us before, when I really wasn't coping on any level. I pace between the front desk and the patch of gravel in front of the main door, not wanting to go far. For the first time since I arrived, the rain has dried up and a few intense rays of sunshine penetrate the thick blanket of cloud. *Mr Sunshine has come out to play, Yaya.* I lift my face towards the sky, staring directly at the concentration of light, until black spots form and spin. *Wheee! Spinnies.* My body aches.

I check in at reception every five minutes. 'You'll call me on the loudspeaker when they arrive? I can hear it outside.'

The girl nods. 'That's the fifth time.' She picks up her book and covers her face with it. *The Secret.* That whole 'you can be anyone you want to be, have anything you want to have' reductive crap. Doesn't it directly contradict the whole concept of twelve-step 'surrender' and trusting in a Higher Power's divine plan? A familiar scratchy contempt builds up as I watch the girl's impassive face soak it all in.

A gravelly voice pipes up behind me: 'It's ten to five. Unlikely at this stage.'

I turn around to see Big J, or Jimmy – who I recognise from the meetings, though I've never spoken to him before – with bowls of stolen milk stacked in both hands. This is the man who apparently spent eight years behind bars for no one knows what. I've become fascinated with him, his air of danger and, by extension, glamour. He's small and burly, perhaps in his late sixties, arms covered in tattoos, a Celtic cross and the word 'SAOIRSE' above a fist within a star inked on his forearm. He tells the best stories ever, but I never know if he's lying or simply exaggerating. Impossible to tell with anyone in here. A brain that's been pickled in booze is a tricksy, slippery thing, prone to bouts of grandiosity and fantasy. Which, I guess, if I'm honest (if I'm capable of being honest), I can relate to. I think of all the tall tales I spun in school – my stepmother is a swinger, I'm adopted, my sister died of cot death, my mother died giving birth to me, my baby brother died in a house fire – each one contradicting the last; I never could remember who I told what to and inevitably got tangled up and caught out.

Was I, even then, destined for this?

'Want to come see the kittens?'

I follow, like a child being lured by a stranger with a promise of sweeties. They're not coming.

The shed where the kittens are housed doubles up as the smoking shed.

'Alright?' The men outside, puffing on their Marlboros or Rothmans.

Jimmy goes inside and kneels, croons at the creatures sleeping in a fleece-lined box under a bench. 'Come on, little fellas, come to Dadda.' He lifts them gently by the scruff of the neck and places them at the lips of the bowls. 'Little buggers can hardly see.'

'Where's their mum?'

'She hasn't taken to the role. Wild, like the women in here.'

He's pretty funny.

'So, no visitors?' he says.

I shake my head.

'You probably deserve it. We all do. Try to see it as a blessing, a way of getting you "on your knees".'

Not this false-humility stuff again. What loving God would want a little boy separated from his mother? He watches me struggle with all the conflicting impulses I know are playing out on my face.

I'm completely see-through, which may have made me a very fine actress, though not such a fine player at real life.

'The Man Above has a Higher Plan for you. You don't know what it is yet, but there's a reason they didn't come today.'

I find my head doing a crazed upwards, downwards, side-to-side motion. Yes, no, yes. Higher Plan, Man Above. Yes. I blink and swallow, looking towards the ceiling. And I want so badly to fall to my knees, but don't want it witnessed, and it isn't a worshipping, it's annihilation.

His face and voice soften. 'They'll get over it in time. Actions speak louder than words, and action takes time to prove.' He wipes his eyes with his frayed, yellowed cuffs, then squares his shoulders, checking himself. 'Ah, would ye look at the cut of this little one?' A marmalade tabby, tiny, is nuzzling into the palm of his hand. 'I shouldn't admit to favourites, but by God...'

For the first time since I arrived, I feel like I'm in the presence of someone like me. I've heard him speak in meetings about his flashes of temper, his extreme emotions, and this: his maudlin love for animals. This is real. I sit in silence and watch him stroke the tiny creatures between the eyes with his thick fingers. He kisses the kittens on the same spot on the tops of their tiny heads.

'Do you treat them for fleas and worms?' I ask.

'Contraband,' he says. 'First thing on my list these days. Some of the lads say the worming tablets give them a great high. None of them want to try the fleas stuff. Side effects too serious. Like blindness.'

Laughter flies out of my mouth and it's not caustic or judging, not a front for something else.

'Can you get me something for the jangles, to help me sleep?'

'No, I don't mess with any of that stuff in here. The cold-turkey approach is best. These sisters know what they're doing.'

There doesn't seem to be a sniff of irony in how he delivers this. And yet, how many times has he been back in? The rumours go: dozens. He is the most common reoffender.

14

At the meeting that evening Linda surprises everyone, including herself, by speaking out. 'I know he's my heroin, but at least he doesn't make all my teeth fall out.' She laughs, over-bright and shrill. No one takes the bait. 'I'm not me when he's in my life, but I'm not me when he's out of it either. Know what I mean?'

The rest of the room falls silent; a few of the men look shame-faced, knowing this is exactly the effect they have on their women. A few of them look angry. Why would you go throwing your love at idiots like that? She deserves what's coming to her. The women look away. The silence is heavy and loaded, a latent violence clinging to its contours.

Another voice claims the space, making no allusion to Linda's comment. The conversation is steered expertly back to comfortable territory: 'It had me in its grip, every waking moment obsessed.' This is Linda's story too, only the 'it' in her case is a 'he'. Her sunken cheeks are puffed up and purple-puce, like little plums.

I wait until the last speaker rounds off his familiar tale with 'but God has me in his hands and in his sights now. God knows what's good for me.' There is a sanctimonious piety to this statement that infuriates me and prods my sleeping creatures. I can feel their wings beat against my ribcage, desperate to be let out. *Disturb and disrupt.*

'This is my first time sharing.' So far, so polite. A big clap erupts. I breathe deeply. 'I often wonder at our capacity for self-delusion.' The perfect pitch, the lowered voice: come into my orbit. All my acting skills are coming into play, and a rush is released. I am holding the space, my audience entranced. 'I've heard a lot of honesty around substance abuse and our pasts forming us, yet very little about the havoc we wreak on other people's lives.' The swarm flies free from my mouth: 'The stuff our parents did to us we're repeating. It's not all about what was done to us, it's what we're doing to those around us, particularly our children.' The air is sucked from the room. Noisy thoughts float and collide, clogging the airwaves. A static hum reverberates in the silence. I have done it, poked all their darkest places.

I don't like how exposed I feel. That was not all about *performance.*

'Thank God I'm not a parent,' one auld fella pipes up, blessing himself. 'Thank God this will all stop with me.'

Another guy says, 'Speak for yourself, missus. Enough of the "we"!'

At the end of the meeting Linda finds her way through the hugging men and stands in front of me. 'Brave.' She blows on her own hot cheeks, flapping the stale air in front of her face with an ineffectual tiny hand.

'You too, Linda. You too. Not sure it's entirely true, though, when you said yer man Mark couldn't make you lose all your teeth.'

She snorts. 'Did anyone come for you today?'

'Nope.'

'Probably for the best. Early days.'

I bite down on the inside of my cheek, taste the metallic tang.

I feel a wallop of a clap on my shoulder. I wince, turn to see Jimmy beaming at me. 'Good on you. All this self-congratulatory whingeing. We're a downright ugly bunch, when it comes to it. Needed that dose of honesty.'

Linda smiles at me. 'Big J is a fan!'

I smile back. It doesn't hurt.

15

Another visiting day comes and goes and no news, not even a message. Almost a month now. How have I stuck it? Perhaps a tiny inkling of what it is to be sober, the beginnings of a reckoning, a grappling with honesty, a delicate, burgeoning *connecting*. And now it's time for yet another unrequited phone call home.

There is, of course, a long clacking queue in front of me. I plant my feet, root them firmly to the ground and breathe deeply, as Jimmy told me to do when surges of rage pulse through me. Apparently this creates a moment of pause, enough to interrupt the reactivity, which in some people is so turbocharged it can lead to murder. 'It's called grounding. Or a sacred pause. Something as simple as that could've saved me from prison.' I doubt that. From the moment he was conceived his life was one big trauma, involving social services and state 'care'. No one ever hugged him as a child. When I heard him share this in a meeting it had *truth* all over it. My airways constricted, and I had a job staying upright. Was I overcome with sorrow for him, the little boy he was, or was it for myself? I can't remember anyone holding me either, which is why I overloaded on the hugs with Tommy. But was it for him – or for me? I wonder what those hugs will come to mean to him in later life. Those suffocating hugs.

At least Tommy was never ignored. It's the worst kind of punishment, being ignored. Reminds me of fifth class when Dana DC, the new girl with the blondest hair and whitest teeth, decided that I was Queen of the Untouchables, a lonely, strange, story-telling girl without a mother – ugh, what could be sadder than that? Silent protests were organised, military-style, when I'd enter the room and the girls would turn their backs, pretending not to hear anything I said. Since my unpopular speech in the meeting, I feel the same freeze from the guys in here.

I'm at the top of the queue. I dial; unexpectedly, someone answers. *Breathe, control, contain.*

'Dad?' I sound like I'm eight, my voice caught in the back of my throat from the effort of straining to look up at him.

'Hello, Sonya?' Lara's voice. 'How are you doing?'

'Is Dad there? I don't have much time.'

'Your father is out.'

'Right. Is this not his mobile, his private number?'

'Your father gave me permission to answer. He told me to ask you if you'd like a visit this weekend?'

'Tommy?'

'Not Tommy. Your father and I.'

'Have you seen him?'

'Your father has. He's doing well. Lovely people, by all accounts.'

'People – what people? Do you mean Mrs O'Malley?'

'He's with people better suited to caring for his needs.'

'What? Who? Who? Where?'

'I'm afraid I don't know that, Sonya, but he's being well looked after.'

'If you had let Dad take him in in the first place, this wouldn't have happened.'

'Your father doesn't have the energy for a toddler, you know that.'

Rage rises like a burning, beating thing – it might knock me out with the force of it. The wings are fluttering, the creatures frantic. No amount of swallowing can stop their flight.

I hear a sigh, the sigh of the long-suffering martyr.

'Are you enjoying this?' Then a white-out. I think I hear words spilling, words like 'interfering, jealous, possessive cunting cow...'

The phone cuts dead. A hand taps me on the shoulder. I don't turn, don't react, just rest my head against the cool metal of the phone box. How can I continue to attend meetings where nothing is relatable, continue to pray to a God I cannot conceive of, continue to inhale my room-mates' stench, their gossip, their noise, continue to fashion wood into shapes meant only for Tommy, if I cannot see him, talk to him, reassure him?

'Love? You alright, love?' The swarm thickens behind my eyes. My knees buckle, my head hits the lino.

When I wake, I'm lying on the ground, Jimmy standing above me.

'Still detoxing this late into the game? Something not right there, not right.'

Am I? Detoxing from my son? Is this what this is, the roiling seas beneath my feet, Tommy's voice inside my head, his eyes following me?

'Have you been taking something?'

I find I can't speak, or don't want to.

'Can you sit up? C'mon, now, you're scaring me now, acting all cuckoo. I'm going to get help. Don't move, now.'

Above my head I see a kaleidoscopic display: triangle to oblong to square to itty-bitty bits twirling. *Beeootiful, Yaya, flakes of fiery snow.*

The doctor questions me: Have you been taking anything you shouldn't? Could you be pregnant? Last time you ate? Any history of seizures? No, no, can't remember, and no. He's an older man, stooped, pot-bellied, brown-blotched skin, hues of yellow. He takes blood samples, rough with the needle, jabbing it in like he wants to hurt me. Or maybe I'm imagining it. He takes my temperature, presses his pudgy fingers into my stomach. 'Any pain?' Way off, not even in the right region. How could I say my brain's just been attacked by a swarm of my own making? I really might end up in the loony bin then.

'Open wide.' He sticks a thermometer under my tongue.

He removes it, shakes it, reads. 'All perfectly normal. Are you eating?'

'A little. I'm a vegetarian. Not much choice here.'

'A woman your age needs red meat for a bit of iron, protein, keep your energy up.'

'I need to see my son.' My voice is scratched and skipping.

The man recoils. 'I can arrange for you to see someone.'

'Can you find out where he is?'

'I'll be back to check up on you in a few days. Eat and rest. I'm putting your name at the top of the list to see a counsellor.' He taps the back of my hand, which is resting on top of the sheets, intended as reassurance perhaps, but experienced more like a ruler, remonstrating. *Bold girl.*

The voices are building in intensity, issuing conflicting instructions, cancelling each other out: leave, go, find him, make it worse, they won't let you have him back. Need to prove your sobriety, your ability to stay on the straight and narrow, to think straight, sit up straight. Thoughts all bendy and circuitous. Apply a ruler to level out. I see myself bent over my copybook, intent on drawing that straight line. No amount of application ever made it right. It shot off up to the right, or down to the left, the ruler like a piece on a Ouija board. I was possessed, even then.

Two fitful days pass in the infirmary where I battle with myself not to bust out of the place, but my dizziness is still intense, and anyway, where would I go? 'How typical, couldn't go the distance,' Father would say. The sound of the rain is constant, at times a soft needling, at others a torrential downpour – a soundtrack of deluge. Tommy always worries about Herbie getting wet, and I'm sure he's outside in it now and Tommy is inconsolable. *Hole in me, Yaya.*

16

On the second evening in the infirmary, Sister Anne enters with a tray of tea and scones and butter and jam, which she lays out on the bedside table.

'How are you, Sonya?'

'Ok now, Sister, thanks. That hasn't happened in a while.'

'You should've told us you had a condition.'

'It's just low blood sugar.'

'The doctor says it hypoglycaemia.'

'Same thing.'

'Tea?' The nun gestures to the tray with its teapot and dainty china cups, a delicate daisy pattern dancing on their surface.

'No thank you.'

Sister Anne pours the rich golden brew in silence, her concentration intense. She slowly adds the milk, stirring with full presence – a ritual that seems somehow holy. I consider telling her about the baby calves separated from their mothers at only a few days old, both mother and baby crying themselves hoarse. I study the nun's relaxed face, her evident savouring of the contents of the cup, and decide against it.

'Scone?'

I shake my head.

Sister Anne stops her stirring. 'Are you really finding it so difficult in here, Sonya?'

How can I tell this woman of my latest mind loop: my son and his best friend being ripped from each other? *Catastrophising*, the guys call it.

'I haven't touched a drop in a month, Sister.'

'But it's bigger than that, Sonya, this addictive state. You still seem to be fighting everything – the "system", as you see it.'

'I'm sober. Isn't that the point of being here?'

'Have you found any relief in prayer?'

How honest can I be?

'I don't know who I'm praying to.'

'Does that really matter, Sonya? Think of prayer as a bridge between longing and belonging.'

I quite like that concept, abstract and romantic as it is.

'Or another way of looking at it: think of it as a transformational current.'

I wonder why they don't give us this kind of context before shoving us into large groups of people incanting words that have no meaning for them.

As if reading my mind she says, 'The literal meaning of the prayer doesn't really matter; what matters is the line of communication you open up, the connection with a Higher Power.'

'But Sister, how can the rosary have any relevance for people in the modern world?'

I wonder have I pushed it too far. She seems to give this some thought.

'The Hail Mary can be a portal to your Divine Mother. Think of it that way.'

The word 'Mother' brings about a complicated reaction in me: a grief, I think, a judgement, definitely.

Sister Anne continues: 'Have you made a connection between your addiction and a severed belonging, Sonya?'

Severed belonging. I immediately think of Tommy.

'Sister, I'm seriously worried about my own child.'

'You're here, Sonya. That is the best thing, for him, for you.'

'I don't know where he is.'

'You do know that it's the family's prerogative to take as long as they need away from the alcoholic?'

'He's only four, he's not capable of making that decision for himself.'

'Perhaps your father feels he needs a break.'

'He hadn't come to see me once in the previous three years. I think he's taken enough of a break.'

'Oh, I see.' She closes her eyes, lost in the moment, savouring the tea, reminding me of Tommy's little face at moments of such bliss. *Yumptious scrumptious.* He always had something of a little Buddha about him.

'I'll pray for you, Sonya.'

Is that it?

After some moments of contemplation she says, 'Actually, I think it would help to see your little boy. Tommy, isn't it?'

How can she know that? Does she remember all the details about everyone's lives in here?

'I can't promise anything, but I'll see what I can do.'

'Thank you, Sister. I'm really grateful.' I whisper, 'I'm afraid he's been given away...'

They're lovely people, by all accounts.

'This can happen, Sonya, though usually not without the mother's permission. Sometimes family members just can't cope.'

How did my father get around needing my permission to place Tommy with strangers? I think of that poor manic kid I used to see running around barefoot on the road where I grew up, like an urchin out of a Dickens novel. The adults used to say things like, 'Poor guy, God knows what's going on at home,' and yet no one ever did anything about it.

'I need to go find him.'

'I don't recommend you do that, Sonya. I'll find out what I can for you. If you leave now, Tommy will be deemed at risk. You need to finish the programme to get him back. You also need to finish the programme for you, so that you can be the best mother he deserves.'

I almost bless myself at this pronouncement and I don't know if the impulse is about taking the piss or if it's coming from a different place, a deeper place. I don't fucking know.

'Don't you think it's weird that his grandfather didn't take him in?'

'It sounds like relations were strained, Sonya. And maybe he felt he wouldn't be able to cope.'

'Bullshit. He has a cruel streak, hasn't even got a message to me to let me know that Tommy's doing ok.'

Sister Anne turns to me and looks me straight in the eye. 'I can only guess at how that feels, Sonya.'

She gets up, touches me on the arm, scoops up the cups and the tray and leaves – a trace of something warm and reassuring in her wake, like the smell of the freshly baked scones, which I would dearly love to have now they're gone.

17

Dear Dad,

I start to write a letter during a rare moment of alone time in the bedroom.

Dear asshole, motherfucker, shithead, lame-ass, twittlefuck, so-and-so...

I scratch that one out. Breathe, take my pen again, blow on its nib as if to cool it, and try again.

Dear Dad,

I hope you're well. (Better than the sharks swimming beneath.) *I am making great progress in here, and look forward to seeing you and Tommy very, very, ~~very, very~~ soon.* (I scratch out three 'very's.) *Visiting days are now every second Sunday between two and five, the second and fourth Sunday of every month* (but then I'm sure you know this). *I have tried calling you many, many, ~~many, many~~ times, but to no avail. I do apologise for how I spoke to Lara the last time* (Sister Anne suggested this would be the best course of action, though I feel nauseous writing it) *and hope you understand I was under considerable stress at the time. I was very very very* very *disap-pointed* (the editing can wait till later, lest I lose my flow) *to hear her voice, and not yours. I wanted (so very much) to talk to you and to hear all about Tommy. My writing is becoming increasingly jagged, that spidery, childish hand my father tried to straighten out. How much of my meaning is hidden in my hand? Father used to say it was an impatient hand. Nothing much changed there, then.

Lara said something about him being with 'lovely people'. Does this mean he is no longer with Mrs O'Malley? And Herbie? My thumb is starting to twitch, violently, and I wonder if this is the beginning of some rare neurological condition. Could this be why I am the way I am? All jangled and out of tune and harsh? I clamp my left hand over my right thumb and hold it a few moments, closing my eyes, trying to access that place I dip into sometimes during the rosary, when the chatter has subsided and there is only a background drone of others chanting. Try incanting the Hail Mary, but it just intensifies the jitters.

I quickly check the corridor to see that no one is coming, then go back into the bedroom, give myself a vigorous shake, climb under the quilt, stick my twitching thumb in my mouth, curl up into a tiny baby shape. 'Oh, for God's sake, Sonya' – I can hear my father's voice – 'less of the histrionics.' I sit upright, push back the quilt and try again. Find your adult, Sonya. Be an adult.

Where was I? Ah, yes. Tommy... And Herbie? Perhaps you could be so kind as to let me know where are they, how they're doing? NO, scrap that. I don't want to know second-hand how he's doing, and my grammar stinks. I need to see him for myself. Perhaps you could arrange a time that suits to bring Tommy to see me? I'm sure it would be very good for him to see me again... You could at least let me know WHERE they are, HOW they're doing. WHY do you feel this is a good idea? WHAT is it about me that you feel the need to do this? The tears are flowing hot and salty and I lick them, in case they fall on to the page. Won't be sending him this draft anyway, might as well cover it in snot and tears and, hell, blood if I like. I push the nib of the pen into the page, the pressure tearing the paper.

I hope you and Lara (I cover her name in little devil's horns, which makes me surprisingly giddy) *are happy and healthy. Again, I extend my apologies to Lara* (won't say sorry, no way) *and I look forward to hearing from you v v v v v v v soon, you motherfucking, lame-ass, twittlefuck, shithead asshole so-and-so. So there.*

Your murderous daughter,

Sonya.

One round of anger therapy out of the way; why does no one suggest writing uncensored vile shit to people; why is the focus always on being contained and serene – when what led most people here in the first place is a pent-up ravening rage? Anger is considered a 'defect of character' and some of these guys who are sitting on decades of unexpressed legitimate stuff then beat themselves up for feeling it. I know the whole place is sitting on a silent scream – I also know I wouldn't want to witness it.

I make a list: my father (check), Lara (YES), my dead mother who left me way too young, those bitches in school, especially Dana DC, Mr O'Grady with the ruler, that stupid doctor, my fair-weather agent, Howard the abandoner, Roberto the seducer, the user... I resolve to vent until it's all gone. It's fun playing the victim – I used to be so good at it; only problem is that now instead of being applauded for it, I'm told to 'get off your pity pot'. Father would approve of that one.

Whatever happens, I must affect a polite, detached, almost disinterested tone in the real letter I'm to send. Any sniff of emotion and he'll clam up. I try again.

Dear Dad,

I write the same words as before, without the hyperbole and florid cursing, and sign off: *Your loving daughter, Sonya.*

Before I can change my mind, I go to the shop, buy a stamp and leave the letter in the basket, which is almost empty, for that day's post. Quite a few of these guys never learned to read or write, which I found inconceivable the first time I heard someone admit it in the meetings. Then a flurry of sharing disclosed the same thing: the failures of the family, the system, society at large. Maybe I should offer to write their letters for them. Just as I'm tussling with this alien seed of altruism, Jimmy claps me on the back so hard I nearly fall.

'Coffee? Ten minutes before the meeting. Still time.'

'Tea'd be great. Black.'

I sit at a table by one of the windows looking out over the measly vegetable patch with its withered carrots, brown beets and yellowing, shrivelled lettuce. No wonder I'm half-starved in here.

He comes back with two hot-cross sticky buns.

'You alright now? You scared the crap out of me the other day.'

'Low blood sugar thingy.'

'Well, then.' He pushes the plate in front of me.

I can't be bothered telling him that it's all the sweet stuff I've been eating that made my sugar levels spike and then plummet. I had to work that one out for myself. I nibble a corner of the stale bun.

'I'm outta here on Friday.'

My chest tightens. How am I going to stick this place without him here? I'm scared of what's coming next, so I speak before he can: 'Congratulations, Jimmy. You're a real example to us all.'

'Will you mind my kitties for me?'

Oh, Sweet Jesus (another of my newly appropriated aphorisms). How could I trust myself?

'Your boy will love to visit them, when he comes.'

My vision blurs; I rub my knuckles in my eyes.

'Don't know if he'll be allowed to come.'

'You want me to pay the motherfuckers a visit?'

I allow the scenario to play out: Lara cowering behind my father at the door in the face of Jimmy, Big J, all five foot eight of him, biceps bulging, Celtic tats on display, etched in beautiful calligraphy on his forearm. *I told you it would come to this; I told you that daughter of yours would bring trouble down on our heads.* Lara's positively whimpering. How satisfying.

Jimmy smiles wryly at me as if he shares my fantasy.

'Back to those kittens. I don't trust anyone else with them. And anyway, with my track record I'll be back in here before you'll even know I've gone.'

I wonder if maybe this is it for Jimmy. He's respected, pretty much runs the joint, and as long as he's here he's not in prison.

'Why don't you train to be a counsellor, Jimmy? You'd be brilliant.'

This compliment seems to hurt him in some way. He takes a huge bite out of his bun, holds it in his mouth without chewing, stares at something across the room.

'Will you come see me, see us, on visiting day?'

He wipes his sleeve across his rheumy eyes and pulls himself to his full height. He swallows, with difficulty.

'Let's see what's first. Me relapsing, or visiting day.' He walks away, shoulders in a straight line, almost level with his ears.

18

The numbing routine continues – they really don't believe in unstructured time in here, which, I suppose, is the point – AA, rosary, meditation, desserts-for-dinner, chicken-coop cleaning, egg collecting, group therapy, Linda's snores, full-on insomnia, ferocious headaches, woodwork, over and over, and people, people, people. Day thirty-eight, and it's time for my first individual counselling session. What's the point? What's the point of any of it if I can't see Tommy, talk to him? Has anyone ever died from the sheer force of missing someone? I might; I really might evaporate from longing.

The room is tiny and overlit, with windows sealed shut. I can't breathe. I climb on to the table beneath the window and am trying to pull up the handle, which won't budge, when the door opens.

'Hi there. Can I help?'

I nearly topple but steady myself by leaning my forehead against the cool glass for a moment, before stepping back on to the chair and the ground.

'Bit stuffy in here.'

I could be describing the man in front of me, with his shiny loafers, his chinos, his jumper slung around his shoulders in an effort to look casual, though the symmetry is just right: the exact same length of sleeve dangling on either side, tied neatly in the middle. A tickle builds in the back of my throat. Something familiar here: the polished slip-ons, the cheekbones, the voice. What is it about that voice? I need to leave.

'Ok if I get some water?'

'Sure. I'll wait for you here.'

My mind must be playing its tricks. He couldn't be who I think he is – my memories of that time aren't exactly reliable. But what if it is him? I'm not in the mood to be lectured or reminded of my former maternal failings. Anger has built a permanent home inside me – I heard one of the men describe it that way, and I like it: it's poetic and theatrical and it fits. And my anger is justified, of course it is – that father of mine… and as I see his face I feel my creatures start to stir. Starve one and another raises its head immediately: *fuck him, fuck them* – the moment of calm after Sister Anne left didn't last long. But at least I felt it, at least I know what shape it could take. This is something else entirely: sharp, cold and deadly, and I feel I could slice Mr Cheekbones with my tongue.

In the kitchen I run the tap, rinse the glass, fill the glass, tip its contents, repeat, before I'm satisfied the glass is clean and the water cool enough. My father's obsession with germs seems to have finally caught hold of me. It's the incessant sharing of everything.

I swallow my full glass in one, then fill another. I suppose I'd better go back.

A wave of stale trapped air meets me. He's standing by the window, trying to open it.

'It seems to be stuck.'

Of course it's stuck, what did he think I was doing on the table – lap-dancing? I have to stop myself throwing my water all over him, which I recognise is pretty extreme, but something about this situation is making me feel panicked. Back in the day I could channel these impulses into my characters, or later I could dampen them with a bottle, or two, of whatever medicinal gloop was in the fridge. Now I have to feckin' 'ground'. I can hear Jimmy's voice in my ear telling me to ask the Man Above for patience. I look towards the stained ceiling, searching out any divine intervention, any message in the cracks. I don't see any zigzagging lines; I can't even play that particular game.

'Would you like to sit down?'

He goes to pull a plastic chair from the table. So absurd, this show of 'gentlemanliness' – so patronising.

'Thank you.' I sit politely, arranging my skirt, pulling it down over my knees. A demure ingénue.

'So, how are you doing, Sonya?' He sits in a too-small plastic chair looking anything but at ease, his long frame spilling over its edges.

'Fine.' I sip my water delicately.

He nods, not taking the bait. He knows exactly what that word means in a context like this. He extends his hand. 'David Smythe.'

Is he pretending not to recognise me? I'm not sure I'll be able to contain this now. The swarm is dangerously close to erupting. I swallow the remnants of the glass in one gulp, which dilutes the bastards and stops their flight, momentarily. I study his long, tapering fingers, his sculpted, strong hands. He looks down and consults his notes. I wonder who told him what? Did the doctor itemise my *neurotic* tendencies? Sister Anne? What would she have said? I find I really do care.

'I believe you've been through a difficult period.'

'Obviously!' I try to smile. 'Or I wouldn't be here.'

'I mean in here.'

'Well, the food is pretty crap!'

He doesn't smile. 'Where are you now? Almost halfway?'

Does he really not know that I am the same person he gave his card to the day before I was forced to come here? He doesn't look me directly in the eye. Something shifty about that, or awkward, or just shy.

'Congratulations on your sobriety to date. That's quite an achievement.'

'I didn't exactly have a choice.'

He stays looking at his notes. 'What do you mean, "exactly"?'

'I was threatened with my son being taken away from me if I didn't come here. And now I'm here, they've taken him away anyway.'

'Who are "they", Sonya?'

I really don't want to answer any question this man asks me about my son. He has seen the worst of me. I cast my mind back to that moment in the pizza place: I was jittery and pissed and without boundaries and he could see that Tommy wasn't in safe hands.

'Are you pretending not to know who I am?' I can't help myself.

He shifts in his seat, a red flush creeping under his collar. 'I didn't think it would help to make reference to that time, Sonya. I'm just as surprised as you are that you're now sitting in front of me here. Surprised and also, I guess, relieved for you and for the boy.' He almost mumbles the words. He looks up, though still not directly at me.

'That girl that works in that place is such a little bitch.'

He fixes his collar, pulling it high as he says, 'Of course, if it makes you uncomfortable, we can arrange for you to see someone else.'

I think back to how kind he was to Tommy, and how he didn't feel the need to quiz me or patronise me, like that other asshole. He paid for our pizzas, for Christ's sake.

'I'm not sure, to be honest.'

'That's ok. You can take some time to decide before your next session.'

A silence descends. My heart speeds. Seeing this man here, this fragment from my past, means there can be no denial now. I was a pisshead mother and I deserve exactly what has befallen me. *Sonya, you're not playing a part now. This is real.* I still don't know how this separation, which, ok, maybe is my just punishment, is in Tommy's best interests. The familiar torturous questions swirl: Who's minding him? Are they being good to him? Can they understand his quirky little ways? Is he managing to eat anything? Is he able to sleep without our bedtime stories, without Herbie? And Herbie? I can't seem to follow that line of thought any further. I'm terrified of what my father might have done with Herbie, who is, after all, only a dog.

'Would you like to talk to me a little about the feelings this enforced separation is bringing up in you?'

Something about him tells me that he's not a father. He has an aura of someone who spends a lot of time alone, a self-regard, a self-containment, an air of *selfishness*. I wonder how old he is. Older than me, for sure – mid-forties? Well preserved, toned. I wonder how long he's been in recovery, and how bad he was before. He seems so upright, so uptight, so repressed, so absolutely *sober* in every sense of the word that I have a hard time imagining him off his head. How I'd like to see him out of control; see his perfectly coiffed hair all over the place. I surprise myself with this thought.

'Would you like to finish our session now, Sonya?'

Would I? I like how he says my name, the way he puts the emphasis on the second syllable, like a character from a Chekhov play, like how Tommy says it. Ya*ya*. I am brimming with my name, its music, its latent possibilities. Son*ya*.

'No, sorry, just feeling a bit hemmed-in here.'

He rubs the backs of his fingers against his stubble, a sound like sandpaper scratching. Shoulders wide and solid, forehead high and domed, brain helmeted. He looks intelligent, except for the preppy clothes. I imagine him in tweed. Much more satisfactory.

'Would you like to go into the grounds for a walk, get some air?' he says.

I nod. We walk down the grim corridor to the front door. The receptionist glances up for a beat, sees me looking at her, then buries herself back into her dark *Secret*, her cheeks flushing. Maybe one of the twelve-step devotees told her she shouldn't be reading that blasphemous trash. I want to shout at her to stop looking for answers inside the pages of some stupid book written by some equally stupid fuck.

'Fresh, after all that rain,' he says.

I look up at the sky, which is dense with cloud, as usual. We walk out into the gravelled driveway, past the tarnished statue of the Virgin Mary with her flaked, aged face and bleeding brown-red lips, past the chicken coop with its rusted barbed-wire fence, *hello, cluck-clucks!*, past the clusters of smokers, mainly men, gathered outside the kittens' shed. I look at their lined, thread-veined faces. Even those whose lives are a wrecked shambles have visitors, a kindly sister, a girlfriend, someone they knocked about a bit. Even their children come, some of whom were genuinely at risk.

I can feel David regarding me.

'Do you have children?'

He looks surprised, caught off guard. 'No, not yet.'

As usual my insight into other people is uncannily accurate, which, instead of making me feel superior, as it normally does, just depresses me. The overwhelming greyness of the scene around us: the sky, the concrete ground, the crumbling, breeze-block walls. Recently my night-times have been filled with the ghosts of the orphaned children who once lived within these walls, still trapped. They are grey, broken children with blank stares, sometimes wearing Tommy's face. His hands beating on the window, his face pressed against the pane.

'This place was once an orphanage,' I say.

'Think that might be an old wives' tale.'

I don't say anything.

'Are you experiencing any relief in here, Sonya?'

'I haven't touched a drop in thirty-eight days.'

'And the head?'

The head, my *head*, what do you mean exactly? You try living with the torture of not knowing where your child is, the callous indifference of that, on the part of someone who is supposed to love you.

As if he can hear my thoughts (I hope I haven't spoken them aloud; am pretty sure I haven't), he says, 'Sister Anne said she left a message with your father. Seems pretty tough that he hasn't let you know where the boy is.'

'It's raining,' I say.

He nods, looking towards the sky. Neither of us makes a move to go back inside.

'Almost refreshing, were it not so fucking relentless,' I continue.

He laughs, surprising himself.

'Can I ask you a question?'

He looks at me sideways, suspiciously.

'I'm curious: is there the same level of relapse in a private facility as in here?'

'No one has documented that, not that I know.'

'I bet the price tag puts people off reoffending in a private rehab.'

I can hear how my words are speeding up, becoming garbled.

'Reoffending? Interesting term, Sonya.'

A warm, giddy feeling is building inside me. 'It seems every second person I talk to in here has been here before, and not just once.'

'Do you believe the twelve-step approach works?' he asks.

Is he trying to draw me into some shared complicity, or is he trying to catch me out?

'Not sure about the one-size-fits-all philosophy.'

'Have you found anyone in here you can relate to?'

'In a way.' I think of Jimmy and the kittens.

He stops walking, turns and looks in my direction. 'Unless a person gets honest, it doesn't matter where they go.'

My body is in his shadow. I look over his shoulder, seeking the light.

He moves away, sits on a mossy wall. I sit beside him. It's damp.

'How's the meditating going?'

How can I tell him that focusing on my breath sends me into a heightened sense of panic? There is nothing calming in plugging into the internal mechanisms of my body, or my mind. I seem to inhabit an inner life sewn from the fabric of dread.

'Have you found a sense of a Higher Power?' He seems embarrassed to be asking me this. It feels invasive and somehow ridiculous.

I shrug, like a teenager.

He quickly changes tack: 'Have you been exercising?'

'Swimming is my thing.'

'Right, well, when you get out, make sure to incorporate a swim into your day.'

Oh yes, and how might I do that, a single mother, on benefits? I don't say anything, just sit on my hands, which are trembling.

Watery sunlight filters through the trees, dappling his face, accentuating his cheekbones, the animal-likeness of him. The light is moving across the planes of his face. The urge to chase that light with my hand, to trace its path, to land on his stubble, the smooth skin above. I imagine him reaching out and taking my hand, his big, solid one encircling mine.

19

My name is called out over the loudspeaker. As I make my way to reception, undulating lines appear in front of my eyes. I move towards the phone as if towards an unexploded grenade, terrified that whoever it was has hung up, and even more terrified of hearing his voice. I pick up the heavy receiver, wipe it down with my sleeve – God knows how much spittle this thing has accumulated – breathe deeply and dive in.

'Hello?'

'Sonya, is that you?'

Stay on script: the suitably chastised daughter, the subdued recovering alcoholic.

'Yes. It's me. Good to hear from you, Dad.'

'I heard from Lara you had a bit of an outburst.'

Exhale. 'All I said was that I wanted desperately to see Tommy. And you. I miss you both.'

'I thought it was best to allow you time to settle in. And reflect.'

Silence crackles like static electricity down the line. Careful not to ignite the charge. I squeeze my hands together, imagining someone else is exerting a calming pressure.

'I've had that now. Dad, I need to see Tommy. For his sake. He needs to know his mother hasn't abandoned him.'

Tommy's face, serious and bewildered, floats in the spaces between my words. I know how much that feeling of being pushed away, of getting the crumbs off a parental table, sets up a hunger that can't be sated.

'I took professional advice, Sonya.'

'What were you advised to tell him?'

'That you had gone away, for a bit.'

Gone away. Tommy wouldn't buy that one. I would never go anywhere without him. I can imagine the whirrings of his overactive mind, tossing up alternatives, each more morbid than the last. I remember being fed the same line when my mother died, when adults were revealed to be liars. 'When is she coming back?' Over and over I'd repeat these words, until eventually Uncle Dom said, 'For God's sake, tell the child the truth. Her mother's not coming back. Tell her.'

'Is that wise, Dad? Tommy is a very intuitive child.'

Could they not have told him I was not well, in hospital. At least then he'd have some chance of understanding. But 'gone away'. Jesus. It's not a euphemism. It's an outright cruelty to utter such words to a child.

'Dad?' This is hard; I can hear how high-pitched my voice has become. 'Where is he? What happened with Mrs O'Malley?'

My father moves away from the phone, or places a hand over the receiver, blocking any line of communication.

'Who's looking after him?'

'It was too much for Mrs O'Malley. He's being looked after by people who know about these things.'

'What things, what people, Dad?'

'Sonya, trust me. He's in good hands.'

I look down at my own hands and my ragged nails, nibble on my right thumb. 'Did Sister Anne call?'

The receptionist taps her watch.

'I don't have much time here.'

I find myself shouting a little down the unresponsive line. I hear him clear his throat, trying to formulate the right response.

'Yes, Sonya. I spoke to Sister Anne. I will bring Tommy to see you next Sunday.'

'Have you seen him?'

'I have been advised not to interfere.' His voice drops a notch, as if he doesn't want his next words witnessed, as if he's ashamed. 'He doesn't really know me, Sonya.'

And this was your chance to change all that.

'What are you going to tell him when you see him? What is this place?'

'I don't know yet, Sonya.' His voice is becoming fractious. 'I'll take advice from the experts on that.'

Experts. Who are these people?

'Tell him exactly how long it will be before I'm out of here, Dad. Tell him I've been unwell. Getting better...' Nothing they say can explain this away.

The receptionist waves at me. 'Time's up.'

'See you Sunday. Between two and five, remember? Come at two?'

He mutters that he will see me then.

'Bye, *Dad*.' I almost choke on the word. I throw a final insincere 'And thank you' down the line, which reverberates back, an empty echo.

The next few days are exhausting, my nights being taken over by bolts of manic energy, my dreams and waking state at 4 a.m. jumbled together, one indistinguishable from the other. Surges of adrenalin rush through me, making me want to run. At home I'd masturbate, before Tommy came along, for a kind of release. Here, with people either side of me, it's impossible, so I lie rigid, eyes open and staring, trying to block the livid images that snarl and unsnarl behind my lids any time my eyes close.

'You ok?' Linda asks early one morning. 'Crazy dark circles under your eyes.'

'Can't sleep.' I push myself to sitting, arranging the lumpy pillow behind my back.

'Is it my snoring? Maybe you should ask to be moved, or I could?'

Funny how Linda's snoring has become a strange nocturnal companion, a welcome distraction from my own chasing, circling thoughts.

'Fuck, no. Don't think I could do this without you.'

Linda responds so well to any kind of compliment that I can see how easy it must be for Mark to manipulate her. Her cheeks flush and a broad smile reveals her yellow teeth and wide gaps between them. It's endearing in a way that a toddler's gummy mouth is. A longing so powerful to hold my boy floods me and I close my eyes to stop the tears.

'What's going on?'

I lie back on the pillow, spent. There's the crack, directly above my head. It doesn't seem to be offering any out, any portal to another world.

'Tommy,' I manage. 'I'm going to see my little boy on Sunday. It's been so long I'm scared he won't recognise me, that he'll make strange. Scared of hearing him talk about Herbie. I've no idea what's happened to Herbie.'

'You've never spoken about him before.' Her voice is shaky and small. 'He another boy?'

'Our dog.'

'Fuck's sake, you had me worried there for a moment.'

I'm not even going to bother trying to explain how much like a second son, or big brother to Tommy, he is.

Linda rolls on to her back and the two of us lie there, staring at the dirty smudges and a bad paint job at the corners of the ceiling, before she says quietly, 'I had a little girl taken away from me.'

'Jesus… Linda…'

She holds her hand up to silence me.

'How old was she?'

'Three. Never told anyone that before,' she says, before she gets up to go into the bathroom and turns on the shower, the sound of the water running almost, but not quite, loud enough to drown out the sound of her choking back sobs.

20

My stomach's loud and cranky, like my thoughts, and my ankles are chafed in my shitty Converse. I've been circling the grounds for the past two hours, having skipped rosary, and lunch. He won't come. He wouldn't even bother calling. Why expect anything else? One of the nuggets I've taken from the meetings is this idea of lowering expectations – life rarely gives you what you want, and anyway, lemonade is for pussies. A leaf falls from the sky and lands on me. *Wake up, dummy!* I take it and put it in my pocket. And then I see them.

My voice rips out of me, any attempt at presenting a respectable front gone. 'Tommy!' – wild and desperate. All heads turn in my direction as I crash past my father, pushing Lara – what's she doing here? – aside to get to my boy. I lift him high in the air, expecting to hear squeals of excitement.

'Spinnies?' I say, catching him under the arms.

'Careful with the boy.' My father's voice slaps me.

Tommy's face is scrunched up, eyes squeezed shut, and not in the ecstatic way I remember. I place him gently on the ground and stoop to kiss his forehead. He flinches. Lara is staring at me.

'Come, now. It's all a bit much for the lad. Why don't we get a nice Fanta or sweeties in the shop over here?'

What the hell does she know about what's too much for my son? How does my father allow this blatant intrusion?

'Dad.' I look directly at him. 'I'd like some time alone with Tommy.'

'Son? Lara and I will be just over here.' He points to the shop. 'Tell your mummy when you've had enough, ok?'

This false posturing antagonises every jangling nerve ending, wires dangerously crossed, likely to flip that switch. I rest my eyes on Tommy's form, so small and angular, constrained in his skin, as if he's holding something inside that's too big, as if his bones might crack from the weight of carrying it. I drink him in, smelling his sweet marmalade scent, disguised with somebody else's brand of washing powder. He's so quiet, not the lively little man I remember. Are my memories of him filtered through the lens of the red-rimmed, melancholic boozer's eyes?

He nods at his grandad, sombre little fellow, then looks off into the distance.

'Not too long, now. Don't want to tire the boy out.'

My mouth fills with every obscenity I've ever uttered and some I've never given shape to before, but some functioning part of my brain intercedes before the explosion. I have to force down all that hot, bubbling bile.

'Come, Tommy, and I'll show you around the place where Yaya's been staying.'

I hold my hand out and he doesn't take it. I smile at him, gently, I hope. *Come back to my orbit, little man.* I want to stick my tongue out and roll the sides off each other but know how that would look.

'No more than thirty minutes. We have to get him home.'

Did he really just use that word?

'Tell your mummy about the lovely lady you're staying with. Clare, isn't that right?'

My tongue worries the inside of my already bitten cheek.

'Half-hour tops,' he says before turning, Lara's arm snaking around his lower back, as if, without her support, he might topple over.

'Would you like to see a giant statue?' I ask, careful not to demand too much too soon, even though my body is craving to hold him close, feel his heartbeat next to mine. Rat-a-tat-tat.

We walk. Single file.

'This is Mary,' I say when we get to the oversized statue in the grotto. 'You know... the mother of Jesus?'

I almost bow my head. He looks blankly at the carved stone figure. Of course he hasn't a clue; I hardly prioritised his religious instruction.

'Look at her robin-redbreast cheeks and lips!' I don't mention the flaking, peeling paint job, which makes her mouth look as if it's bleeding. I don't mention the whole mother-of-God stuff, certainly not the Immaculate Conception stuff, sure to bamboozle him and fill his head with nightmares, as it did mine.

'Hey, were there any lady giants like this one in the Land of Nod?'

He shrugs, kicks at the ground. He tracks a large black beetle as it makes its lumbering way across the path.

'Big fella, huh?'

He picks up a twig and bends to prod it.

'Maybe not, Tommy. How would you feel if one of your giants started poking you?'

He doesn't stop, just flips the beetle over and crouches low for further inspection.

'Jeepers creepers, how many legs does one tiny creature need?'

I'm trying to reach him when he presses the twig down hard into the centre of the beetle, its innards flying in all directions, a sickening crunch.

I can't help myself: 'Did that make you feel better?'

He doesn't answer, just throws the twig down and puts his hands in his pockets. 'Tommy...? Tommy. Look at me.'

His eyes. Dug out with a spoon.

'I'm sorry, darling. Yaya's sorry. I didn't mean for this to happen.'

I kneel in front of him. How can someone so young have so little light in their eyes? Were they always this deep-set, or are they grooves from tiredness? No person this little should have eyes like these. A replica of his mother, who deserves the bruises she sports.

I'm careful not to touch him, reading his signals that this is close enough.

'I was sick, Tommy. And now I'm getting better. I'll be home soon.'

He looks down, scuffing the toe of his trainer on the ground.

'We can all go home soon.'

There is an unspoken absence hanging between us.

'The first thing we'll do the day I get out of here is pick Herbie up.'

At the mention of the dog's name his eyes well and he blinks hard.

'We're almost there, Tommy. Over halfway. Only five and a bit weeks to go. We can do that, can't we?'

He walks on ahead of me, shoulders hunched, a silent shrunken old man.

'Would you like to see some kittens, Tommy?'

His head makes an imperceptible upward-downward movement.

'Follow me,' I say as I sweep past him, woman in charge.

When we reach the shed a number of other visiting families are there, cooing over the little 'fur babies', as one girl calls them. 'So cute they make me want to cry.' Tommy looks unimpressed at her histrionics and seems to want to leave. I push to the front and reach in to lift out the small, inquisitive tabby. 'Look, Tommy. A marmalade cat.' His two favourite things rolled into one: animals and orange jam. For a moment he seems to forget his hurt and reaches out to stroke the kitten between her eyes. The episode with the beetle crosses my mind and I'm careful to keep a close watch. The Tommy I left behind would never willingly kill any other living creature, even buzzing bluebottles as they'd bang against the window, crazed. I remember him shooing them out through the opened windows and doors, crying when I squashed one with my thumb. I ooh and ah at the tabby, overcompensating, sensing the other parents staring at me.

'Would you like to adopt her, Tommy?'

He looks up at me, a tiny glint in his eyes. 'Would Hewbie like her?'

There. His voice. And it almost melts my bones.

'Herbie's such a gentle giant. I'm sure he'd look after her.'

'Five weeks is long, Yaya.'

'Yes, darling. Too long. Ask Grandad to bring you next week and the week after and the week after that. Six more visits and then we can go home, with our new friend Marmie.'

He repeats the name: 'Marmie'. Nods, satisfied that it is a good name. 'Where is Hewbie, Yaya?'

I think fast. 'He's in a lovely house with other dogs and he has made a new friend, a big spotty Dalmatian named Hugh.'

Tommy looks away, an expression of disgust clouding his features. He never liked to be lied to.

'Yaya?'

'Yes, darling?'

'I want to go now.'

I can sense the interest from those around me intensifying, wondering how I'm going to handle this obvious rebuff.

I decide on a magnanimous approach: 'Of course, sweetie. Let's go get creamy ice.'

I take the kitten from his hands and place her gently back down among her siblings.

'I want a kitty too, Mam,' says the same little girl who said she could cry they were so cute.

Tommy looks at her slyly out of the corner of his eyes. 'Not ours. You can't have Marmie.'

The girl starts to wail. 'That's the one I want.'

A switch seems to be triggered inside his small body and I can see his impulse to smack the girl before it happens. I'm forced to grab his hand as it flies in the air. I hold on to him firmly and pull him away from the shed.

'That's not ok, Tommy. You can't go around hitting people.'

He looks at me, like *Who are you kidding?* Heat rushes to my cheeks.

'Would you like to see the room where I sleep?'

He shrugs, hands deep in the pockets of jeans I don't recognise. Who bought him clothes? Did they take him shopping? He hates the bright lights, the thumping music, the crowds, just like me, hates the 'stupid' other people. Do the folk minding him know this about him? Do they let him grab anything orange he likes off the shelves? Underneath his favourite fleece hoodie (the one I stole for him last year) he's wearing a new orange T-shirt. Jealousy grabs me by the throat, rattling me around.

'What's she like, Tommy, the lady who is looking after you?'

He almost disappears inside himself, his head hunched low.

I look towards the sky.

'Where has Mr Sunshine gone to today, Tommy?'

He looks up, his focus intense, seeking out the concentration of light behind the thick membrane of cloud. His eyes dart all round, never alighting on one spot. After a few moments he gives up. He has never not managed to find the spot where Mr Sunshine is hiding.

I point, over his shoulder. 'There. See?'

He shakes his head. 'He's gone away.'

'He hasn't disappeared, Tommy, remember? He's up there somewhere. It's up to us to find him.'

His eyes are cast down towards the gravel path beneath his feet. What does he see?

'It's only a matter of time, Tommy, before the sky is blue again. You know that, right?'

He doesn't respond, seemingly irritated by everything about me.

'What colour is the room you're sleeping in, darling?'

He actively scuffs the front of his trainers, a long, deliberate, provocative scuff.

A part of me wants to smack him, another part wants to crush him close, sing in his ear over and over: *You are my sunshine, my only sunshine...* He has no interest in seeing my room, and anyway, what was I thinking? I don't want to show him the four institutional beds in the dreary, stuffy room. What kind of an image would that plant in his mind? Why has he not asked me any questions: what, who, when, why? His enquiring mind never used to stop questioning, sorting, labelling, packaging. Have they given him some sort of sedative? Is that why his eyes are as dead as any addict's in here?

I stamp my feet into the ground, shaking my head – push that one away. A leaf floats loose from one of the sentinels: a skinny, anaemic-looking fellow. Mr Droopy – how's that one, Dad? That's a new one!

'A magic feather, Tommy!'

He reaches out to catch it, regards it closely, examining the veins, running his thumb over the lines. I remove mine from my pocket.

'Look, Tommy, two autumn leaves for your scrapbook.'

He worries the one in his own hand, rubbing it between his thumb and forefinger, crumbling it into tiny pieces before letting it fall to the ground. My offering lies vulnerable in my palm. He reaches out, as if in slow motion, and takes the leaf, which has dried even further since it fell only moments ago. I expect him to shred and stamp on it, but instead he kisses it and puts it in his pocket.

'Would you like me to kiss it too, Tommy?'

He looks at me, his face registering first distaste, then consideration, followed by a tussle: yes, no, no, yes, stupid, yes, before he pulls the leaf out and offers it to me. I take it, kiss it, and put it back into his pocket.

'Be careful not to tear it, Tommy. Remember how fragile it is?'

He nods, tapping on the outside of his pocket.

'You can kiss me goodnight every night now.'

His face closes down, an expression I recognise from my father.

'Would you like some ice cream, Tommy?' I look up at the grey, cold sky.

I wonder what he's eating now. Have they made him swallow meat? He doesn't look like he's eaten much. Has he developed my fascination with blanking out, spinning from lack of food? I long to reach out and rub his belly, cover it in butterfly kisses. *You will never have to look after your mummy again.* He needs to learn to be a little boy, he needs Herbie by his side. That dog has been there since his beginning, and even if I was passed out or otherwise off my head, Herbie's soft animal bulk was a constant presence. An ache pushes behind my eyes; the mist is rising.

I walk ahead of him, determined not to let him see my building panic. I need some soothing music but am terrified of what I might conjure.

'Have you been to the beach, Tommy? I miss our outings to the sea.'

I turn around and see him shaking his head ferociously as if trying to rid it of terrible things. Have my creatures made their home inside him too? I gently hold his head in my hands.

'First thing we'll do when I get out of here is pick Herbie up, go to the beach, throw skimmers, paddle, eat our creamy ices, and then we'll all eat our fishies on the couch together.'

Does he buy it, trust me?

'And Marmie? Can she come to the beach too?'

'Why not?'

'Can we get a lead for her? She wouldn't like to be left home when we go for walkies.'

'What a great idea. I think she'd like that!'

I picture our motley group being stared at, judged. I wouldn't give a damn – let them stare, they have nothing better to do.

'Yaya?'

'Yes, darling?'

'Have you been very sick?'

How do I answer this one without adding to his overspilling anxiety?

'I have been sick, darling, but I'm nearly all better.'

He nods, a kind of a half-nod, as if trying to convince himself. We're outside the shop now, seconds away from another separation.

'Would you like a hug, Tommy?'

I risk it, terrified of the possible rebuff my question might give rise to.

He's weighing it up, turning over the possibilities in his mind, when I hear my father's voice beside us: 'Ah, there you are. We were getting worried. Come on, young man. Time to get going.'

He grabs hold of Tommy's hand, which goes limp, while the rest of his body turns hard. Lara is right behind him.

'Bye, darling.'

He says bye, then walks away, his hand still caught in my father's grip. Just as they've almost reached the car park he breaks free, and runs back towards me, hurtling his body against mine, nuzzling his head against my stomach. I bend down to kiss the top of his head, which smells of anti-dandruff shampoo, or is it anti-nit? It smacks the back of my throat. I picture him getting his hair washed by someone else, eyes scrunched tight, soap dripping in. That shit stings.

21

I'm not sure I'll be able to contain this mad fluttering thing in the centre of my chest now. I need to run, to fuck, to fly, need an outlet, release, soothing. So I run. In my shitty Converse, with my shin splints, I run around and around the circumference of the grounds, visitors still present – who is that mad bat? *That mad bat is me!* I want to shout at the top of my voice, and I think I see her, my imp, in her gaudy gear, gearing up. And I'm tempted to engage, I really am. It's all going on in there: love, longing, loss, rage, looping, cranking itself up. *Lara*… I mean… what was Father thinking? Dear God, how is this in Tommy's best interests? How? You saw him. The pain of him, his shrunken little self, his confusion, his look of bamboo-zlement, his fear, his *abandonment*. And yet – to have seen him makes happiness explode inside me like fizzy sherbet. Still, I run.

I only stop when I might puke. I'm dizzy, which is kind of nice; I'm back in my body, heavy and exhausted, shins sore. No sign of Lady Madcap now. I walk, slightly limping, heart thumping. Try to gather the disparate parts of me. I draw on everything I've learned in here. Feel the ground beneath my feet, look around me, try to see, to really see, what is really here: the shedding trees, the leaves underfoot, the murky sky above. I breathe slowly, attempt to access my Higher Power: a kind parent, or that part of me that wants what's good for me. A nurturing cheerleader, not that high-kicking fiend who's only out to cause chaos. One foot in front of the other, one breath after another, and I find I am a little bit calmer.

And I'm starving.

In the cafe I scan the room and see Jimmy, centre stage. He catches my eye, grins like a schoolboy, throws his hands in the air in an expansive gesture. I shouldn't be this happy that he's back. I weave my way through the room to his table, noting how the men around him freeze at my arrival. I'm probably still palpitating, and no doubt my hair is plastered to my head with cold sweat.

'How'ya, Jimmy?'

'Cheers.' He raises his water glass. 'Nice job with the kittens. Seem to be thriving.'

'Ah, they missed you, though. Even though you were only gone, like, what? Ten days? Didn't think they took boozy bods back into the fold so soon.'

His grin expands to consume the whole lower part of his face so that he looks like a scrunched-up hand puppet, the ones made of foam that I used to love to manipulate when I was little. 'I'm not just any old boozy bod,' he says, tucking into a tough old piece of steak with relish.

If there were baby calves in the shed, would he treat them with the same tenderness he does the kittens? So strange, that disconnect. It's not his fault.

'You want to join us?'

The others shift uncomfortably. I try on a smile. A whis-key-weathered farmer, the one who bellows at night like a bull, so the rumours go, scrapes his chair back from the table, agitation in his eyes. 'Well, I'm off.' Probably the smile that did it, that smile that used to put Lara into paroxysms of rage. 'Don't you dare... like that.' Like what? 'Wipe that snarky smile off your face, or else.' Or else—?

Now the others are all leaving, a scene reminiscent of the class-room, with the bitches all freezing me out.

'Something I said?'

Jimmy laughs, waves his fork in the air, points it at me.

'You going to get some grub inside you? Can't have you keeling over like that last time.'

He's right, I could plummet, so I go to the counter and ask for anything vegetarian.

'Still on that crazy diet?' the tiny woman with the hairnet says. She dollops three scoops of lumpy mashed potato and a watery mush of turnip and parsnips on to my plate. 'Bon appeteet.'

'Aw fuck, you really gonna eat that?' Jimmy says.

I nod, hold my nose and fork a mouthful in, and down the hatch. *Vrrrrrrrooooom, Yaya!*

'Good girl. Only two more mouthfuls, and then it's time for sweeties.' He pushes a crusty-looking strawberry-jam roulade in front of me.

'So, I heard you had a visitor. How'd it go?'

'Complicated.'

'He's lucky to have you.'

I push the food away, suddenly nauseous.

'Look, you're here, you're tackling this thing head-on. He's young enough to bounce back from this.'

My eyes wander to the window above eye level. If I concentrate hard enough, above the din and clatter of the other tables, I can block his voice and hear the rustle of wind in the trees.

'Even as a baby I was flooded with adrenalin, pissed on fear. I never experienced a calm moment before coming here.'

The leaves are shushing, whispering, accusing.

'I can hardly remember my own being born. Don't let your life slide by in a blur. For your boy.'

Heat rises and courses through me, followed by a bout of intense cold. My internal thermostat is haywire. I don't want this unsolicited advice now, these reminders of my failings as a parent; I want to revel in that hug. I rub the spot on my stomach where he pressed his head.

Jimmy pushes his chair back, goes to the canteen and asks for three helpings of dessert.

'Call me Sweet Tooth,' he says, winking on his way out.

Do teeth really taste like sweeties, Yaya?

It's an expression, Tommy, like when I call you Munchkin!

Do sweeties really make your teeth fall out?

Well, too much sugar rots your teeth, Mr T.

Is the fairy that collects the out-teeth a good or a bad fairy?

There's no such thing as a bad fairy, Tommy.

Yes, Yaya, there is, you know there is.

22

A week later and I see him again: Mr Sober Smythe, sitting by the grubby back window in the cafe. I've just come from chicken duty and have ten minutes before my next group session. I watch him a moment, cradling his cup, blowing on it, but not drinking from it. Those hands. I debate with myself a moment, then walk over and ask if I could join him. He nods, coolly, I think. I wonder who he has been counselling and am surprised to find I don't like that thought.

'How are things, Sonya?' He stays sitting.

'I'm sorry I didn't arrange another session. Until I get my son back I'm not able for any of this.'

'Ever heard that one about putting on your own oxygen mask first?'

Ah now, I'd have given him more credit than that.

'Why are you here, Sonya?'

'Because I have to be. For Tommy.'

'See?'

'He's four, David, four. He doesn't have a father. I'm his world and without me he can't function.'

'How do you know that's true? Maybe he's functioning much better without you around?'

That is pretty fucking harsh and out of order and out of line and all out of whack. David seems to recognise this as he says in a much softer tone: 'I'm just trying to make you see how much better he'll be when you're in his life in a stable capacity.'

I sit on my hands. This man makes me sit on my hands. How dare he presume to tell me how to think, how to live, how my son operates? This whole 'recovery' operation stinks of that corralling of self, of instinct, into a small, tight, constrained way of being. Start your day on your knees, pray for guidance. 'Thy will be done', for mine is warped, maniacal. And yet.

Sometimes I exhaust myself. I just wish I could do life, in the ordinary sense. I wish I was on a date with this good-looking man, being *normal*, instead of discussing my need for recovery. It seems unfair that he saw me pissed, with my child, when all I know of him is this upstanding version. I wish I knew the other side too, to level off the playing field.

A young guy about eighteen, a new recruit on work duty as a waiter, approaches our table.

'What you having?' he says to me.

'Peppermint tea. Thanks.'

The boy sucks in his lips. 'Doubt they have anything like that in here.'

'They do, actually.'

'Right,' he says as he walks away, looking as if he'd like to rip someone's windpipe out.

David smiles at me, conspiratorially, I think.

The boy returns with my tea, which he throws down on the table, liquid sploshing over the sides. David jumps, his thighs scalded through the soft cotton of his chinos.

The boy's hands form into automatic fists, every muscle and sinew in his body straining.

'Don't worry about it,' I say, trying to catch his eye. 'Can happen to any of us.'

David looks furious. He goes to the bathroom.

'Are you new here?'

The boy's mouth is a hard line.

'This place is a joke.'

I don't contradict him.

'Would you like me to show you around later? Have you met the kittens?'

'Has no one drowned them yet?'

It's only bravado, he's still a boy, and yet I sense an undercurrent of hurt that needs to hurt in return. I watch him walk away, his prowling back.

David returns.

'You ok?'

'Bit scalded, actually, but I'll live!'

'I don't think he meant it.'

David looks at the boy, studying him like he's a rare exhibit in a zoo.

I suddenly want that gaze on me.

'Tommy came to see me last Sunday,' I say, in a spurt.

'Did he? That's great. How did it go?'

'Difficult, and lovely.' I allow myself to relive the *lovely*. The moment with the leaf, the kissing it, the final hug at the end.

David sits up straighter in his chair. Neither of us have touched our drinks.

'Did your father place him in care?'

I can sense my joy as an external thing – a pink balloon with 'LOVELY' scrawled on it – floating loose from my grip. I have to stop myself climbing on the table to draw it back down.

'It can be a difficult process to get a child back once they're in the system.'

He piles a teaspoon with sugar, then tips it back in the bowl. He lifts the cup to his lips, then stops short of sipping, puts the cup carefully back into its saucer.

'Are you paid to say stuff like that?'

Above my head is another sort of balloon. I sit back in my chair, slumped and heavy. No point in engaging with any of that.

He picks up a napkin and folds and unfolds and folds.

'Sonya, I only wish you all the best with everything, I hope you know that.' He stands up, pushes his chair away from the table.

And before I have time to think of something to say, he's gone.

The sight of a back again. I think of all the times when my father turned away. The turning away when my mother died and I was only eight; when I was a hormonal, grieving teenager, crying my heart out over my first lost love; when I was off to London to pursue my dreams; and then, back in Dublin, when I was most likely mired in post-natal depression. Has the sight of my father's back set up some kind of psychic imprint? Every man I've tried to love since has turned away too.

The boy is standing at the counter, staring straight at me, smirking, before he too turns his back. I squeeze my eyes shut. Behind my lids a kaleidoscope of various shades and patterns of darkness play out. The creatures stir and rouse themselves, a kinetic force of nature, a flock programmed to fly thousands of miles, even in inclement weather, even if they might be flying to their death. My eyes open just as my mouth does. This shouldn't happen, not while I'm sober, and not in front of this angry, wretched boy. It's all I can do to witness the stream of abuse I hurl at the world, the boy, who turns and observes me in a detached manner, as if he's watching a play, and maybe he is, and I'm entirely taken over by the character I'm playing.

23

Sometime after my white-out (I've no idea how much time has passed), I find myself sitting in front of Sister Anne in her office, sipping tea heaped with sugar. The nun is playing with her hands, seemingly fascinated by them. 'How do you feel now, Sonya?'

I look out the window at the squiggles of rain that hit the glass, little translucent worms, and think of Simon the torturer, my childhood neighbour who used to dangle earthworms in front of my face until I'd cry – for the poor worm. I draw my attention back to the room. Is Sister Anne scared of me? The way she's sitting, tensed, at the edge of her seat, ready to bolt, suggests she is.

'We have seen this kind of behaviour before. Usually in men with violent tendencies. When they can't use their fists, their tongues will have to do.'

'I have never hit anyone.' I feel my colour rising, my hand starting to itch.

'Have you ever lost control like that around Tommy?'

'No, no, never with Tommy.'

'How can you be so sure? You're not in control of yourself when rage takes over, or when you're under the influence of alcohol, surely?'

'Sister, it's because I'm away from my boy that I feel this angry. It's like part of me has been cut away.'

'What about your blackouts?'

'Blood-sugar levels dropping.'

'Or perhaps it's a way of the mind shutting down when things get too much?'

Perhaps, but I just need to learn to control myself. I thought I'd be better able to do this now I'm not drinking, but then the booze, alongside being an aggravator, is also an anaesthetic. There it goes, my mind: tossing up plausible reasons, intellectualising, interpreting, excusing, justifying.

'Sonya, that was a very serious incident.'

How weird that my school principal said these exact words, just before I was expelled, when I eventually reacted to the bitches ignoring me and lashed out at the puniest of them, a fury of fists and feet. My father was called. *Unacceptable behaviour.* He agreed, of course, didn't even ask to hear my side. A director wrangled this story out of me when I was trying to access a heightened state during rehearsals for my strung-out modern Nora in *A Doll's House.* How pleased he was, rubbing his hands, a parody of glee. 'A real-life rebel!' Somehow, in this life, this reality, I've found myself cast as a mother, and I'm terrible. That casting director was right – what did she say exactly? 'Too angular and febrile.' *Too something, alright.*

'Sister, I'm sorry. It won't happen again.'

Sister Anne nibbles on the corner of her biscuit. 'We have strict guidelines we have to adhere to, Sonya. You know this.'

Seems pretty unlikely that no one else in here has lost it on occasion. Sister Anne gets up and moves to the window. She looks out, seeking something in the patterns of the rain, some guidance from the Man Above. Her lips are moving, muttering a silent prayer.

'Sonya, some part of me believes in you, your capacity for change.'

I'm flooded by relief and a desire to go and hug the nun's small, compact body. These urges – they're not normal, are they? I resolve to question every impulse before I act, to never pay heed to the strong inner prompts.

'Thank you, Sister. I won't let you down.'

'Can you promise me something, Sonya?'

'Yes, Sister?'

'That you try to be more gentle. Eat more, breathe more, soften yourself. Loosen and soften. It's the only way the spirit can get in.'

Loosen, soften: such strange words for a nun.

'And Sonya?'

'Yes, Sister?'

'Try simple prayer. Start with a "Please help".'

I look at her, willing her to provide more guidance.

'This is an official warning.'

'Yes, Sister. Thank you, Sister.'

That feels like a prayer: Thank you.

'You may go, Sonya…'

Please help, please help, I incant over and over as I walk down the dimly lit yellow-stained corridor, where the lingering smell of traces of smoke transports me: a woman with high colouring, fine blonde hair like mine, cigarette dangling between her lips, 'Dance, sweetheart, dance,' her eyes narrowed into slits, her lipstick bleeding, make-up flaked and peeling. Mother Mary, Mother of God… Mary, Mary, quite contrary. My father's voice: 'Christ. Leave the girl alone, can't you? Let her sleep.' A sensation of spinning, of being held high and jiggled, stardust falling, off-pitch singing in my ear.

24

Sipping my tea in the cafe, I'm relieved to see the boy isn't there today. 'Has he left already?' I ask the girl who serves me. 'That fella? Gone. Just walked, thank fuck.' I stare at the mildewed, splotched windows, trying to divine a sequence and meaning that isn't there. What will happen when I finish here? Do I get a certificate of completion, a licence to be a sober, fully functioning mother? The marks on the window start to swirl.

The tea is scalding and I swallow, barely registering the burning sensation on my tongue. I clamp my hands tight around the thin enamel mug, feel mild pleasure. I wonder if they'll blister.

'Hello, Sonya.' David Smythe's voice registers in my left ear. 'Looking very serene, sitting there in contemplation.'

Did he just say 'serene'? Amazing that gap between how someone looks and what's really going on, something I've learned so much about since coming here.

'Not too long to go now,' he says.

'Ten days.'

'Congratulations. That's quite a feat.'

'Thanks for agreeing to see me again.'

'That's ok, though I don't have much time.'

I wish he hadn't said that.

'How are you?'

'Tommy didn't come again this Sunday.'

'I asked about *you*.'

I look at him as if he's stupid. He gets this.

'Your father has to follow the guidelines.'

'He's his grandfather. He promised me he'd look after him.'

'It was a big ask to expect him to look after a four-year-old.'

'I didn't ask. He insisted I come here.'

My father complex is a hugely unattractive side of me, pointed out by Howard enough times: 'Grow up, Sonya. Not all Daddy's fault,' or some variation of this.

'I know how disappointing it is to feel let down by the people we love.'

This is so much less harsh than a Howard-swipe, yet it lands. A thump to my windpipe.

'Fancy a walk?'

I nod.

On our way down the corridor, I stop at the dispensing machine. 'Think I'll get a Coke. Feel like something fizzy today.'

'That shit affects the body's enzymes, pushes the brain into over-drive.' He sounds so patronising.

I drop the coins in, loudly. First time I've ever done this: a new departure! David pushes the front door open, holds it for me. The light outside is grey, flat. I shake the can up and down a few times before I pull back the ring, the pressure inside exploding, foam cascading over the top, spray flying in all directions. I know I should get centred, contact the earth beneath my feet, but sometimes a girl just wants to fly. Must be the bubbles: they always have this effect. A kid's kick. Speed is building up inside me, making me want to run, jump, high-kick, cartwheel, 'Wheee, look at me!' I hear my father's voice telling me to be careful, to stay on terra firma, to stop making a spectacle of myself.

'Don't think you need that stuff,' David says, gesturing to the can.

'Nope, I guess not.'

I run my tongue over my teeth, which are singing.

'Can you tell me what happens when I leave? With regards to Tommy?'

'You'll have to present yourself for assessment, obviously.'

'Any idea of a time frame?'

'Each case is different. They have to see you can maintain your sobriety, that you're not a risk.'

'So, breathalysers, that sort of thing?' I take another gulp of the sticky, gassy liquid.

'I imagine so, yes. They will do everything they can to reunite a child with his mother. Unless the child is deemed at risk, of course.'

How did my father get around needing my permission to have him placed in care?

We stop in front of the grotto. Neither of us genuflect or cross ourselves. He looks at me sideways.

I try it, silently. *Hail Mary, Mother of God, pray for us sinners, now and at the hour of our death...* Not working.

'Anything that helps, I guess,' he says.

'She looks like an old, pissed *Mona Lisa*,' I say.

He laughs, the sound of someone laughing at a funeral. Too loud, all wrong.

'You look well, Sonya.'

Where did that come from? First time he's mentioned anything about my appearance. I regard my clothes: the elbows of my synthetic jumper worn and shiny, my jeans faded and baggy. Maybe he's referring to some 'inner glow' of which I'm unaware. Probably the Coke.

'Thanks. You too.'

'You'll be ok,' he says, looking down.

'Hope so, for Tommy's sake.'

'And yours. Your life is important too, you know, Sonya.'

He looks directly at me for the first time. Eyes a flecked hazel. I thought they were green. I look up: the wispy clouds are gathering into solid shapes, the outline of sheep. *Baa baaa black weep…* Sheep, Tommy! *Yes sir, yes sir…* The sun is obscured, again, obscured.

I try to be casual as I say, 'Ok to continue seeing you the other side?'

'Not in an official capacity, but feel free to check in.'

That feels weirdly transgressive. I wonder how Sister Anne would feel about that. *Not in an official capacity.*

I don't tell him I still have his card in my wallet.

'Sonya, have you figured out your triggers?'

'Yeah, yes, I think so.'

I don't mention Sister Anne's insight into whether my drinking might be related to becoming a mother. What am I meant to do with that, anyway? Can't avoid that one. My mind turns to my own ghost mother, to my smudged memories of her, to the absence of any sense of safety in my recollections.

'Don't isolate. Get to meetings.'

'I imagine that'll be one of the conditions of getting Tommy back.'

'Yes, and that's a good thing.'

My lack of support outside is dizzyingly worrying. Being in here has made me reckon with the scale of the task of trying to navigate parenting solo, sober. Any notion of romance has melted away.

Who will babysit? I look at this man in front of me. How mysterious that our paths crossed the way they did. I tell myself to be careful not to build castles in the air.

'Well, Sonya, I have to go shortly, so all that's left for me to do is wish you the very best of everything.'

That sounds terribly final.

'Thank you. For everything.'

He looks like he wants to say something in return, but he extends a handshake instead. We pump each other's hands, dry, formal, no eye contact. I drop mine first, turn, so I don't have to watch his back retreating, and wave, a little jazzy, frisky one, a final upbeat, defiant gesture of goodbye.

25

I have always hated things ending. Every play that ever ended was experienced as a sort of intense grief. Only seven more nights to go, six, five, four, three, two, one. *Blast off, Yaya!* And then I'd be left alone, without the bright lights to blind me to myself and the clapping that would allow me climb back inside myself, even for a brief, fleeting moment.

Much as I have spent most of the three months resisting my time here, willing it to end, I now find myself clinging to the familiar surroundings, experiencing a surge of maudlin emotion towards my fellow 'inmates', particularly Jimmy. Even though I'd like to convince myself we'll stay in each other's lives after, I know we probably won't. We only fit in this set of circumstances, like a holiday romance who turns up in real life on your doorstep, all false intimacy and *amore*, in the exposing light of daytime.

The closer Sunday creeps, the more terrifying the prospect of leaving becomes. Everything about this place takes on a kind of sepia-toned hue, steeped in longing, a view already filtered through a lens of nostalgia. I want to hold tight to every person I encounter. The bitten inside of my cheek has become a gaping hole, my tongue incessantly prodding and stretching its limits. Every relationship that ever ended, even those I didn't feel meant anything at the time, comes flooding back. Even though it was me that was doing the pushing away, it was rarely what I wanted.

I'm swinging with delirious daydreams of my reunion with Tommy and Herbie one moment, and then smacked in the face with reality – who can even tell me where our beloved Herbie is? I find myself following Sister Anne about, then trying to conceal this fact. The nun regards me with a new level of unease and wariness, or so I think. I think I feel things, then feel things I can't conceive of – I try to hide them in a box and tie them neatly with a ribbon, but the ribbon is satin-slippery, and unravels, and the box opens. Although I don't want to admit it to myself, the cravings have started up again, the whisperings. The closer it comes to leaving, the more my mind fills with an image of my old pal, my soother, my true-blue cure. I really want to knock myself out.

The day of reckoning finally comes. There are three of us leaving today, including Roddy, the guy in the pink pyjamas from the first day. I'm glad to see he has graduated to wearing his tracksuit. He is very loquacious about all he learned this time. His fifth time, he tells the gathering, which is met with a rambunctious round of applause. Christ, how I miss that sound.

Cold, cold, cold. Empty, empty, empty. Terrible, terrible, terrible... Like a captive flung into a deep, empty well, I know not where I am nor what awaits me... I am Chekhov's Nina, bathed in the spotlight, transported, transporting – my performance in *The Seagull* regarded by the critics as 'an absolute triumph'.

This final meeting is meant to be a testament to our shared recovery, to our commitment to continuing the journey together outside. This fostering of codependency is a makeshift raft, leaky and likely to go off course. The two boyos seem hopeful, excited even; they say they are looking forward to the next chapter of their lives, when all I can feel is a fluttering of wings. In spite of this, or maybe because of it, I declaim loudly to my captive audience, spouting the expected terms: gratitude, humility, experience, strength and hope. My words ring out hollow and false. *I am a seagull – no – no, I am an actress... I never knew what to do with my hands, and I could not walk properly or control my voice...*

Sister Anne is watching me closely. I think she sees.

'Ok, young one?'

Jimmy is standing in front of me, his arms outstretched. I move into his circling arms, head pressed against his chest.

'Now, we have one last goodbye.'

'Not sure I'm able.'

'What about the promise you made to your little boy? The little tabby?'

'Don't think so, not right now.'

'No more broken promises, Sonya.'

'We'll come get her another time.'

'By then it might be too late. She'll be wild. You have to do this, for your boy. Good for you to have a little creature on the outside. It won't be easy, the first few weeks...'

He takes me by the hand, gripping it firmly. I feel Sister Anne's eyes following us. We leave via the front door and the receptionist is someone I've never seen before. I wonder where Ms Bookworm is. I hope she's living her life.

'Nice day, all the same,' Jimmy says, for something to say.

And it is. A November-fest of reds, ambers, rusts. The leaves are golden in this light.

The guys are standing outside the shed, smoking, their grey faces lifted towards the sun like withered plants. Jimmy goes inside and I follow, my eyes struggling to adjust to the gloom.

'There she is, hiding, under the bench.'

'Ah no, Jimmy. This is far too traumatic for her. Leave her with her tribe.'

'You'll give her a great life. She'll have a new family, settle in in no time.'

The tabby is lifted by the scruff of her neck, squealing and clawing at the air.

'Here…' He thrusts the kitten at me; I hold her against my heart. 'Ok, little one. We're going to take very good care of you.' The cat seems to relax in my arms, purr a little.

Something seems to have shifted in the cat's bearing, much as it has in mine.

'Remember, Sonya, breathe, pause, practise patience. *Patience* is where it's at.'

'Sonya Moriarty to reception, Sonya Moriarty.' My name is called on the tannoy, well articulated by the new girl, who sounds like she's had speech and drama lessons. I should set her straight.

'Someone here to collect you, then. That's good,' Jimmy says. 'I'm going to say my byes here… Go on, now, get. And remember to eat, and feed that little girl, will ya?' I go to kiss him on the cheek, but he moves away. 'See you around so.' He's on the ground, head stuck under a bench, inspecting the remaining kittens.

'Bye, Jimmy, and thanks.'

He grunts.

I move slowly across the grounds, feeling as if I'm pushing against an invisible weight. Drag my trainers along the concrete, scuffing them, like Tommy.

My father's sitting on the bench inside the front door, his face hidden behind a copy of the *Irish Times*. I watch him, the receptionist watching me, before the paper twitches and lowers. 'Hello, Sonya' – as if this were just a normal, everyday occurrence, as if he saw his daughter every Sunday for a brunch and catch-up. 'You look good.' He stands. 'Where are your bags?'

I gesture to my one half-empty suitcase, memories of that morning hurtling back when I'd had no time to pack.

'What's this?' he says, taking in the bundle of fur.

'This is Marmie.'

'Well, aren't you going to put it back with its mother?'

'She's coming with me. A new addition to the family!'

I recognise that suppressed eye-roll, that swallowed sigh. He holds himself in check, lifts my suitcase, turns and walks stiffly towards the car.

'Off home now, Sonya?' Sister Anne's voice behind me.

'Yes. Thank you, Sister – for everything.'

So many thank yous. Since when did I become so *grateful*?

The nun looks at me and the kitten. 'Take good care, now. I'll pray for you and the little creature and Tommy.'

I look towards the ceiling. The better actresses are those that don't cry; those that fight the tears.

'Well, then.' Sister Anne extends her hand and encircles my free one.

'Well, then.' I bite on my cheek. I want my hand back.

'Don't want to keep your father waiting, Sonya. Go easy on him, now.'

I nod, turn.

'And you,' she says to my back. 'Go easy on you, Sonya.'

Don't look back, don't look back, a display of emotion might follow, and I can't let that happen in front of my father. I look down at Marmie's sweet, bewildered face and kiss her on her button nose. 'Don't worry, baby. I'll look after you,' I whisper as much to myself as to the cat.

As I follow my father's stooped back through the cars, I see a figure moving towards us, waving. I watch my father appraising the clothes, the bearing of the man, as he comes into focus.

'Sorry I missed your leaving ceremony, Sonya. I meant to make it. Terrible traffic on the N9. An accident or something.'

'I wasn't expecting you.'

'I didn't want you coming out alone. I know how vulnerable this time can be.'

Something like real gratitude lands, a spreading warmth in my chest.

He turns to my father, extends his hand. 'David Smythe.'

'My counsellor,' I say.

David looks in my direction.

'Well, sort of,' I say.

'Duncan Moriarty,' my father says, ignoring my last statement, looking intensely relieved. This man presents in the right package.

'What's that?' David asks, taking in the little creature in my arms.

'That's Marmie, my new kitten.'

'What about the big dog? Won't he savage her?' He's trying on a jokey tone, although the mention of Herbie makes my father stiffen.

'Herbie is the biggest softie that ever padded this planet!' I say. 'Can we go pick him up now, Dad?' I'm trying to keep my voice

160

light. If he treated my son so carelessly, or in his view *carefully*, then what would he do with a big shaggy dog?

A taut silence ensues, which David punctures by saying: 'Probably best to settle in the little kitten on her own first. Don't want to expose her to too many new things too soon.'

I can feel myself float above myself, surveying the scene from a safe distance, allowing for perspective. Don your cape and fly the fuck away. Is this recovery in action? My old version would've flown into a white rage at this point, lost all ability to focus on the bigger objective of the scene: to get my boys back.

'Good idea. Marmie and I will go home and settle in together first.' Allowing my father to untangle from the hook.

David offers his hand. 'A pleasure to meet you, Mr Smythe.'

Is that his business card Father is slipping to him? They shake on it. Jesus. Wept.

'Sonya. You know where to find me.' David nods at me, keeping a professional distance. I don't watch him leave.

My father breathes out, as if his body has been hostage to a held-breath dread. He holds the car door open. I climb inside, settling Marmie's purring warmth on my lap, and press my cheek against the cold window. Close my eyes, wait until I feel my father is seated and hear the click of the belt buckle, before I speak: 'I'm grateful to you for coming, Dad. Means the world to me.'

Those words are both insincere and the truest thing I've ever said.

26

My father drives deliriously slowly. He's being beeped by drivers behind us and I wonder was it this bad on our outward journey – or was I just so off my head I didn't notice? His hands are gripping the steering wheel, his body bent close to it, allowing him to peer myopically through the windscreen, a sheen of sweat on his forehead.

'Did you forget your glasses, Dad?'

He doesn't answer. I shift my head at an angle that allows him to be observed without him realising. His skin is mottled grey and red, spots of high colour on his cheeks, a raised dark stain of pigmentation on his forehead, disappearing under his receding hairline into his scalp. I wonder at the circumference of the thing. Has he had it checked? His large frame seems diminished by his hunched posture, his hands suddenly an elderly person's hands: brown-splotched, high-veined, knuckles protruding. A blast of one of Mahler's symphonies in a minor key. My thoughts are suitably pitched: how much of Tommy's growing have I missed? Has he lost all his miraculous toddler pudge?

The drive back home is stretched and strained and the view is shit ugly: long expanses of three-lane motorways, both directions, flanked by industrial warehouses selling electrical appliances and second-hand cars, giant traffic lights looming overhead, pointing in seemingly endless different directions. All I want to do is run back to Sister Anne and beg to be reinstated in my nylon bedroom.

It doesn't help that my father seems as bewildered as I am. For once we share the same fogged-up outlook. The grey sky starts to spit. The kitten meows, her little body tense, as if she might pounce.

'Shut that thing up,' my father snaps. 'Having a hard enough time concentrating here as it is.'

'I'm trying my best,' I say, sounding pathetic to my own ears. I try to soothe the distressed kitten by holding her close to my beating heart. *Boom boom boom, Yaya.*

My father turns Lyric FM up even higher and a modern, discordant tune fills the spaces in the car, climbing inside me, aggravating my restless, slumbering creatures.

'Dad, that's dreadful,' I say as I reach across to turn down the dial.

He doesn't disagree, just lets the silence ring out, until the kitten's bleating interrupts.

'I hope that thing will be ok,' he says. 'I hope you know what you're doing, Sonya.'

Soon the car is cruising, or doddering, alongside the canal-bank path that leads directly to the stretch of Sandymount Strand closest to home. The view opens up to include huge numbers of city swans, gliding proprietarily over the oily black slick of the canal. For a moment, there is white. *Stop them, Yaya, they're hurting her.* The incident at the duck pond flashes in my mind. The cat jumps free of my grasp and throws itself at the window, hissing.

'Fuck's sake, Sonya.'

Did my father just curse? A first. And all it took was a kitten and a gaggle of swans.

'Sorry, Dad.' Another first. 'I have her now.'

At the top of the road we turn right, and the slate-grey body of water reveals itself. The canal becomes the edge of the sea. I long to roll down the window and inhale the salty air but think better of it with the bucking bundle between my palms. The sea is flat and serene, the sky too, as they merge and blur into one. A ten-minute drive along the seafront, then a turn to the right, to the left, to the left.

'Here we are, Sonya,' he says as we pull up outside the shocking-pink door. 'Must be nice to be home.'

Home. He lifts my case from the boot and opens the front door with his own key. Inside everything is shining, clean and ordered, smelling of polish and bleach and camphor. 'We had to blitz. There was a bit of a moth problem when you were away.' What a sickening picture: dark flying particles of dust alighting on my life. I place the wriggling kitten on the carpet, where she proceeds to piddle immediately. I lift her, trailing pee through the living room and kitchen as I struggle to open the back door.

'Maybe should've put it outside first. Semi-feral, by the looks of things.'

I check the parameters of the yard. Is it a safe, enclosed space? I didn't have to worry about Herbie as he never ventured more than a pace behind Tommy.

Father has turned on the kettle, taken down two tea bags, two mugs, and goes to pour milk in mine. I hold a hand up. No milk in this house. Shit, I can't put the kitten's health in peril because of my personal beliefs. What about Tommy? Maybe Mrs O'Malley was right; maybe I did put him at risk of rickets because of my own skewed relationship with food. Anxiety mounts, the whispers start. That fucking fridge. I think of one of Sister Anne's nuggets: 'Contemplative eating and drinking. A way to interrupt the mind-less devouring mentality of the addict.' Cradling the cup of tea in my hands, I consider the shifting liquid, the way it slides up the sides of the enamel and down my throat, the aroma, the texture, all its own thing.

'You look well, Sonya.'

'Thanks.'

I watch the kitten running in circles, sniffing, pawing the ground. This is good, this sitting with my father, sipping tea, a frolicking kitten in the kitchen. Maybe 'good' is all I need.

'Right, Sonya, better get going…'

Of course this moment was coming. I gather my reserves of strength and dignity and say, 'Sure.'

'We brought in all the basics, except cat food. Didn't reckon on that one.'

Who's this 'we'? Mrs O'Malley, or Lara? Neither option fills me with much pleasure.

'Thanks, Dad. Chat tomorrow?'

He lifts his heavy grey overcoat from the back of the chair, lumbers towards the door, one hand pushing into the sleeve, the other dangling awkwardly.

'You going to be ok?' he says.

I nod; a trooper. Just as he's turning to go, he hands me a card. 'Tommy's social worker's number. Maureen Brennan. She's expect-ing a call from you in the morning.'

'Thanks.' Then I ask in as casual a tone as possible, 'Do you have the contact details for the one who's actively minding Tommy?

Clare, or something? She might be very glad to hear from me. He could be being a handful.'

'Sonya, that's not how this works. This Maureen Brennan is your contact.'

The torture of having to get through a night here without either Tommy or Herbie.

My father kisses me lightly on the cheek. 'You did it, daughter.'

We are both surprised by these words and the surge of moisture in his eyes. Emotion has finally caught up with him, taken residence inside him – I wonder if this is a sign of him getting old.

'Talk to you tomorrow.'

And he is gone, the door shut firmly behind him.

27

I look around the recently scrubbed cottage, take in the biro marks on the walls, the spills on the once-cream carpets. I walk into the bedroom, the kitten following; settle her on the bed beside me and get out my phone, still plenty of data available on my last top-up, seeing as it hasn't been used in three months. Tap in the words 'Dublin pounds and rescue centres' and spend the next hour calling each one in turn.

'A big shaggy black carpet of a dog, all sorts, huge tail, long sloppy ears, beautiful eyes, you'd know him if you met him,' I say to one young woman who sounds like she's smoking, chewing gum and painting her nails all at once.

'Nah. Sorry. Nothing of that description in here.'

'What about three months ago?'

'Well, if it was that long ago, he'd be gone by now, missus. Either rehomed, or sent to a rescue, or euthanised.'

I throw the phone down. I'm going to have to ask my father directly, though I want to avoid having that conversation as much as he does. I lie on my side, curled in on myself, my nose touching the tip of the cat's. Rest my hand on her fur and close my eyes, imagine Herbie and Tommy snuggled up against me. *Breathe in, out, in, out, Yaya, it's safe to go to Nod with me and Herbie here.*

Sometime later I wake to the sensation of a sandpaper tongue licking my cheek. I open my eyes and see two dark pools staring at me. 'Ok, kitty.' Push myself to sitting, check the time on my mobile: ten past five and already pitch-black outside. My stomach's rumbling, so I head into the kitchen, pour a saucer of milk for Marmie, pushing aside the crowding images, and open a tin of beans. Eggs? The carton says 'Free range' – but are they really, or are the birds kept their entire lives in cages in cramped agony? At least my chickens got to run around and see the sky. The soft gooey centre of a boiled, poached or fried egg – which? Too much choice. Anxious whirrings start up; I've lost the ability to make decisions, having been institutionalised for too long. I eventually settle on fried, but when I serve them I can't stop fixating on the rheumy white encasement. I scrape the eggs into a bowl for Marmie. Having lost all appetite, I stare into the fridge at the yogurts and cheese, and that one glaringly empty shelf. *Please help.* I look upwards. All I can hear are the echoing whispers. I imagine the sensation of being stroked, soothed, emptied out, blissed-out.

You can have MiWadi like me, Yaya. It doesn't make you go all flop or your voice all gooey.

I turn on the TV: its flickering images, its disconnected voices, its bodies with their ridiculous posturing, its too-bright colours, its tinny sounds climb inside me, setting up a jarring jangle. Turn off the racket, place my hand on my heart, feel the crazed flight, pray. *Help, please help, Mother Mary, help.* Nothing. Grab my keys, bag and Marmie, wrapped in Herbie's blanket, and open the front door, rage assailing me at the sight of my treacherous neighbour's front door – I'm going to have to learn to look the other way.

I sit in my car for the first time in over three months. The engine starts, the kitten mewls, I step down on the accelerator.

There's an hour to kill before the meeting in the church hall closest to my house. Sister Anne printed out a list of local meetings and folded them into my pocket before I left. 'Not optional, Sonya,' she said. I drive hard and fast, summoning up Roberto, foot to the floor, the engine's roars blocking out Marmie's bleating. At the seafront I pull to a jolting stop, get out, pick the kitten off the back seat and make a sling for her out of the blanket. I pull my shoes off and run on to the cold damp sand, my feet losing themselves in the soft suck of the sea foam. Exhilarating, wind in my face, sea spitting, cat's claws scraping. My face must be red-welted. 'Ok, kitty, ok.'

I run until it feels as if my insides are coming up and out, snot is streaming, breath caught high in my ribcage. Stop abruptly, sit, and Marmie jumps loose, running in distracted circles. I lie on my back, make angel shapes in the sand. The kitten comes to sit on my chest and settles there. Watch the clouds shape-shift above my head and raise my arms to orchestrate their movement. *Let's sweep away the clouds, Yaya, and find Mr Sunshine!* I angle my face towards the concentration of light, eyelids close and dots spin. I sit up, holding the kitten lightly. 'Come on, sweetie. Time for my medication.' Drag myself reluctantly towards the car, and this time drive at a reasonable speed back towards the local church hall.

I walk in, ten minutes late, and position myself at the back, Marmie squirming in her makeshift pouch. The woman to my right leans in and smiles. 'Adorable.' The man to my left makes a disgusted face, stands, scrapes his chair loudly, muttering. Necks crane, faces turn, expressions holding the full spectrum of human outrage and delight. I'm doing it again, *making a holy show of myself* – a Lara favourite that prompted one of two responses: a desire to run and hide, or to make a further spectacle of myself on stage. The whisperings intensify. They're not saying anything distinct, just a soft susurration, like a snake charmer, hypnotic and powerful.

'The worst times for me are the evenings, when the ache kicks in. Typical empty-nest syndrome. Since James left, it is, quite simply, agony. I don't honestly know if I would be here if I didn't have these rooms to come to.'

The woman is in her sixties, white hair in an immaculate chignon, black polo-neck, tailored trousers, small studded diamonds in her earlobes.

I catch her eye and am greeted by an open smile.

'What's the kitten's tipple?'

The room laughs and a warmth seeps in. Permission granted.

'She's partial to the Pinot Grigio.'

Uproar, hilarity, grown men and women weeping with laughter. Nothing in moderation in this room.

'Welcome,' the elegant speaker continues. 'That white witch in a bottle casts a very strong spell. She's a hard bitch to escape, clad as she is in all her finery.'

I have a flash of the two of us, sipping a chilled, crisp, dry beauty with hints of elderflower and lemongrass, in the woman's pristine white marbled kitchen with views on to the conservatory and lawn.

The meeting closes, a cup of tea materialises, Marietta biscuits and general pleasantries are bantered about. The woman stirs an ancient memory in me. Something about her scent, notes of mouthwash and rosewater, and the timbre of her voice, saccharine-sweet, yet containing within it its opposite. She offers me her card: 'Jean Cullivan, piano teacher and masseuse.'

'Call me any time,' she offers after hearing that I have just been released from a rehab facility. 'But then, I'm sure you've been given a list of numbers your arm's length.'

The only number I have is David's and I don't want to call him too soon. I could call the communal phone in the hall, but think of the endless queues.

'Not really, no.'

'I never understand how they let people out of those places with no proper supports in place.'

'They don't have the resources, I guess,' I say.

'This fucking government,' Jean says politely. 'Fucking shower of crooks.'

'Nothing to do with the government, actually. The place I was in was run by a religious charity.'

'Well, exactly. My point exactly. My commiserations, by the way.'

I smile, with no thought of the desired effect. 'Actually, the old bats weren't so bad.'

'God, you'd have to drag me to a place like that kicking and screaming.'

Feel heat rise to my cheeks, ashamed and inflamed. 'I didn't exactly have a choice.'

'We always have choices, dear. To think otherwise creates victimhood.'

No point in explaining any of it. I'm back in the real world and this is how it rubs up against me. Just another bossy, intrusive older woman, with her judgements. Would my own mother have been as disappointed in me? 'Better get the little mite home. Thank you for the number.'

'You're welcome. Call any time, I mean it.'

This invitation sounds more like a command and I feel my body stiffen and shut down. 'Kind of you, thank you.' Manage to avoid any of the obligatory hugs, the kitten a shield.

'Tend to that little yoke as you would your inner child,' a discombobulated voice shouts out after me.

And that was supposed to make me feel connected, to loosen the shackles of 'self', to interrupt the patterning that used to drive me to stealing and glugging, to help calm the voices, counteract the frantic urges.

28

I settle myself into the driving seat, Marmie on my lap, and turn the key in the ignition, allowing the thrum of the engine to vibrate through me. Imagine Roberto snaking his hand up my thigh, his fingers opening me up as he drove at full throttle. My driving is chaotic and aimless, the void in my stomach creating a dizzy, edgy sensation. Must get the kitten something to eat. Pull the car to a stop outside the sliding door to Tesco, park in a disabled spot, hear Marmie's squeals as I run. The lights are too bright, the trolleys too shiny and sharp, the shoppers too pale and pasty, too fat, their scent too chemical, the muzak too ugly, too artificial, the aisles too stocked, the world is Too.

I find myself in the booze aisle, but not before I've managed to find the cat food, fish fingers. Progress. Feel a tug at my hair shaft; haven't felt that in a while. I sense rather than see my imp. She's there alright, trying to bust through. The guys in rehab who relapsed said it usually happened in week two or three, when a certain confidence kicked in, a lowering of the guard, which led to them believe the burbling voices: Just the one, can't do any harm, will never go back there, no siree, can handle it this time… I've never heard of anyone going straight back on the batter. But then maybe no one would admit to that. The Shame. Fingers rake through my scalp, a tightening, a constricting, vision tunnelling, perception narrowing to a single end point.

My heart is pounding so loudly I'm sure others can hear it. Run to the car, drive it to a dark corner, open my bag: a motley assortment. Not sure whether I paid or not, the moment foggy in my mind. Unscrew the top of bottle numero uno – a feminine, jaunty little number – sniff, tentatively sip, inhale: sharp and sweet, citrus and candyfloss. Funny how little resistance there is, how my mind is not at war. All forces are galvanised towards the moment, all troops employed. A directive – steady and clear. No tormented decision-making process, just pure clarity, pure seeing. Sipping, delicately sipping, supping of my nectar, tracking my flight from heart to honeyed heart, from Tommy to Herbie to Marmie. I lift the little girl and kiss her on her precious button nose.

The car drives itself home. Now it's taking on the contours of the place I left: hazy and soft. I float up the path. Key slides in the door, well oiled and pink, I'd forgotten how pink – a bright tap-dancing fuchsia. And there She is, in her full technicolour glory. No ignoring her now. A thrumming music in the air. Manage to carry all the bags, the three full remaining bottles, into the kitchen, the kitty rubbing my ankles, her purring mingling with the gentle piano chords. Limbs like syrup, mind sedated, creatures doused, unable to stir.

The kitten's mewling intensifies. *Greedy guts, Yaya, feed Marmie!* I fork Whiskas into her bowl, which is emptied, filled, emptied, filled, the same number of times as my glass. How much can the little one's tummy hold – and mine? Swells, with the music. Crescendos. Am I sated yet? Numb, yes, emptied out. I get it now, that expression the guys used: wiped. I'm wiped, I've wiped all semblance of myself off the planet.

The wave crashes over me and I let myself be tumbled, swallowing gulpfuls of the sea. What is it, Tommy, what do you see? Is it that seagull? *The colour of ice cream*, he says, licking his lips, my lips, my cheeks. Come here, Tommy, come here. I reach out and press his body close, too close. He wriggles free, like a little sprite – like everyone in my life, he manages to escape my fierce, needy grasp.

I wake to a tiny bleating sound. 'Ok, little kitty, ok.' The kitten is trapped behind the fridge. I can see Jimmy's horrified face staring at me. Jesus wept.

'I know, I know, but I told you I wasn't up to this.'

I stand gingerly and reach in to free the cat, wavy lines dancing in front of my eyes. *Selfish, selfish, selfish, selfish, selfish, selfish, selfish, monstrous, selfish.* Tommy's anxious eyes following me. What was that? Weakness, greed, testing, obliteration, giving up, giving in, madness, indulgence? Think back to the moment of 'choice', the moment of choosing to buy the booze, and all I can recall is an out-of-body sensation: giddy and high. Blackout before the booze, now there's one I haven't heard before. *Bullshit, Sonya, excuses, excuses.* Awful how sudden and sober and acute the thoughts that come are. How long have I set myself back with Tommy? How long before I can be breathalysed, give a sample or whatever I'll be expected to do?

There they are: three empty bottles winking at me. The fourth stands proudly, defiantly, chest puffed – a dare. I smash it against the inside enamel of the sink; it splinters into shards and cuts into the centre of my palm. Turn on the tap and stick my hand under it, watch the water running pink. I try to sip a glass of water, hoping to rehydrate my scratchy eyes and extinguish the fire in my gut. Most of it comes back up. This is just perfect. A beautiful homecoming.

The rest of the day is spent in 'recovery' mode, resting and attempting to swallow mouthfuls of food. Somehow I manage to short-circuit the cow's milk thing and eat two of the yogurts my father left for me. Both my head and my cut hand are throbbing. I periodically open the back door for Marmie, terrified for her. I don't remember feeling this level of panic around Herbie, or even Tommy, as a baby. There was always the sense that both of them could look out for themselves, and to an extent for me.

By day two after my 'slip' – a sly word, a liar of a word – I'm right-minded enough to attempt to make some calls. Find the number my father gave me.

'We were expecting you to ring two days ago. We were worried.'

'Sorry. I wasn't feeling too well.'

'Are you better now?'

I can hear the edge in the woman's voice. She'll have heard all the excuses, and then some. I decide against further explanation; it'll only dig me in deeper.

'Yes. Thanks. When can I see Tommy?'

'My diary is full up until Friday. When I didn't hear from you...'

No arguing with that. Probably for the best. If I keep flushing out my system, I should be totally alcohol-free by Friday. Two more days. My commitment was to never get drunk around my child again. I haven't broken that vow. And I won't.

My phone is hot in my hands. I dial David Smythe's number. He doesn't sound surprised to hear from me. We arrange to meet later for a walk in the park.

29

The day is cool enough for a coat and hat, a crisp November day. I strap Marmie to me, inside my good camel overcoat, a throwback to my former glory years. He's sitting on the bench by the bandstand when I arrive, two cups from Insomnia in his hands, a layer of froth above his upper lip. What is it about the shape of his mouth?

'Still drinking tea?' he asks, extending the cup towards me.

'Thanks. Properly addicted now.' I sit myself beside him, Marmie squirming and purring.

'I see you brought the kitten.'

'Don't know what to do with her. She cries if I'm even in the next room. Such a needy little thing.'

'You sure this is what you need right now?'

'She's for Tommy. I promised.'

We sit in silence as I reach in to release Marmie and lay her on my lap. He scratches her tummy. 'Cute.' I'd like to lean my body against his, rest my head on his shoulder, and crazy as the impulse is, I'm scared of how vulnerable I feel. I move a little closer. 'Cold.' He nods, his body softening, legs splaying, thigh touching mine. I wonder why he agreed to meet but don't want to ask.

'This is the bench I was sitting on the last time,' I say instead, 'when I noticed Tommy running up and down by the edge of the pond, remember I told you?'

'Yes. And you think you blanked out? Something about an old man and a duck attack and hissing swans?'

'That's it. Yes, and I'd put his shoes on the wrong feet. He kept tripping over them and I didn't even bother changing them.'

We both sip our drinks, David absently rubbing the kitten's tummy.

'What did you see that day in the pizza place?'

A blank space opens up between us. He shifts his body infinitesimally away from me. 'Not sure how to answer that, Sonya.'

'Why, was it that ugly?'

'I could read the stress in Tommy.'

I don't know which would have been worse: had he said I looked like a drunken sot, or this, this focus on Tommy's distress. I remove the top of the cup and contemplate the dark depths. Yes, this is worse. The shame creeps across my skin, tingling and biting.

'You could see that Tommy was a stressed little boy?'

'He had these big frightened eyes, and you seemed kind of manic, strung out.'

I cast my mind back. I hadn't eaten in days and I'd had a binge and my boy was starving. Can he see that I'm post-binge now? I don't feel manic, just tired and disappointed and emptied out. And if I'm honest, and if I let it in, the guilt might just undo me. I should have worn my big Jackie O glasses; I'm sure I'm sporting the same dug-out under-eyes my father had in the years following my mother's death, the same hollows my son wears since my abandonment of him. I hope the whites of my eyes are not yellow. What other signs? Amazingly, my hands aren't shaking, although my fingers are periodically twitching. The smell could be reeking off me; it does that, even days after. *Stinky-stink, Yaya!* Tommy used to come into the bedroom with a toothbrush and paste, and a glass of water. Jesus fucking wept.

I check my clothes – anything chaotic there? Odd socks, surely, but they can't be seen. I brushed my hair and fixed my face before leaving, but as my eyesight dims in the days after a blow-out, I probably look like a mad old bat with caked, blobbed mascara and streaky, dried-out foundation. I'm lucky I didn't kill the kitten or set the house on fire.

Imagine Tommy being so scared that a stranger could see it in his face. I think of the woman on the beach and Mrs O'Malley.

'Are you ok, Sonya?'

'Did I smell of it?'

'Booze? I could smell the attempts at disguising it.'

What about now? Can you smell it now? I don't expose myself to this line of questioning.

'Have you made contact with Tommy's social worker?'

'Yes. Meeting her on Friday.'

'That's good. Will give you some time to compose yourself.'

So. What does he see? Has he ever had a 'slip'?

'Have you been to a meeting yet?'

'Walk?' I ask, not wanting to continue where this conversation is headed. I pick up the kitten and place her inside my coat.

'You should get that cat a leash!'

'That's what Tommy said.' I don't know why, but this makes a bubble of happiness swell inside me. We fall into step, circling the pond, no words shared or tossed between us. I have an image of us, in twenty or thirty years, walking like this, my hand in his, or his gently resting at the base of my spine. There's something of the old-fashioned gentleman about him, and this doesn't make me want to toy with him, or run away from him, as I would have in my earlier incarnation. Is this my 'post-recovery' self, one who just had a blip, a sober person who can appreciate the quality of silence, the breeze touching my cheeks, the rustling trees, the ripples in the water, the sleeping ducks bobbing peacefully? Today there are no duck attacks, no swans hissing. All is serene, and I don't feel the need to rip the fuck out of the fabric of that peace.

'Have you spoken to your father yet about what he told social services?'

The mention of the words 'social services' immediately leaches any remnants of calm.

'You may need to hire a solicitor.'

Talk about blurring boundaries. Is he angling for a job here? I don't need this right now; what I need is forgetting time. Still too shaky and vulnerable after my bender to be able to grapple with this.

'You've gone very quiet. Hope this isn't too much of a shock to hear. I'd have thought your father would have made you aware of the legal situation and its ramifications.'

Ram your ramifications up your arse. Silently hum the tune to a waltz I danced to in an avant-garde production of *Pride and Prejudice*. Picture myself on set, wearing a corset, a crinoline-style dress, shot silk, pale blue, and suspenders.

'I think the whole middle-class thing will work in your favour.'

This is going to be the hardest acting job ever. All the characters I have played up to now were able to give full vent to their passions and furies. My new character is called Ms Sanity, and Sanity has to hide her truth at all costs, Sanity has to smile and suppress, Sanity has to present a neatly packaged front to the world. My audience would no doubt be bored of Ms Sanity within minutes.

30

'Dad?'

'Sonya, it's very early.' His tongue sounds thick with tiredness.

'Sorry. Can't sleep. Need to know which pound you put Herbie into.'

'Wait a minute, can you?'

I hear him rustling about, careful not to wake Lara beside him. Sound of his footsteps padding downstairs, then the tap gushing.

'What did you say, Sonya? Are you aware it's not even six a.m.?'

'It's my new regime. Where did you leave Herbie?'

'A decent sort I know from golf took him in.'

'Can you give me his number?'

'I thought you'd be glad that the dog has found stability.'

'Dad. Please give me this man's number. I need to get Herbie back.'

He whistles through his teeth. 'Have you been drinking, Sonya? You sound wired.'

'I'm not going to even dignify that with a response. The number, Dad?'

'Let me call him later, at a reasonable hour, and see what he has to say.'

'Dad?' I can feel a hot fiery FUCK YOU forming in my mouth, but I suck it back down and say sweetly, 'You're the best.'

He grunts, sips his recently poured brew and says, 'I'll call you after I've managed to make contact.'

'It will be so good for Tommy to have his best pal at home, when he returns.'

'I'm not promising anything…'

'I know you'll do your best. For Tommy. Thank you. Chat later?' I disconnect, congratulate myself on my astounding acting, until I notice the kitten staring at me disconsolately, mewling in the corner.

Tea and toast and marmalade jam, tea and toast and marmalade jam, tea and toast and marmalade jam. *Yummy sunny oranges in a jar, Yaya!* Three rounds, before showering, dressing 'appropriately': contrite sober mother part, over-the-knee skirt and high-necked polo, hair scraped back. The tea makes me piss, which is good. Force glass after glass of water down me, hoping this will be sufficient to clear out any remnants of booze from my system. David calls to wish me luck.

Maureen is a big, buxom woman, though not maternal, as her body would suggest. There's an impenetrable wall around her, a cast-iron casing around her heart. I admire her bullshit-proof bearing, and instinctively know not to lay it on too thick. We exchange a few curt pleasantries before she offers me tea. My fourth of the day so far. The building is surprisingly bright and cheerful, freshly painted with excellent fake plants dotted around. I run my fingers over their leaves to make sure they are not, in fact, the real thing. The air smells of synthetic lavender, gentle background music wafting, not muzak – Satie, I think.

The conversation moves along well-worn tracks: how did you get on in rehab, do you think you're fit to take Tommy back into the house, are you open to home visits? Will you breathe into this for me? The question, when it comes, though expected, is an affront. I nod and blow. I hold my breath as Maureen reads the results. She says nothing, her face remains impassive. I know better than to ask; the story is that I haven't touched a drop since first going into recovery. My pulse thrums loudly in my throat, please, please, please let there be no alcohol left in my system. There's no mention of a court hearing, which has to be good. I tell her that it was my wish that Tommy went to his grandfather – an unfortunate situation, I explain, and rather badly handled on my father's part, as there are no other family members who could've taken him.

'Are relations that strained in your family?'

I think about that. I don't know if I have any cousins; I don't know if Aunty Amy is dead or alive, or indeed Dom. I don't know where Dom is. I hope he's ok.

'My mum died young and I never knew her parents' – the first time I've said that out loud – 'and my mother's only sister didn't get on with my stepmother, and my father stopped talking to my uncle.'

Maureen looks at me in a way I can't read. Does she think I'm a liar, an attention-seeker, an actress?

'So you can see why I felt my father should've taken Tommy.'

'Your father expressed regret that he couldn't manage the boy, but he said he exhibited some behavioural concerns.'

I feign nonchalance. What the hell did he say?

'Do you know about his fascination with fire?'

I think of his face lit up by the flames that night, his enthralment with anything bright and burning. Mr Sunshine, Mr Flickering Fire. Has this built to something more dangerous? Is my little boy a potential arsonist? I almost laugh; he's not yet five. And still.

'I know he likes to look at bright, flickering things. He's like his mother in that way.'

'Did he ever try to set anything on fire before?'

'No. He just liked to watch it.'

'And you let him?'

'Only under supervision.'

'What about when you were blacked-out?'

Maureen's reading from a report. Penned by whom? There is no psychiatric report on me, as far as I am aware.

'I never left Tommy alone in a room with a lighter.'

'Did you teach him to strike a match?'

'No, I don't keep matches in the house.'

Maureen checks her watch, clears the bundles of paper on her desk.

'Did something happen? Did Tommy cause an accident?'

'Nothing serious, Sonya. We can talk more next time, and we'll arrange for a supervised visit next week.'

'Great, yes. Does that mean I can pick him up today?'

'I meant that you can visit him here with me, next week.'

'Oh, I see. So when will he be coming home?'

'That depends on how the next couple of weeks pan out. We need to make sure you're committed to staying sober. You need to work with us on this.'

I find myself nodding furiously. Yes, yes, I understand, yes. Too submissive, not convincing, hollow words ringing out. Maureen has seen it all; I know to check the tears.

31

'They have a great big garden,' Father says of his golf buddy, who, apparently, would be 'devastated' to see the dog go. 'He has settled in very well, Sonya.'

I'd like to ask Herbie what he thinks about that situation, Dad. Not a good move as far as presenting Ms Sanity goes. 'Just let me speak to them.'

He looks trapped, like a well-behaved schoolboy who has been caught smoking behind the school sheds, his one act of rebellion. Lara is bustling about at the kitchen counter, pretending to look busy. You'd think she'd make herself scarce, give father and daughter some time alone together – who am I kidding?

'Can I have their number, Dad?' I can't stay another night under that roof with only my scattergun brain and the bleating kitten for company.

'Not a good idea, Sonya.'

Lara coughs, a code for her man. 'We need to get going for your medical appointment.'

'Yes, yes, that's right, yes.'

Poor, pathetic man.

'A friend from golf, did you say? D'you mean Gerry and Olive? I'll pop in on them on my way home. Not too far out of the way.'

Lara clatters dishes loudly.

'You'll do no such thing,' my father blurts. 'It's not them, anyway.'

'That dog has landed in a great big house,' Lara says as she spritzes and scrubs. 'Ken Dunne, the solicitor. You should be grateful to your father and not hound him like that.'

My father stares at her as she mutters under her breath, 'Don't draw me into this.' She used to love taking that stance, particularly after she'd stirred a dollop of hostility and a sprinkling of venom into whatever row was brewing, and then would sit back to watch me lose it with one of my tantrums.

'Look, Sonya. It's not wise that you go barrelling in there, ok? Trust me. I'll handle this my way.'

'Two days, Dad. Forty-eight hours. That should be plenty of time to get him back. Now, I'd better leave you two to get to your appointment. Nothing serious, I hope?'

'Just a routine check-up.'

'Right so. Thanks for looking after Tommy so well, that day.' I put emphasis on the last two words, so as to give shape to the absence of all the other times.

My father kisses me hastily on my cheek, as if he's guilty of being disloyal.

I step down on the accelerator, the act as much a celebration as a desire to get back to Marmie, whose cries have been filling my ears. Having Herbie back will make all this so much easier. He'll tend to the kitten as well as he did to Tommy. There were occasions, just a few, where I left the two them of alone, when I had to run to the local shop for supplies and couldn't face the fact of leads and buggies.

Marmie is trapped, this time under the settee. I drag the couch away from the wall and as soon as I lift her she relaxes in my hands. I research 'separation anxiety' in puppies and kittens and it nearly kills me the pain they go through when separated from their pack. Need to get the little thing used to the idea of me coming and going, so I try the trick of going out for five minutes, then twenty, then two, then forty. Confuse and reassure. Arrange favourite treats, pieces of cheese, tuna, stuffed inside socks and plastic containers, turn soothing classical music on. I can now leave the room without being greeted by a shivering wreck on my return. Call David, arrange a walk in the park. This time I'll demonstrate how 'normal' I can be by leaving the kitten at home.

32

My overzealous application of perfume, a sweet flowery concoction – perhaps it's gone off? – swirls about me in the wind, gathering in intensity. My lank hair is whipping across my eyes, making them water, my cheeks more red than usual. I have noticed more broken veins on my delicate skin recently, and the application of old, caked foundation does little to tamp down my high colour. I see him, pacing along the edge of the pond, hands deep in his pockets, and have to fight a desire to bolt. My voice, when it makes itself heard, is a bubbling cauldron of unmediated bullshit: 'Hi there, great to see you, windy day, nippy too, kitten home alone, getting Herbie back, cleaned the house in preparation, beyond excited, will he take to the kitten? – hopefully they'll be pals...'

David nods, in amusement or bafflement, I can't tell which.

'Hi, Sonya.' He bends to pick up a conker. 'What a beauty, and I thought the season was over.' He's scrutinising the chestnut. 'Like polished mahogany.'

Is he staring at his reflection in there? I sidle up to him, peer over his shoulder, experience a strange jealousy at the object of his fascination. 'Hmmm, shiny alright.' The strain of playing Ms Sanity is beginning to show, the seams of my character fraying at the edges.

'The kitten is on its way to being trained; doesn't shit now every time I leave the room.' What am I doing? He doesn't respond, just takes out another white starched handkerchief and wraps the conker in it. Does he have a nature table at home? Uncontrollable laughter rises.

'What's so funny, Sonya?'

He regards me from a wary distance, then surprises us both by tickling me in the ribs. I wriggle against him like a little kid. A charge is ignited between us that has nothing to do with being a kid. Inhale him, his signature citrus scent masking salt and sweat.

And just like that, he invites Elation in. My breath is caught high in my ribcage, my body saturated with beats. Frothy wisps of clouds gambol overhead, grass green and shining, drops of rain still clinging to individual blades, trembling. The air shimmers with music.

'You ok?'

What does he see when he looks at me? An overwrought, strung-out woman of a certain age, too thin, ribs jutting through and all lustre gone from her hair. Washed-out blonde. Washed-up actress. I hope I wasn't humming.

'You seem brighter today, Sonya.'

Is that good? Bright, as in happy-bright, up-bright, intelligent-bright, or over-bright?

'Yes. I guess I am.' I shiver, quite dramatically.

'Cold?'

'A bit. Shall we go inside?' I'm careful not to use the words 'home' or 'to my place'.

He doesn't say anything, just walks in tandem beside me, breath hawing in the cold air, as if we were both chasing down some fantastical dragon.

'That's quite a shade of pink!' he says when we reach the front door. I smile. My fingers feel thick and clumsy; the keys drop, he picks them up, our hands touch. The kitten at my ankles, rubbing, purring. How sweet, how achingly sweet. I pick her up, kiss her, go into the yard. He follows me and leans against the door, observing me observing the kitten.

As I move past him to come back inside, my body brushes against his, one breast accidentally pushing against him. He grabs me, presses me against the fridge, its vibrations thrumming through me. He freezes, pulls away. I draw him back. 'It's ok, it's ok, it's ok.'

'Sonya, this is not wise.'

When have I ever done anything because it's *wise*?

'You're not my counsellor, right?'

He considers this a moment. 'Not in an official capacity, but still…'

I want this man in this moment more than I've ever wanted anything.

'I'm a big girl, David. I'm sober and I'm making this choice sober.'

'Very early days, though, Sonya.'

No more talking. I pull him back to me. I wrap my arms around him, and his stiff body softens. We kind of rock like that for a few moments until the tension becomes unbearable. We're no longer fixed versions of ourselves; we're in the process of becoming something else entirely. David's eyes glaze over as he pulls my jumper down over my shoulder and traces his lips over my hot skin. He seems instantly pissed on the moment; all semblance of control gone. His tongue is inside my mouth, tang of metallic, kick of coffee.

I give myself over to the thrill of being afraid. Fear equals adrenalin equals aphrodisiac. Standing up there in the spotlight, all eyes trained on me, all ears tuned in to my words, the spell I would weave, the orgasmic terror.

This is that: close attention being paid to me. I had forgotten the power of that rush. A kind of obliteration. A moment that seems both holy and depraved. I am turned on in a way I haven't been since I was with Roberto in some forbidden place. We shouldn't be doing this. A *forbidden* encounter! How romantic, and how undeniably sexy.

After, somehow having made it to the bed, we lie in each other's arms, drenched in sweat. I know what's coming, the whirring, the back-pedalling, the wishing it had never happened. Neither of us speak. Outside: a clear night sky, like navy velvet shot through with brilliant diamonds. *Take him and cut him out in little stars.* Where are you, my Mister Man? My breath gets stuck high in my throat and I'm scared I'll spill into tears. This is the part I dread, when I feel as if I have vacated myself. I hate this moment of bare-arsed vulnerability.

David falls asleep easily, his face relaxed, his body twitching involuntarily. I lay a hand on his cheekbones, tracing the line of stubble down towards his jawline. Can't bear the feelings this closeness brings. This is something I've always experienced: this post-coital surge of excess emotion, while whatever partner is lying beside me is out cold. I go into the kitchen, fill a saucer of milk for Marmie and lay it in front of her. The little girl laps at the milk with her baby-pink tongue. I am entranced by her intense concentration, her defencelessness.

David sleeps for a solid seven hours, while I pace, watch telly on low. A Mystic Meg rip-off is on, her phone number flashes on screen. I get my phone, dial, and am greeted by an automatic voice to dial in a credit card number. Fake Meg's bland, pretty, young face fills the screen. The casting department got it very wrong – they should've cast a wrinkled hag with searing blue eyes; this one is as inane as a catalogue model. I wonder at the type of person who would pay for an out-of-work actress's advice at 3 a.m.

Fall at some point into some semblance of sleep on the couch; must do, because when I wake he's standing over me.

'Mind if I do?' he says, as he sits beside me, drawing me close.

My body stiffens; I stink, need to stand under a shower, alone, but don't want him not to want to be with me. He pulls my hair back off my face and kisses my cheek. Who is this carefree version of David? It's as if he transferred all his uptightness into me last night – he should be mortified by what just happened. He should be very worried about what he just did.

'Can I make you breakfast?'

I manage a polite 'I'll do it after my shower.'

'Don't bother your pretty head with that.'

What script is he following now? I walk as slowly as I can manage, when every part of me wants to run. As soon as I'm inside the bathroom I lock the door. The shower is as hot and the flow as hard as my skin will allow. I massage my coconut-and-lime Tesco special-offer shampoo into my scalp, a cheap waft of suds permeating my everything.

I cover myself in a big bath towel, scurry to the bedroom, wishing I could lock the door. What to wear? Decide on a demure look: checked shirt and jeans, barefoot, light touch of make-up. He wolf-whistles when I walk into the kitchen. I'm offended, but only slightly, more alarmed than anything. I should have seen it: he has a love/sex-addict thing going on. Isn't this why there are strict guidelines in recovery? The danger of swapping one addiction for another. David has over ten years in sobriety, so he should be able to handle intimacy, although regarding him now, there's no doubt that dopamine, or some other highly addictive feel-good chemical, has been triggered in his brain. His eyes are shining and faraway and it's obvious he's inhabiting some *other* world.

I haven't worked out the exact shape of his fantasy yet but am certain it involves some form of conquest: Fair Maiden. Has he cast himself as a conquering master, hero, servant, slave? I really want him out of my house. The smell of the eggs is making me sick. He serves me a heap of scrambled on soggy toast, lots of pepper. He doesn't even ask, just twists away at the grinder. Everything about him is irritating: his stupid happy whistling, his long skinny legs, the memory of them wrapped around me, almost choking me, his ridiculous smile. I want the old David back, the one I craved to touch, because he was out of bounds.

'Are you ok, Sonya? You're very pale.'

'I'm not hungry, sorry.' I push the plate away. 'Didn't sleep very well… Not great when I don't sleep.' Trying to minimise the chaotic, jangled emotions that are spilling about.

'Would you like me to go now, give you your space?'

'Might be a good idea. Feeling a little overwhelmed.' The most honesty I've managed in years.

'I'll just finish my coffee and eggs, then I'll be on my way.'

My breathing slows down, the tightness in my chest loosens. He eats and drinks at a leisurely pace.

'Ok so, I'll head off. See you soon. Thanks for a lovely evening.' He kisses me gently on both cheeks.

I'm grateful I don't have to force him to leave, as I had to many times with Howard, particularly on those Sundays when he decided he wanted to hang out with me all day. Sometimes I actively had to push him out the front door. 'Fuck off, Howard,' I'd say. 'Psycho,' he'd fling at me. Then, after he'd leave, I'd spend the day feeling bereft.

'You're miles away, Sonya.'

'Sorry. Tired is all.'

'Chat later. Sleep well so.'

He walks jauntily down the garden path, lifting his hand in greeting to someone on the opposite side of the street. When I pull back the slats on the blind, I see that it's Mrs O'Malley. Good, let her think I'm a woman capable of being loved, or a gigantic slut – don't care which, as long as it makes her back off.

'Thank God he's gone, Marmie!' I change the bedclothes, open the window, fill a hot water bottle, creep back into bed, place the bottle at my lower back, Marmie on my chest. My body closes down, a series of internal doors shutting, locking. I reach down and place a protective hand on my crotch. I'm disgusted by what my body allowed. It's not even a religious thing, or a moral thing; I don't know what kind of a thing.

When I wake five hours later my mind is less frantic. I check my phone: four messages from David. Thank you, hope you're ok, call me when you wake, that was amazing you are amazing. We're ok, aren't we? It's as if I've just released a needy, sex-starved Jack right out of his box.

I get up, eat some dry cornflakes by the handful, wrap Marmie in the pouch and walk to the park. The wind is skittish, the sky a mottled feast of blues and whites. Where is Tommy today? Is he out under this same sky? Is he searching for Mr Sunshine, pretending to wipe away the clouds? I watch a seagull swoop on to the pond and scavenge the ducks' bread. A man claps at the air: 'Shooo.' Silly man, can't he see the seagull needs to eat too? *The colour of ice cream, Yaya!* I wonder if my body will allow me to continue to stand.

33

Forty-eight hours have passed, and no word from my father. Of course. Time to take matters into my own hands. Drive to the 'decent sort' from golf's house, solicitor Whatshisface. I memorised his address that night I looked him up, straight after Lara let the word slip.

It's a twenty-minute drive under cover of early-evening darkness. The house materialises like something out of a fairy tale, all fake Gothic turrets, stucco, soft pink. *A pink candyfloss house, Yaya! A* fountain, two BMWs, a dog pen, a kennel. Heat blasts my body, my skin hot and blotchy, as if torched. I'm surprised to find the electric gates open, but park outside, just in case. My hoodie is pulled high over my ears, despite the fact I might combust with the revving of my internal engine. 'Herbie,' I whisper, 'Herbie, my man?' I think I hear whimpers; he'd be a shit guard dog, in spite of his size; he's a big softie, anyone could tell that. Anyone who cared to look closely.

A mixture of anticipation and dread drives my steps across the shiny black tarmac driveway, flanked by fake grass verges. This preposterous house is grotesque in its affectations. I'm standing outside the pen, there it is, the cage I dreamed of, and there he is, his face pressed to the wall.

'Herbie?' He lifts his head, an ear twitches, then he falls back into his tightly curled position, back to the world. 'Herbie, it's me, it's really me.' How am I going to get him out of here? There's a padlock. What kind of people padlock a guard dog into a cage? Then I realise he's probably only ever let out when they go out. What sort of people—?

I sprint back to the car, open the boot and find the secateurs I bought on a whim in a garden-centre sale last year, when I'd had a fantasy about doing something 'normal', like pruning my wild rose bushes. They're still in the bag I bought them in, along with the gardening gloves that I slip on. A delicious thrill shivers through me. Now I'm the character I was never cast as: the badass criminal.

Back at the cage, I falter a moment. Will this backlash on me? Even if it does, this dog is not going through a moment more of suffering because of me. I focus intently on cutting though the wire mesh; I'd use my teeth if I had to. I cut and cut until eventually one section tears and I make a hole. Herbie is whimpering loudly. 'Alright, old boy, it's only me.' He looks straight at me and I'm sucked into a vortex of such sadness I wonder if I'll ever surface again. 'Darling boy.' He stands, legs unsteady, tail involuntarily moving in a jagged circle as if it's forgotten how to wag. I hear voices at the door. The hole is big enough to clamber through and I crouch in the dark beside my boy, his big head suddenly in my lap. I cradle him: 'Shhh.'

Herbie, it's ok, Yaya's back, it really is the real Yaya!

The voices say their thank yous, marvellous round today, adios, adieu, till next time. 'Come on, ole boy.' We need to get out of here before the electric gates lock us in. I try to push Herbie's bulk through the hole but he seems dazed. I go first. 'Come, Herbie.' I pull the edges of the circle and then like some magically trained circus animal he jumps through the hoop and the two of us run towards the car.

Herbie is panicked, his breathing fast and high, his big lolling tongue trying to grab on to the air to cool him down. I should have brought him a bowl of water. Cast my mind back to the pen: was there any food or water? I imagine throwing a firework soaked in kerosene through the letter box, leaving a poo-bomb on the doorstep, scratching the shiny midnight-blue BMW with this year's reg.

'Herbie?' He seems unsure; perhaps this is playing out like a dream, something he's careful not to trust in case he wakes up cold and alone in his cage. Vow to win him back and instinctively know to take it slow. I wind down the back window, even though it's cold and damp, and he sticks his oversized head out, tongue catching the wind.

'Home sweet home,' I say as we drive up to the house. His whole body is shaking. Poor guy. My heart is full to the brim, bobbing about in there like some unmoored, overinflated balloon, likely to burst at any point. I open the back door; he jumps out, sniffing the air. He cocks his leg and widdles on the overgrown tangle that is my front garden.

I open the front door. 'Marmie? I've a friend for you to meet!' The little cat trots out all confident, sees the huge shaggy dog and bolts, Herbie in hot pursuit. Marmie's squeals fill the air. I hadn't thought of Herbie as a cat chaser before now. He wouldn't do anything if he caught her – would he? – unless his months in captivity have changed him. I pick Marmie up from under the couch, sing snatches of lullabies into her ear. The cat is rigid. The phone rings.

'Yes?'

'Hi, can I bring you over a takeaway?'

His voice, all warm and familiar. I can feel the old creeping coldness.

'Busy later. Thanks, though.'

'Really? Doing what?'

This line of questioning has an invasive quality that powers up my protective walls.

'Important day tomorrow. Going to see Tommy.'

'You might need a listening ear after that. I'm here for you, you know that.'

'Thanks, David. I'll let you know how it goes.' Sewn into the fabric of that statement is the implied directive to leave me alone until I decide to call. 'Chat soon.' I disconnect.

Anxiety is mounting, extremities hot and twitchy. I spend the next hour or so googling 'bonding a cat and a dog' and receive so many conflicting instructions that the mist starts to swirl. The door to the yard is wide open and there's a cartoon stand-off between them, Marmie hissing and swiping at the air, Herbie standing stock-still, fixated. He looks like David last night as he took in my naked body. The first twenty-four hours are the most intense, one post wrote, after that they'll start to relax a little in each other's company. I'm glad in a way of the distraction. Marmie is growing more boisterous, circling him, hissing, then running away. The poor old dog doesn't even give chase, just stares in her direction, panting. Meanwhile the texts keep on coming: Where/what/why/who? Who, indeed! Who are you to ask? Makes me want to go out and fuck a random stranger.

The doorbell rings. The caller presses down longer than is polite. Damned if I'm going to be bullied, and anyway I couldn't trust myself not to lose it. Excitement builds. A voice bellows through the letter box. Herbie starts to bark, Marmie mewls.

'Sonya, open that door. NOW.' I'm moving towards the door to bolt the Chubb when I catch a glimpse of a silver Cortina outside. My adrenalin falls so suddenly I feel as if I might crash to the floor. How I wanted this particular scene to play out: the obsessed, demented, jilted lover who turns up on the doorstep of the object of his crazed fantasies, enacting some beautiful, brutal act. And that, right there, is weird, and I know it.

'Sonya, I know you're in there. You can now add "thief" to the list of your spectacular fuck-ups.'

What has happened to all the old certainties – that my dog would love me and only me, that David would remain a cool customer, unknown, and that my father would always at least affect a restrained, polite exterior? I feel as if I have supped of some concoction in the underworld: that night of lying in the tangled sheets has resulted in a falling-through from one realm to another. Oh look how the kitten has morphed into the Cheshire Cat grinning from ear to ear, how Herbie is wearing a Mad Hatter's hat! And my father? The Queen of Hearts outside, stomping up and down, with no care for decorum.

No point in trying to engage – no point at all. I settle back to watch my father run out of steam through a gap in the blinds, in much the same way he used to watch me as I'd bellow and rant, his motto 'Never feed the tantrum with attention.'

'Unacceptable behaviour, Sonya, really, the worst. I brought you up better than that.' Poor Dad, he really has lost the run of himself. Just as I knew he would, he runs out of steam and strides away down the path, anger in every bunched muscle. I hear someone utter a greeting and his gruff response: 'Not now, Mary.' I turn to my two charges, who seem to have come to a truce, Marmie rubbing her delicious little nose against the dumbstruck Herbie's.

The night is rather lovely, with the two lovebirds staring at each other from opposite sides of the bed. It's comforting having the warm bodies lying there, not wanting anything at all from me. I fall into a restful sleep, with no visitations from the demented dentist, my childhood dolls, nor any of the sensations of falling or suffocating in shit. When I wake I have the impression of being filled with the colour green: trees, grasshoppers, grass, the colour of buds, of new life.

I move through the morning slowly, strangely luxuriating in the further texts from David: Good morning, Good luck today, Thinking of you. This is so unfamiliar, something I could perhaps get used to. The example set by the animals must be making me soft. I take my time with my cup of tea, cradling it, contemplating the texture, taste, smell. Sister Anne was right: the small pleasures in life really can fill you up. Herbie seems shell-shocked, as anyone would, having been released from prison into a warm, scented bed with a gorgeous feline companion.

I dress carefully, force myself to eat toast and a banana, talk to Herbie and Marmie, telling them to be good, to be kind to each other. Now I know that Marmie is well able to hold her own and would probably win out in any scrap, I'm ok leaving them, just. I still can't get certain morbid imaginings out of my head: the kitten in his big mouth, or the dog's eyes scratched out.

34

I pull up outside the shiny building among the dilapidated flats with plenty of time to spare. Adjust my driver's mirror, look at myself, see, yet don't see. My image has always been a kind of a blur, only ever reflected back at me through other people's eyes. My impression of myself is as of a stranger appraising me, not too kindly. Flip the mirror back.

Maureen is there to meet me at reception. How I want to lay my head on her ample bosom, have my hair stroked. I shake my head and stamp my feet as imperceptibly as I can – disturb the patterns, ground their flight. Breathe in: a sacred pause.

'Ok, Sonya?'

'Fine, good, thanks, all good.'

'Tommy'll be here in a few minutes. I'll spend some time alone with him first, then you'll get to see him.'

'On my own, or…?'

'I'll be in the room, just as a formality. Follow me.'

I'm mesmerised by the swaying bulk of flesh that moves with such assuredness, such grace. It's as if different bulges of her are talking to each other, all nodding their heads in calm agreement. In her office I'm asked to blow, and then to pee into the container. Tea is offered, and the phone rings.

'He's arrived. Ok to wait here for a few minutes?'

I nod, clamp one hand over the other. I sit down, as I'm scared my legs might go spastic, give me away.

'Just breathe, Sonya. I know it's hard.'

She walks towards the door, then turns. 'Oh, and Sonya. You're the mother here, remember?'

And she's gone, trailing shame in her wake.

A knock on the door, and a voice cuts in: 'Ok to follow me?'

Already? A small, wiry, grey-haired lurcher of a woman smiles tightly. 'Just in here.' The door is opened and there he is: tiny – so much smaller than I remember him, sitting at the children's table with its purple plastic chairs and bright pink table. He's wearing clothes I've never seen before: a little sailor top and blue corduroys. Somebody has decided on the 'cute' look.

'Hi, Tommy!'

Maureen is sitting as discreetly as her bulk will allow in a far corner of the room by the window. She has a file on her knees and is looking through papers, or pretending to. Tommy doesn't answer me, and I can immediately sense I'm right back to where I was at the beginning of our visit in rehab. I should have brought something familiar from home, but what? He was never a kid that was into teddies, seeing as he had a big, live one by his side.

'Herbie's back!' He looks up, disbelieving. How many times have adults told him lies in the last few months? 'Yesterday – he came back yesterday. Was asking about you!' He looks back down at the table. 'I also have Marmie at home, the tabby kitten, remember? The one you chose that day.'

He's struggling now to contain excitement, I can see the battle playing out: don't trust her, not safe, and yet some part of him wants to bust out of his skin and run to me and bury himself in me.

'They like each other. I think poor Herbie is a little bit in love.'

He squirms on his plastic seat. 'Don't be silly, Herbie is much too big.'

My heart, a tight fist, lands with a thud in my stomach. Since when has he been pronouncing his perfect 'r's? Where has Hewbie gone to? Someone must have spent time with him, correcting his baby speech. I'd like to punch that someone in the face.

'And dogs can't fall in love with cats, silly.'

Silly? D'you mean Yaya? Say it, please say it. I will the word to fall out of his beautiful rosebud mouth.

'They sure look like they're going to be good pals, though.'

He pretends to be uninterested, picks up a book from the pile on the table, flicks through it and settles on a page with a kangaroo and a baby in its pouch.

'I made one of those for Marmie!' blurts out of me.

He raises his face to study me.

'We went to the park with her and people were laughing and pointing, but you know what I always say…?'

Tommy looks back down at the book, pretending to read.

'…Who cares what other people think? Let them stare; they have nothing better to do.' A slight smile plays out on the corner of his mouth. Maureen's attention shifts; she sits upright, her antenna twitching. What kind of a mother feeds her son with antisocial, verging on paranoiac, sentiments like that? The desire to shock builds in me, Maureen now cast in the same category as all those bossy old biddies who were forever butting in. Heat builds and I want to pull my top off, reveal my toned body to the big worn mattress of a woman, soft in the middle, who's making surreptitious notes on me. What would a 'good' mother say now?

'Only some people, of course, Tommy. Only some people have nothing better to do than stare.' Digging myself in deeper here. Why wasn't I handed a manual on good mothering when he was born? I search and search for memories of my own mother, concrete ones, ones that don't have that woozy quality. I mean, I was eight, not eight months, when she died, but there's nothing there, beyond that spinning sensation, beyond my own fabrications. Didn't they know I didn't have a clue that day they let me go off on my own from the hospital? The only support I was offered was a harried public-health nurse who said on occasion, 'Are you sure you're coping on your own?' I'd nod, tears in my eyes, greasy hair (probably), and say, 'Sure, I'm fine, just fine' – then, in the sixth month, the nurse promptly disappeared. *Maureen, teach me things, be like a mother to me so I can know what to do.*

After a strained silence Maureen says, 'Tommy, tell your mummy about school. What did you learn at school today?'

School? I don't remember giving permission to send him to school. I don't want him bullied, and he's too small.

He speaks in a low, colourless voice: 'Learned to spell "Mummy" and "Daddy".'

Did he say that on purpose, just to get a rise out of me? My hand itches. I rub it hard. This is exactly why I don't want him being contaminated; he will not grow up comparing himself to other people.

'That's great, Mummy, isn't it?' Maureen prompts.

Who is this 'Mummy' of whom she speaks? I nod, manage a swallowed 'Yes' and then: 'Great boy. Clever boy. Mummy always said you were a bright boy!' How forced I sound, how like a caricature of a 1950s housewife smiling inanely at the camera while secretly high on Valium and gin, raging at the injustice of the role she has been trapped in.

'I told them I don't have a daddy,' Tommy says. Maureen's gaze is boring into me. I'm going to have to reach for the right script here.

'You do have a daddy, Tommy, of course you do,' I try. 'Remember I told you that your daddy loved you very much?'

He looks towards the ceiling and beyond, into the celestial sphere, with that dreamy face I know so well, and sticks his thumb in his mouth, then removes it guiltily. I'm so relieved to see his old habit still has a hold over him – he hasn't been totally eradicated, repackaged. I notice that welt at the joint and I want to reach out to kiss it.

'My big guarding angel in the sky,' he says.

'That's right,' I say, reinforcing the lie in front of a professional.

God knows what repercussions will flow from this one, though to be fair if you were to put any mother and son in such an unnatural position every mother out there would fail on some point. *I'm only human*. I try speaking to myself in a soothing, non-critical voice, be that loving parent I never had growing up. This is what a lot of the guys said in the meetings: it's the hypercritical voices, the ones full of self-loathing and judgement, that make them liable to fuck it all up in a moment.

'They asked us to draw a picture of our mummy and daddy,' he says. At least he's talking to me, but I can't help feeling he was planted with these prompts, is testing me in some way. How dare they assume – I mean, surely in this day and age? Test-tube babies, one parent, two fathers, two mothers, all the variations of 'family' dance in front of my eyes. I'm catapulted straight back to my own experiences in the classroom, my attempts to make up a mother figure with a halo above her head, the others sniggering or, worse, freezing me out. I will not have him subjected to that level of ridicule.

'What did you draw, Tommy? Did you bring the picture?'

He shakes his head. 'I told them my dada is in the sky. I drawed you, me and Herbie.'

That's my boy, good lad, be yourself.

'Herbie? That your doggie?' Maureen asks.

The floodgate bursts: he jumps off the chair, pushes the table away from him, the book tumbling to the floor, its spine broken in two.

'When can I see Hewbie? When, Yaya? Now?' The old terms of endearment fall out of his mouth and I want to fall to my knees and kiss the perfect feet of him. Instead I stand tall, plant my feet firmly on the ground and say, 'Soon, darling, I'm sure Maureen will organise that you come home very, very soon.' I look at Maureen as I say this.

'When, Maween, when?' Tommy goes to her and tugs at her sleeve.

Maureen looks down at her notes, composes herself a moment, then speaks in a low, reasonable voice: 'Soon, Tommy, soon, just like your mummy says.'

'Now,' he says quietly at first, shaking his head over and over. 'Not soon, not soon, not soon. Now, I want to go see Hewbie now now now now.' He's getting all worked up, red in the face, hot and blotchy like me. Having found his voice, it won't stop spilling: 'Home now Yaya now Yaya now...'

Maureen seems quite calm in the face of the outburst. I want to join in his dance of outrage, but I need to maintain at least a semblance of equanimity, so I go to him, put my arms around his hot, shaking little body and feel him go limp. He nuzzles into me, sniffing and shuddering.

After some moments, Maureen speaks in a calm manner: 'Ok, now, Tommy. We have to go. Say goodbye to Mummy now. You'll see her next week.'

I disentangle from him, place him gently on the ground. He clings to my knees, pushing his head against my skirt, trying to disappear up under it.

'I think it would be best if Tommy came home with me now. He's been through enough.' I know that this is impossible, and Maureen doesn't have the authority, there are boxes to be ticked, protocol to be followed. From now on, Tommy won't see me as the woman who rejected him; he'll know he is wanted by his mother. Let him turn his anger on this other woman, on his foster carers, on the world out there.

'You know that can't happen today, Sonya,' Maureen says in a tight voice.

'But why why why why?' On and on he continues, an eruption of incomprehension.

Once this 'Why' has planted its seed in him, its roots will grow tough and deep, and no amount of digging will unearth them. I should know.

I bend down to him and whisper in his ear: 'Darling, it won't be long now. We can count the days together.' I turn to Maureen, follow the internal direction to minimise the drama. 'Can you tell us roughly how long?'

'I'll let you know next time, ok, Tommy? Only seven more sleeps till you'll see your mummy again, ok?'

He sniffs, rubs his nose with his sleeve, looks into my eyes with such a lack of guile it might break me in two.

'There, Tommy, seven more sleeps. We can do that, can't we?'

He nods, tries to be a big boy, a strong boy, all those labels I bet have been placed on him. He reaches his hands towards me and pulls my head down to his level. He flutters his eyelashes on my cheek. A kiss like butterfly wings.

35

The restaurant is loud and bright, busy and bustling with a forced joviality that makes me want to back out the door the moment I've arrived. Tang of microwaved metallic tomato sauce on the air, matching napkins with walls, striped lime green and deep purples, try-hardy. Low pop on the airwaves – some she-wolf young one, one of those sexually liberated 'feminists' that writhe in their underwear in a cage. Something about broken dreams, about bastard men that 'steal' their hearts away, about yeah, yeah, yeah, I'm so sexy, sexy, sexy…

'A treat,' he said. 'Let me take you out somewhere nice.' It's been so long since I've been dressed up, on some man's arm, out in the public arena, that I allowed a frisson of excitement to live in me for as long as it took to get ready, even as I knew this was the greatest fantasy of them all: the greatest addiction containing the greatest high, and everything that follows. Coming home to the clean house, the feel of my son's eyelashes on my cheeks, the dog and kitten lying sleepily on the rug in the living room, I could almost imagine a world where good things happened and continued to happen. Then he rang. I agreed, in my moment of rose-tinted weakness. And because the fridge was beginning to whisper to me.

I decided to go for a walk in the park beforehand, noting with intense concentration the beauty of the fallen leaves, crisp underfoot with frost, and the silhouettes of the almost-bare trees against the high, domed, almost-blue sky. Present-moment awareness: an antidote to craving. Marmie looked so sweet with one of Herbie's heavy corded leads attached to her tiny collar with its loud ringing bell. She has taken quite well to the lead, considering her feisty nature. There were, of course, lots of stares, but this time they were accompanied by smiles and oohs from various children: 'I want to do that with Snowy, Mummy.' Mummy smiled indulgently as they passed, then spoke in a whisper that carried on the clear, crisp air: 'That's just plain odd.' *Who cares what other people think, Yaya?* I smiled and shook my tail feathers.

Now, dressed in a fifties vintage-style dress – a testament to my previous incarnation as a London leading lady – I am standing in the queue of this overlit, straining, faux-Italian franchise in suburban Dublin, when I see him coming. My hope, situated somewhere in my chest cavity, a beating, pulsing thing, pitches forward, as if it were plummeting down the track of a Giant Dipper. He looks overdone, smells of a clean chemical concoction that climbs into my nostrils; the waistline of his jeans is too high. Sanitised and shining. He moves towards me, smiling possessively, and kisses me on the lips.

'David Smythe,' he says to the receptionist, a young, pretty, unformed girl, who flushes from her chest to the roots of her hair.

'Follow me,' the girl says, smoothing her skirt over her spindly hips and rump as she leads us to a booth by the wall, to what should be a cosy alcove except that the light dangling overhead is as white and glaring as in an interrogation room. I slide in across the leatherette surface, sticky and hot against my thighs in their 40-denier tights. In spite of my judgement of the blushing girl who has skipped away, a timid fawn, my own blood is rushing too fast to the surface.

'You look gorgeous,' he says, which makes my skin angrier, that probing light irritating.

A waiter arrives and pours iced water into my glass. I gulp greedily, wanting to remove the ice cube and rub it on my inflamed skin. I sit on my hands.

'You seem a bit jumpy,' he says. 'Did today go well?'

How to bat the question away without causing offence? I attempt a smile. 'Good, great, no time at all now, you know. You? How was your day?'

'I had a great day, actually. A day where I could be of service. Called in to do an intervention on a young lad, his family sick with worry, twisted and reactive with worry. Amazing how the presence of a neutral, skilled facilitator can defuse a charged situation.'

He positively bloats with self-importance as he relays the facts of his successful 'rescue' operation. The air buzzes around my head with judgements, and some of them must land. His hands start shredding a napkin. My own are hot and itchy. I shift my weight so that they can't escape my body's heft.

The waiter reappears. 'Ready to order?'

'I'll have a vegetarian pizza and a mixed salad,' I say, as there are no other options.

'Just give me a minute,' David says as he reads with intent, his finger running beneath the text. 'I'll have a steak au poivre, rare.' His voice booming in the confined space.

'Anything to drink?'

'We're fine with waters, thank you,' he says.

'Actually, I'll have a Coke.'

'Right so.' The waiter leaves.

'Are you really eating beef? Hardly humanely reared cows in here, I imagine.'

He looks down at his fingers, which continue to fidget and shred. 'I'll eat what I like.' I let that hang. He sounds so childish.

'David, have you ever been married?'

'I'm not sure what relevance that has to anything,' he says.

'We're not in a therapy session here. Simple question.'

'Yes, Sonya. Briefly. You?'

'You know I haven't.'

And I think how unbalanced this all is; how much this man knows about me, and how little I know about him. He seemed very uncomfortable at the mention of his marriage.

'Are you still working as a solicitor?'

'What is this? The bloody Inquisition?' he says, smiling, trying to flirt a little.

The food arrives. It's as bland and tasteless as this place. I look at his steak with some disgust. David can't seem to manage to swallow more than three mouthfuls, my comments about the cow's dubious lineage still ringing. I shake my head, looking to create a clearing. I'm ruining a perfectly good evening. 'You're always looking to destroy something good' – one of Howard's refrains. He was right, and he was wrong: there was no conscious decision on my part, it just happened, the voices happened, the images spilled, the creatures awoke. I'm well on my way to furrowing that same groove now; I know I'm making that face.

David studies me. 'I wonder why you feel the need to be so prickly, Sonya.'

'Sorry,' I say, sounding anything but. 'I guess we're just not compatible.'

He laughs.

I'm shocked out of my dramatic interior musings. 'What's so funny?'

'You are: Just. Not. Compatible. Why? Because I called you prickly? Is that the best you can do?'

This isn't a tactic I've encountered before, and I feel as if I've been manhandled and thrown to the floor, all bets on me, now an unexpected loser. Why is he bothering? Why doesn't he just piss off and leave me alone, like the rest of them?

'Well, I'm just not into this, just not into you. How's that?' I say, obeying a director who's pushing for a Liz Taylor moment from *Who's Afraid of Virginia Woolf?*

'You're so see-through. Not going to get rid of me that easily.'

Go, stay, go, stay, go, stay, go, stay, go, go, go, much easier if you just go... 'Classic Groucho Marx shit, Sonya.' I can hear Howard's voice.

'Think you may have underestimated my staying power,' David adds quietly, smiling.

I want to place his hand between my legs. I want to rest my head on his shoulder.

36

Three weeks pass, punctuated by my visits with Tommy and my conflicted toying with David, that familiar push-me-pull-you routine, which doesn't seem to faze him, and which makes me think I may finally have found my match. He doesn't give much of himself away, except in bed. I ask about his childhood, his work, his ex, but he deflects all my questions all the time. Funny how I'm constantly revising my opinion of him: Mr Sober, Mr Solid, Mr Safe, Mr Slippery, Mr Sexy. He is the perfect candidate for my naming game. Mr S. He is very serious (Mr Serious!) about my recovery, monitoring my attendance at meetings.

As there's no way I'm going to jeopardise getting Tommy back, I turn up at the meetings, zoning in and out. 'Take what you like and leave the rest' – I hear Jimmy's voice in my head. Sometimes something touches me, pierces my self-absorption, makes me feel part of the human race. Sometimes somebody says something, and I feel that rarest of things: kinship. Usually this relates to the voices in the head, the hypnotic instructions, the addiction to danger, the fuck-you-world attitude. Although no one directly says they see their embodied sidekick, their demented imp, I know they do. I also know this is something there is no shared language for.

As for solutions? The whole 'I can't, God can: let him' thing still feels like a cop-out. Some part of me still believes in willpower, the need for it, to exercise it. And yet I know it's bigger than weakness, this addiction, it's bigger than any human force of will. Prayer? I quite like the whole 'transformational current' thing Sister Anne floated to me, but I can't feel the charge, no matter how hard I try. What was the other thing she said? – something about prayer being a link or a bridge between longing and belonging? That's good too. One to try to grapple with. And God likes good manners. My prayer is that I will never get pissed around my child again. Please and thank you. That is not flippant: I am wrestling with what it means to be a good mother. David says *parenting self* has to come first. Sister Anne said finding a sense of a loving parent is the only way to be one. God the loving father, the kind mother.

No date has been given for Tommy to come home. How can this be in his best interests? He is becoming increasingly withdrawn and has shown no emotion since his first outburst. He wears his silence like a shield.

It's my fourth 'supervised' visit today. The sky is heavy and low, the light has that milky quality that makes me nauseous. I steady myself outside the building a moment. Fluttering in my chest, my throat.

Inside, the reception is empty and I sit, stand, pace, sit, cross my legs, uncross, cross again, let my hair loose, pull it into a ponytail, open my handbag, slick some gloss on, and then I notice Maureen standing there – how much of that spectacle did she witness? 'Hello,

Sonya. Come with me.' We walk, out of sync, dead air between us, through the heavily disinfected hallway, painted a brilliant white, smeared with traces of small fingerprints.

'How are you, Sonya?' Maureen doesn't wait for an answer before she plunges on through the list of obligatory questions, then the humiliation of the breathalyser, although she barely looks at the results before saying, 'We think you're ready.'

Really... amazing... but what? No... really? The creatures have stirred and are beating their tiny wings against my windpipe. Frantic little fuckers. I place my hand at the base of my throat. How can Maureen know I won't suffocate Tommy with my need, set the house on fire, white out, black out, blank out, starve him? How can they say I'm ready when I've never felt less ready? Exactly the same feeling I'd get just before I'd go on stage, I remind myself, and then I'd be up there, being brilliant. I don't have to be 'up' anywhere, being *brilliant*, though – just present, just sober, just normal.

'I see... When?' My voice is a wheeze.

'Next week. We need to prepare him, and you, of course.'

Maureen is distracted, already moving on to the next case.

'Clare has spoken to me about some concerns she has for him, particularly his building obsession with fire. We'll need to monitor that.'

Obsession. Bit of a histrionic word – even for me. He's only an almost-five-year-old. What to get him for his birthday? A fire hose? Feel the wrong sort of laughter building. *Not now, Sonya, not now.*

'Sonya? Did you hear me?'

'Of course, Maureen. Thank you for alerting me.'

This ability to manage myself is growing. Like last night with David when I told him we needed to slow things down. All very adult and civilised, and he seemed fine with it. So unlike my usual going cold and withdrawing. Am I learning how to communicate, to connect in a real way with someone who might actually be good for me?

'Sonya…? We're letting Tommy go back to you earlier than normal on account of your father. He says he can vouch for you, and that he will keep an eye.'

A pretty waltzing number wafts from the speakers, and I can't for the life of me fathom what it is. Father would know. My father, who has been in communication with this stranger, but not once in the last three weeks has picked up the phone to me. Has he really promised to 'look out' for us? I can see how easy it would be to believe him. I experience a familiar rage, and yet, even if he never shows up in our lives again, he has orchestrated this early home-coming. Perhaps he does, on some level, care, perhaps he carries some buried guilt after all.

'Sonya, did you hear a word I said?'

'About my father vouching for me, yes.'

'And after? Obligatory aftercare for both you and Tommy.'

'Yes, yes, of course…'

Maureen looks unconvinced, but not all that bothered, which makes me suspect my instinct was right – she's overworked and under-resourced. I study her slack face and body, burrow deeper: she's seen it all. Here she is, letting a little boy go back to a woman who's capable of suffocating him with a surfeit of love – or is it need? The memory of that night twitches in me, terrifies me. Was it the booze, or will I be worse without it?

I go to the plastic spider plant on the windowsill, perfectly placed to drink in the sun's rays, and rub my finger and thumb over its shiny surface.

'Very lifelike,' I say to Maureen, who doesn't look up from her paperwork. I lean in to smell it. Artificial. Toxic. Obnoxious. What's the point of such a thing?

A polite knock on the door interrupts.

Maureen looks up from her file. 'He's here.'

I nod. Don't know where to look, what to do with my hands, how to stand. *I am a seagull – no – no, I am an actress.* My seagull has broken a wing and is thrashing about in the undergrowth. Feed me the lines, someone, please. A recurring nightmare in the run-up to opening nights. A prompt, please.

Tommy is ushered in by the lurcher-lady from last time, who doesn't even bother to exchange a hello, just gently pushes him in, leaves him there. He seems swamped by the space in the room. He's wearing a new tracksuit, all synthetic shine. Who thought that was a good idea?

'Hello, Tommy.'

He shakes his head, hands deep in his pointless oversized pockets.

'How are you, sweetheart?'

He stuffs his hands further in his pockets, as if he'd like to lose himself in them.

'Herbie and Marmie are the best of friends now!'

His eyes dart around the room, alighting on nothing.

'Marmie?' Maureen asks.

'Our kitten.'

Maureen looks back down. 'That'll be nice, won't it, Tommy?'

He says nothing.

'They can't wait to see you, T.'

'Sonya, are you going to tell Tommy the good news, or will I?'

I'm building up to it; trying to establish a connection first.

'Tommy?'

219

I will him to look at me.

'Maureen has said you can come home with me next week.'

He scuffs one of his ridiculous new trainers, with flashing lights set into the soles. What sort of a person—?

'Tommy, don't...' My voice is high.

Maureen audibly sighs, and I can't blame her. Some mother's instinct.

'Did you hear that, Tommy? You get to go home with Mummy next week?' Maureen asks.

He says nothing.

'Are you ok with that, Tommy?'

He's four – shouldn't have to answer questions like that.

'Is everything ok, Tommy?'

'Yes, thank you. Can I bring my Jupiter?'

'Jupiter?'

He makes a sound like a fire engine in a cartoon: nee naw, nee naw.

'Ah yes, Fireman Sam's fire engine.'

The irony of that isn't lost on me. They've been indulging his obsession, it seems, feeding it.

'Of course you can, dear. Can't he, Mummy?'

'Sure, yeah, sure.'

'So, we'll see you both here next Friday and you can go home to your furry friends, Tommy. Sound good?'

No matter what Tommy were to say now, the box is ticked and the boy is on his way home. I think of the barefoot boy on my street growing up; the boy in the cafe; Linda's Mark, the abuser, as a boy; Jimmy, the adrenal-overloaded boy; the boy who watched his father throw himself into the canal; the boy who got pissed with his father at eleven, who shot up with his mother at thirteen; all the boys the world fashions into versions of hard, broken, swaggering men. My own father? David – as a boy?

And here is my boy, wearing the wrong clothes, living the wrong life in his flashing trainers and polyester tracksuit. He'll never even know his own father.

We say our awkward goodbyes and hasten away from each other. The car can't drive fast enough today. The whisperings start: *Sup of me and I will offer thee succour*, or something like that. Poetic licence.

The prospect of being at home scares me, but the prospect of a meeting scares me even more. I should go, but I can't bear to be in a room full of intense, damaged adults bemoaning their pasts, handing their will and lives over to some fairy-tale deity. I know this isn't fair, nor is it a realistic appraisal, but fuck it, it's how I feel right now. Too much honesty, too much introspection. Thank God (He/She/It) for animal therapy: the two love-struck hairies provide great entertainment, Marmie holding the power, circling, swiping. The big old boy is driven to distraction. The phone flashes. Not in the mood. Stick the telly on, flick aimlessly, settle on a replay of *Grand Designs*, an episode I've seen with Tommy, where a couple make a house out of reclaimed tyres, which we both loved the idea of: 'A house on wheels that won't go anywhere.' We both laughed until we cried. I allow myself to feel the full force of the five months of missing him, and it rains down on my body like punches.

37

David calls and calls again. Feck's sake, not very perceptive for a so-called 'counsellor'. I thought I had clearly articulated my need for space, and I thought he had heard me. He sends a text: Worried about you, am calling over. Something about that feels so wrong and yet so right. Perhaps this is my opportunity to let someone in, let someone care. Or it's another opportunity to tell someone to fuck off. The usual tensions, and I can't deny a frisson of excitement at the thought that he just won't give up. Have I, at last, found that pair of arms that will hold me, even as I'm kicking out in a bratty tantrum?

Find myself in my bedroom rubbing pearly lipstick on my cheeks and lips. I change my clothes three times before deciding on what I was wearing initially: tight-fitting jeans and a long-sleeved T-shirt. Stand in front of the mirror, turn. A blur looks back at me. Go into the bathroom and brush my teeth, stick my tongue out and scrape it clean.

The doorbell rings. There's something unnerving in the fact that he never seems to be more than ten minutes away. I don't even know where he lives, which I try to convince myself is not that weird.

We've only been seeing each other a few weeks. I open the door, the dog barks, the kitten mewls. He walks in.

'You need to let those animals know I'm welcome here.'

His voice has an edge I haven't heard before.

'Want a coffee?'

'No.'

'Everything ok?'

'I have great difficulty being ignored, Sonya. Remember we spoke about this?'

'I wasn't ignoring you. I told you I needed some space.'

'You didn't really mean that, though, did you?'

'I did, actually. Trying to process some stuff around Tommy. He's coming home on Friday.'

'Well, then, even more of a reason for you to reach out.'

His tone is pious and intensely irritating.

'I told you I feel we need to slow things down.'

'Now I know you don't mean that.' He moves towards me, smiling possessively.

I move away.

'How was your day, David? What were you up to?'

'Busy day as ever, you know…'

'Not sure I do.'

'Busier than you, anyway.' He smiles, softening his words.

'Actually, I was visiting Tommy today.'

How did he do that? Twist it back on me, so I am the one who ends up justifying and explaining myself?

'David, I was thinking… I'd love to see your place sometime.'

'Why?'

'Pretty normal request, I'd have thought. I don't know where you live.'

223

'I prefer it here.'

Is that supposed to be a reasonable response?

'You look gorgeous, Sonya.'

'I'm thirsty.' I go into the kitchen, pour myself a glass of water, gulp it down.

'Aren't you going to offer me one?' he says as he reaches across me and opens the cupboard. In spite of myself I feel that charge between us. A dragging sensation in my pelvis, painful and intensely pleasurable.

'David, I'd love to know a bit more about you.'

'Would you, now?' He moves towards me, clinks his glass off mine as his free arm draws me close.

My body is being played. I try to pull away from him. 'Have you any brothers and sisters?'

'Not that I know of.' He puts his glass down, takes mine from my hand, leans in to kiss me.

'Are both your parents alive?'

'What is this, Sonya?'

He starts to kiss me more intensely, his tongue probing my mouth, making it impossible to talk.

I push him away, half of me meaning it, the other half leaning in towards him. 'Are you still working as a solicitor?'

'Don't I have my hands full?' he says, stroking my hair, which makes me feel young and vulnerable, and cared for. I don't remember anyone ever stroking my hair.

'David, do you think this is a good idea? Do you think *we* are a good idea?'

'Not sure I'm up to much thinking right now.' He pulls me to him, wraps both his arms around me and starts to sway. Herbie and Marmie move closer to me, as if guarding me.

'What do you think Sister Anne would say if she saw us now?' I whisper.

'I think she'd be mightily jealous! That nun has a little spark for me.'

I wonder about that. Sister Anne seemed so bullshit-proof. I'm pretty sure she'd be appalled if she found out about this.

He places his hand on my inner thigh. Herbie starts to growl, intensifying the drama of the moment, which both scares me and turns me on.

'Sure you're ok with this?' David says, not waiting for an answer. He starts to pull the zipper on my jeans, his fingers feeling for me. The usual battle plays out for a moment: you know where this will lead, pull it back, take it slow, make it real, take it slow… before I am expertly steered into territory where there is no more thought.

What follows is anything but slow. He handles me with an urgency that borders on aggression. He stands at some point and shoos the animals back into the hall, closes the kitchen door and lifts me on to the countertop, then the floor. He turns me over, as if he's determined to mark every part of me. What fantasy is this? I feel myself fly away, watching from a distance. There is silent resistance in my body, a stiffness that he doesn't pay heed to, that I don't pay heed to. I wonder was that some kind of punishment for all the questions.

He lifts me then, like a child, and carries me into the bedroom, lays me gently on the bed, kisses me all over. Throughout it all I say nothing, my mind shocked into silence for a brief interlude. He falls asleep easily, while I lie motionless beside him, the animals scratching the door outside. I hear an indistinct susurration, a dangerous beckoning. Place a pillow over my head and roll away from him, curl up at the farthest edge of the bed.

'Are you ok?' he whispers, and I wish he wouldn't. He sidles over to my side of the bed, reaches out for me.

'Hmmm-mmm.' I turn my back.

He snakes an arm over my ribs. Boa constrictor. I lift it off me. 'Too heavy.'

'Sorry. Hey, I'm starving. I'll go get us something, I guess your cupboards are bare, as usual?'

I nod, desperate to get him out of my space. He gets up, dresses fast, kisses me on my cheek, tidies my hair behind my ear, blows into it.

'Don't go anywhere. Stay right where you are. I'll get us a nice veggie pizza.' He sounds as if he's speaking to a child, or an invalid. 'You ok?' My head moves up and down, yes sir, yes sir, a submissive. He kisses me gently on my forehead and leaves.

As soon as I'm sure he's gone I call my two pets into the bedroom. Both of them are shaking with stress. We're all in need of distraction. 'Walkies?' Howls. I dress in layers of comfy, slouchy clothes, and set out to the park, pull my hood over my head. I wonder at myself, what this all means. I walk and I walk and I walk. It's dark. Tommy? Tommy, where are you, how are you doing, little man? All I can hear is my own breath in my ears.

38

After a night battling my demented dentist armed with a pneumatic drill, my Pierrot dolls issuing gleeful instructions, *Open wide, dear one*, I find myself in a sleep-addled state, standing in the kitchen in a concentrated pool of sunlight, the crazed laughter still ringing in my ears. Kettle on, tea on its way. David wasn't there when I got back, which triggered that familiar feeling of abandonment, which is ridiculous, considering I was the one who left him standing on my doorstep for hours. I wonder how long he waited. I watch Herbie and Marmie follow each other around the yard, the cat stopping to pee wherever Herbie cocks his leg. 'Herbie?' He ignores me, keeps the focus on the cat. The bite of rejection stings.

My mobile is hot in my hands. I can't think of a single person I can call. Still too early with my father; I know how he works. And David? Can't even begin to grapple with the contradictory feelings that swirl about. Sister Anne and Jimmy would both tell me to ask for guidance. What the hell? I drop dramatically to my knees, which hurts, try out various versions of *Please help*, then fall into a repetitive incantation of the rosary, which opens up a space, offsets the other speedy-greyhound thoughts racing to a dark, dingy kennel and a sure, early death.

When I open my eyes I find Herbie licking my face. Thank you, old boy! Only two more days before Tommy is home. His voice rings out, a canned cranky theme tune, *Why Yaya why why why but why Yaya why why why…* Seemingly inexhaustible. Need to block it out: I find the hoover and power it up. The cat and dog run and hide and I continue to push the head into dark, dusty corners, fighting the filth.

I go for long walks, trying and failing to be present, everything filtered through a smeared long-distance lens. Attend a meeting, listen but don't listen, hear but don't hear. The Serenity Prayer is helping, though. Soothing words on a loop: serenity and acceptance and courage and wisdom, serenity and acceptance and courage and wisdom. God grant me some of that. I manage to get to Tesco, pick up fish fingers, cornflakes, marmalade, bread, dog food, cat food, toilet roll, bananas, potato waffles, beans – on some level I'm coping, and in spite of the sensation of tugging at my hair, of fingers scraping and pulling, I am able to circumnavigate the booze aisle. No way I'm going to have a repeat performance of that night, no way am I going to jeopardise getting my baby back. Strangely, Jimmy's suggestion of the 'sacred pause' is helpful, the space it creates, just enough to interrupt the circuit before the *blackout before the booze* – which I now know is a thing.

Friday finally arrives. I dress carefully, apply a slick of red lipstick, then wipe it away. I'm feeling the cold today after another night of disturbed sleep; tell myself this is the reason I have the shakes.

Settle into the car, breathe. Roll down the window, poke my head out, increase speed, stick my tongue out, catch the wind and tiny droplets of moisture.

I'm left waiting fifteen minutes in the overheated waiting room. Remove my outer layers.

'Excuse me, could you please find out where Maureen is?' I ask a receptionist I've never seen before.

The young woman plastered in cheap make-up, which is melting in this unnatural heat, speaks without even looking up. 'She'll be with you when she's with you.'

Little hussy. I get up, dramatically stretch, walk to the window, haw on it and draw a heart. The receptionist says nothing. Feel like I'm being watched, turn, see Maureen standing at the door. That woman materialises as if out of mist.

'Just something Tommy and I used to like to do,' I say as I rub away the condensation with my sleeve.

'Sorry I got a bit delayed, Sonya. Tommy seems a little distressed today. Needed some time with him alone. Ok now, though, good to go when you are.'

What? No. Don't I get some time alone with you? Some tips?

Tommy appears, being led by the same wiry lurcher-woman as before.

'Thanks, Sally, I'll take it from here,' Maureen says.

The woman regards me with withering disgust – her only means of expressing her judgement of these selfish, childish, poor excuses for mothers – and leaves. I don't get a chance to communicate that I am in complete agreement.

Tommy is trailing a kids' wheelie bag in the shape of a fire engine. Oh, please. He's wearing the flashing runners, and his old jeans and hoodie.

'Hi, kiddo. All ready to go?'

Kiddo. Where did that come from?

He looks at Maureen, then at me, and nods.

'Herbie can't wait to see you.'

'Go on, now, Tommy, there's a good boy. We'll see each other again very soon, and I have Clare's number if you want to chat to her about anything.'

She's all bustle and business now as she ushers us to the door.

'The meetings are obligatory, Sonya, remember?'

'Yes, I remember.'

'And school must be continued.'

'Yes, yes...'

'Not optional, Sonya. No matter how Tommy feels, he goes. We'll be checking up there.'

'Right.'

'And we'll organise a home visit very soon.'

'Ok.'

'Stay in close contact with your father.'

The irony of that.

Maureen pushes against the door, holds it open.

'Chilly day all the same. Stay warm, and safe.'

Too much emphasis on the last word. Dismissed with a tight smile, a wave, a 'See you soon, Tommy', and then the door closes and the two of us are outside, neither one looking at the other.

'Car is over here, Mr T.' I go to take his bag from him, but he shrugs me off. 'Ok, ok, Jesus...' Wish I could pull back the words the moment they've escaped me.

I hold open the back door, and he climbs in, clutching his new case. Try to buckle him up, but he still won't let the bag go, settling it on his lap like a pet, so I have to stretch the belt over it. Remember to do this: it's a good start. I turn on the radio, fiddle around till I find something 'poppy', inane and upbeat – I'm not in the mood to be ignored. Put my pedal to the floor, hoping to get a reaction.

'Wheee, Tommy, see? Yaya's still the fastest motor racer you know!'

He sticks his thumb in his mouth and looks out the window.

'Fancy a creamy ice?' I shout over the music, even though it's entirely inappropriate in mid-November.

He pushes his nose against the windowpane, squashes it. I sing along, 'Ooh, I'm your baby, baby, baby', until I look back and see he has his fingers in his ears. I stop, feeling slapped. Turn the radio up to block any stinging words that might come flying out of my mouth.

'Home sweet home, T,' I say as we round the bend into the terrace, half expecting claps and squeals of excitement, though not really. He's just not going to give me an inch. I park the car on the kerb, open the front door, and Herbie and Marmie bound out to piddle all over the dead flowerbeds. Tommy climbs out, still clinging to his ridiculous wheelie case, pressing it to his chest. He looks around, dazed, as if blinded by the light after days in a black cell. Herbie goes to him, then backs away. Tommy doesn't engage.

'Tommy, meet Marmie.'

'That's not the kitten. Too big,' he says, before he walks up the path and into the house.

When I manage to corral the other two back inside, I find Tommy in the living room, unpacking and folding his clothes. He places them neatly at the end of the couch. Who taught him to do that? 'Want to watch some *Jeremy Kyle*, Tommy?' Stick the telly on, tune in to the raucous shouting, regardless of his answer. Need to pretend things can be the way they were. Herbie is sniffing the air around Tommy, looking at me then back at Marmie. Yes, Herbie, he does smell different. A persistent tickle in my throat brings on a coughing fit so acute I double over. Tommy doesn't even glance up from his folding, concentration intense. When I used to cough before, he'd be by my side, stroking my hair.

I sit on the couch and pat the surface beside me, inviting Herbie and Marmie up. Tommy finishes his folding, looks at the three of us sitting with space between us and climbs on to the armchair on his own. He never sat in that chair before. Neither of us did – it's a lumpy, ugly, broken old thing, and I determine in that instant to get rid of it.

'Anyone hungry?'

I get up, not expecting a reply, turn on the grill, take out the fish fingers, shout into the living room: 'Marmie loves fishies too, Tommy. We all do.' I stand staring at the grill, not seeing anything, until it becomes apparent that smoke is spilling from its mouth. *Fuck's sake, Sonya.* Hear my own voice, my father's and David's all rolled into one. Reach in to lift the blackened fish by hand, scorching the tips of my fingers, throw it on a plate, and take the smoking grill pan into the yard. Sense Tommy in the doorway.

He moves to the plate of fish fingers, lifts one and nibbles the outer edge.

'Tommy, don't, it's probably still raw inside.'

He swallows. 'Burn.'

'Yes, Tommy, that's right. When does Yaya ever do it any other way?'

He sniffs the air, inhales, closes his eyes. He nods, like he's satisfied with what he smells, then returns to the lounge humming a theme tune I've never heard before. I follow him, not sure how to play this. Herbie jumps off the couch and moves towards him, tail circling then curling under as Tommy studiously ignores him. Tommy settles himself back on the chair and surveys the room as if he's never seen it before, looks at the animals in a way that makes me think of the boy in the cafe. He's only five, Sonya, only five in a week's time. Maybe we should have a birthday party, invite everyone we know. Who – exactly? Clare, Maureen? Probably not protocol. Father? David?

How about his little school friends? School is non-negotiable, Maureen was pretty clear about that. I wonder could I track down that fire-blowing guy I used to date – imagine Tommy's excitement! I look at him pretending to be engrossed in the TV and resolve to give him the best party ever, with fireworks, sparklers and Catherine wheels. There's something about those spinning circles of fire, some trace of a memory as a child, a giddiness, being held high on my father's shoulders, a sensation of belonging to him, to the world. Fire did that for me too, burned the rest of the shit away. I guess a sort of purification. Try to remember more, but it slips away from me, leaving me wide open to the pain of this reunion that has us all acting so cold and wary of each other. Tommy's rejection of Herbie cuts to the core of me. 'A God-shaped hole.' I hear the men's voices from the meetings, and it lands.

39

I call the rehab centre's public line, which is engaged, of course, leave the phone on redial – pick up, someone, anyone, I don't care who, just someone who knows what this feels like. Eventually some bored receptionist answers, tells me they're all in rosary.

'This is an emergency,' I say. 'Page Jimmy Maloney, please.'

'Call back between five thirty and six thirty tomorrow evening.' The phone cuts out.

Perhaps we should eat? I think of one of the slogans bandied about in the meetings: 'HALT – hungry angry lonely tired'. I literally snorted the first time I heard it; now, though, I wonder. A full belly can soothe. I make peanut-butter sandwiches but have no appetite for this kind of fuel. Tommy eats only the centre, leaving the crusts. A giddy, restless feeling rises in me, creatures stirring. 'Walkies,' I say, hoping to deflect. Tommy goes to the spot by the door, takes down the leads and hands them to me. The animals wail as if they've never seen the outside world.

I take the leads from Tommy. 'Thanks, Mr T. Would you put your coat on?'

He does, and wraps his scarf around his neck without my asking.

Outside it's spitting rain and vaguely windy, my least favourite combination: mild and noncommittal. Tommy attaches Marmie's lead, looking delighted in spite of himself, while I have a hold of Herbie, who's straining to be let loose. At the traffic lights Tommy stops, even though there's no traffic coming in either direction. 'Nothing coming, Tommy. Come on, race you' – and I tear across the road, dragging Herbie with me. A hurtling lorry appears and obscures my view of Tommy. Herbie is intent on pulling me back into the road, his wild barking underscoring my panic. Tommy doesn't move until the little green man appears, then he looks right and left before stepping out. Who has moulded this version of my boy? I suck down my curses and run to meet him in the middle of the road, offering him my hand, which he doesn't take. 'Good boy, Tommy,' I say, overriding the other script. He looks like he hasn't heard me. 'Will we go to the playground?' I say, an adult who puts her child's needs before her own. I never brought him there before – allergic to the other families, the stares, the squeals of the kids, the forced fun.

'They don't allow aminals.'

Do I imagine it, or does Herbie look at him?

'Ok. Duckies?'

He nods. I should have brought bread. No more 'should's – another nugget from the meetings. It's the 'should's that set up shame, which leads to self-flagellation, which leads only one way. Sounded so reductive and simplistic in there, but out here I'm clinging to anything that might keep me on the straight and narrow. We sit on a bench, the rain soft but drenching, Tommy swinging his feet. How I'd like to whip those absurd trainers off and throw them in the pond.

Marmie is hiding under the bench, Herbie seemingly staring into space, the stench coming off him, his own special wet-dog waft.

'Herbie? Come here, boy.' I pat the space beside me, between Tommy and myself, inviting him to climb aboard and soak up some of the awkwardness. He doesn't move.

'It's raining,' Tommy says, pronouncing his 'r' as if he's been taught perfect RP at RADA.

I check my phone for messages. Nothing.

'Shall we move to the bandstand, Tommy? It's not raining under there.'

He gets up, satisfied with this plan, and shuffles off on his own, leading the pack.

Will we ever be a pack again? In the bandstand, I dance an Irish jig: *a haon, dó, trí, ceathair, cúig, sé, seacht, a haon, dó, trí, a haon, dó, trí.* 'Come on, Tommy,' I whoop, grab his hands; a misstep, as he backs away from me.

He has moved to the far edges of the railings and is staring at the pond, his back tense. 'Can we go back to the house now?' he says. I notice that he doesn't say 'home'.

I can't go back to the confines of those claustrophobic rooms; need to be wind-whipped, rain-lashed, need space, perspective. 'In a bit, Tommy, ok?' He doesn't answer. I tie the animals to the railings, tell Tommy to mind them, and step off the bandstand into the rain. Start to jog, building into a run, lose sight of Tommy for a moment as I loop the circumference of the park. My imp is there in the bushes, little bitch. Increase my speed, blinkers on.

On my third lap I see Tommy standing in the centre of the field, holding on to the two drenched creatures. One more round. I wave. No one waves back. My heart. I complete two more laps, my tendons aching, shin splints hurting, lungs busting, pulse throbbing in my neck. I stop, do a little puke, feel momentarily better, then walk back towards the trio.

'Right, let's all go home, shall we?'

I catch Tommy throwing his eyes to heaven. I turn and start to weave my way dizzily out of the gate. Despite my physical exhaustion, a bolt of raw fury shoots through me. How dare they take my son away from me and replace him with this sanctimonious, little-green-man-obeying, eye-rolling stranger? I begin to run, and don't look back to see if they're all following. Strike out on to the slippery road, not waiting for the traffic lights to change – when did I ever wait for the little green man? – and continue running until I reach the front door. Turn then, see them all trailing behind me in a line. Swallow. I have to battle a desire to get on my knees and throw myself at their feet.

Once inside the hallway, the four of us freeze and size each other up. Tommy makes a soft tip-of-the-tongue-to-the-palate click, mobilising the animals to follow him. They move as one into the kitchen, the sound of the tap running, cupboards opening and closing. I follow them and see him standing on the worktop, reaching for a bowl.

'Tommy?'

He pretends he doesn't hear me.

'Tommy? That's too high. Let me...'

As I reach past him, he flinches. I lift him off the counter, place him on the floor, fill a bowl for the animals, his plastic cup for him. He turns his back on me.

A whole-body lovesickness burrows inside me, biting and scraping. I find myself moving towards the front door, grabbing my keys, my wallet. Slam the door. The white witch has me in her thrall. I sit in the car, start it, rev it. This is it, the moment of unconscious surrender, but there is some other part of me watching: angels, good and evil, battling it out. Hear voices from the meetings: cunning, baffling and powerful. Ask for help, something outside of yourself, a Higher Power, something in nature, a tree, a member of the group, doesn't matter who or what, just ask. Get humble. Sister Anne? *Please help.* The Man Above just won't do it, the Divine Mother too abstract, the angels too ephemeral… too… insubstantial. Need something solid, something real to hold on to, need to hear a voice to interrupt my own. I take my phone and swipe, overriding my last sense of him. The line connects. 'Can you come over?'

I thought there might be some residual hurt or anger, but he answers without a hint of recrimination. 'Sure, but do you think it's a good idea on your first evening together?'

Words fall out of me, words about not trusting myself, about Tommy's alienation from me, his distrust, my contradictory impulses; words that I have some sense should never be spoken aloud, yet I'm powerless over the anxiety of the moment, the spilling momentum.

I whisper, 'Please come.'

I can hear a register shift before he speaks, and when he does, his old sermonising tone is back: 'Don't go anywhere. I'll be there in a jiffy.'

I get out of the car, open the front door, shout calmly from the hall, 'Just needed to get my sunglasses', which is ridiculous, as there's not a screed of sunlight today. 'Going to have a shower, Tommy, ok?' He doesn't look at me. Water might help.

When I come back out, wrapped in a towel, I see my boy rubbing down the animals, talking low to them, reassuring them. The trio forming a closed circle, with me on the outside.

'Tommy?'

He looks up.

'Will you have a nice hot shower? Don't want you getting a cold.'

He shakes his head.

'Ok, darling. Let's dry you off, get some clean clothes on you.'

The doorbell rings.

'That's just a friend. Go on, now, go into the bedroom and get changed.' I try on the capable, coping mother voice. He doesn't move. Since when did I have a friend?

40

David is standing outside, a pizza box in hand.

'Thank you for coming,' I say, over-bright. 'Is that the pizza from the other night?'

'What's going on?' His voice is my father's voice. This is enough to puncture any lingering craving, my world suddenly pulled into sharp focus. 'You should put some clothes on,' he says more softly. 'Don't want you getting a cold' – my exact words to Tommy a few moments ago.

He steps into the hall. Tommy is standing in the doorframe to the bedroom, pale and stock-still.

'You remember David, Tommy? The nice man who paid for our pizza that time?'

Tommy ignores me, goes into the bedroom, the animals following, and closes the door.

'Understandable, in the circumstances,' David says.

'I'm just going to put some clothes on.'

'Grand. I'll pop the pizza in the oven, keep it warm.'

I think of the smell of burnt fish fingers, the congealed bits in the oven, say nothing.

'Tommy, are you ok with this?' I say as I step back into the bedroom. Am *I* ok with this?

He turns his back and steps out of his wet clothes, uses the same towel he dried Herbie off with and almost flays himself with it. I attempt to laugh, lightly. 'Ok, I think that's enough. Do you want to put your PJs on?' He steps into his jeans, T-shirt and hoodie. I sit at the dressing-table mirror, brushing out my hair before turning on the hairdryer full blast. Both the animals jump. 'Want me to dry your hair, buster?' I say to Tommy, who ignores me, goes into the kitchen, animals in tow. I can hear mumbles. Quickly dress in a slouchy long-sleeved T-shirt dress, apply a slick of mascara, pull my hair back with an elastic.

'Well, don't you look nice. Doesn't Mummy look nice, Tommy?'

David is holding Tommy at the kitchen sink so he can wash his hands. Tommy's body is rigid. David ignores this. I sit at the table while David dries off Tommy's hands with kitchen towel, then pulls out a chair for him.

'It's vegetarian. I know how you don't like to eat animals,' David says to Tommy, cutting his slice into bite-sized pieces, standing over him.

Tommy eats, every last morsel.

'When did he last eat?'

I think of the peanut butter sandwich he nibbled at.

'Before we went to the park.'

'Did you go out in the rain?'

There is no right answer to that.

'This little fella was telling me all about school.'

'I'm sorry you have to go, Tommy.'

'I think you'll find he quite likes it, Sonya.'

'Do you, Tommy?'

He looks out the window, then down at Herbie and Marmie, then back out the window, his gaze agitated, not resting on anything for very long.

'He was telling me his painting was hung at the front of the class-room, and he got a gold star.'

'That's cool, Tommy. I always told you you could be an artist!'

'Or maybe an engineer, an architect, something with prospects?' David says.

Tommy nods, like he thinks this is a very good idea. Does he even know what 'prospects' means?

'Want a cup of tea, Sonya?'

No, I fucking don't. 'Please,' I say, holding my hand up. 'No milk.'

'Ah now, don't you think I know that much about you by now?' He looks at Tommy as he says this and laughs. 'No milk for Mummy.'

Tommy laughs back, aping him, a sound that doesn't belong to him. Has he been guzzling cow's milk from the carton since our separation? I don't think I could bear that.

'Are you eating, Sonya?' David says.

'Oh ok, just a sliver, then, with my tea.' Ms Sanity is making a guest appearance.

'Do you think you could put that dog out?'

'Herbie is an indoor dog. And anyway, it's raining out there.'

'Would you not get it a kennel?'

I look at Tommy, who is staring at me ferociously.

'Absolutely out of the question. That dog has been traumatised enough.'

'Not asking you to get an electric one!'

Tommy gets up and walks into the sitting room, sits on the floor, and for the first time since coming home he puts his arms around his pal. I watch, grateful.

'That's bloody unhygienic,' David mumbles, standing behind me.

'You sound exactly like my father.' I try on a laugh.

'Is that your stock answer when you hear something you don't like?'

I steer him back into the kitchen, attempt to generate a charge, to wrestle some power back, whisper, 'Have you missed me?' There's not a trace of the man who took me on the floor, here, who devoured me. I wonder if I made it all up.

'Sonya, I didn't like your tone of voice when you called. Remember the incident in the park?'

Feel exactly as I used to when I'd tell my father a secret, and he'd look at me in that way, and then later, in some argument, he'd use it against me, or worse still he'd have told Lara and she'd throw it at me: 'No wonder those girls in school don't talk to you.'

'You hinted at stuff, Sonya. And then earlier, your voice, it contained within it the possibility of all that.'

All of what, exactly? What did I say to him? I'd never have driven away, left Tommy on his own in the house. I just need to learn to sit with the urges, to soothe myself.

'We both know what you're capable of, don't we?' he continues.

I think of the guys in the meetings talking about what it means to be a mature adult: discerning, protecting themselves, not exposing themselves to the wrong sort of people. Think of Linda, imagine Mark bamboozling her with his questions, questions none of which she can answer correctly, designed to trip her up, no matter what shapes and sounds her mouth gives form to.

David walks into the living room. 'How's Tommy? This must be hard, huh? Strange being back in your old house?'

Herbie makes a low grumbling sound.

I follow him in. 'Not really, is it, Tommy? Just take a few days to get used to each other is all.'

Tommy is regarding us both in the same detached manner, causing a blockage, a sensation like a rough-edged pill stuck in my windpipe.

'Ok, Tommy, now time to say goodnight and thank you to David,' I say, woman in charge, woman residing under her own roof.

'Would you like it if I stayed, Tommy?' David says.

'Ok,' Tommy says.

'David, can we talk in private?'

I close the door behind us and speak low and, I think, reasonably, with not a hint of seduction, or wheedling. 'Hey, I think you were right earlier, when you said Tommy and I should spend time alone together on our first night.'

'That was before you told me what you told me.'

'You're making this much more stressful than it needs to be.'

'Sonya, you don't want to make a scene, scare the boy even further.'

'What exactly do you think I'd do, David?'

'Do you even remember what you said to me on the phone?'

An insistent hum starts to ring in my ears. Blurred fragments, no conscious memory, none, beyond picking up the phone and a feeling that my mouth should be stopped.

'I'd never forgive myself if I left you guys alone together.'

Breathe, swallow, breathe, swallow. The hum is increasing in volume and makes me want to clamp my hands over my ears. Ridiculous impulse. None of this is what it seems. He's only here because he cares, has my best interests at heart, and Tommy's. And I did ask for help.

'Are you ok?'

'I'm fine.'

'But you're not, are you?' He moves towards me. 'It's ok, sweet-heart. You don't have to do this alone again.' He goes to wrap me in his arms. Mr Sweetness & Light... *Mr fucking Mercurial!*

A part of me wants to soften, to yield, but 'sweetheart' – no man has ever called me that before and it doesn't sit. I'm not that; I've no desire to be anybody's that. I want to push him away, throw him out of the house, but can't risk traumatising Tommy with dramatics on his first night home.

'Thanks,' I mumble against his chest. 'Thanks.'

'Any time, you know that.'

'It was just a moment, *you* know *that*.'

I gently push him away, look into his eyes, fight an urge to shake my head to clear it of the build-up. It's all going on in there now. He leans in to kiss me on the lips; I let him. 'Right, let's tell him you're staying, will we?' He kisses me again.

I open the door. 'Tommy, David's going to have a sleepover. That ok?'

Tommy nods, not by his own volition, as if controlled by a puppetmaster.

'Where does he sleep, Sonya?'

He knows well there's only one bed in this house.

'Maybe you should give the boy his space and you can sleep out here with me?'

Tommy shakes his head, snapping those strings.

'It's ok, Tommy. I'm coming in with you.'

Tommy looks sideways at David.

'Herbie, Marmie,' Tommy says. 'Come.'

And the cat and the dog walk as one, trailing him.

'Time for a bedtime story,' I say to David, who settles himself on the couch, before I too follow Tommy into the bedroom.

Tommy pulls out a large picture book of *Fireman Sam*.

'What about Yaya's made-up stories? Our wave-riding adventures, Tommy?'

He screws up his eyes, shakes his head, then takes his clothes off and neatly places them on the chair.

'Do you need a hand, Tommy?'

His body hardens. I know that signal. Once he has dressed himself and is under the quilt, I invite Herbie and Marmie up. Tommy looks pleased. I start to read about Sam, a minuscule plastic fireman who loves to be on time; when he hears that bell chime, he puts on his coat and hat in less than seven seconds flat! Oh, please. I try to ape the sound of a real-life fire engine but fail spectacularly. I try making up a different, more exciting, imaginary story, throw in a few flying roos and ginormous waves called Walter and Wendy, and far-off lands made of chocolate diamonds, but Tommy stops me.

'That's not it. Start again.'

I sort of fudge the words a little: 'The little yellow fellow with the jutting jaw is the hero next door... He's an avid timekeeper with his bright, clean engine (yes, really!) – whohoo...'

Tommy looks suspiciously at me before he starts to sing his own version: 'Hurry, hurry, Mr Cool and Calm Sam the Fireman... Cos he's gonna save the day...'

I lean in to kiss him on his forehead and continue reading until he stops singing and his breathing slows down. Come on, Sam!

41

David is lounging, socks off, feet on the coffee table, reading *Bonjour Tristesse*. 'No wonder, Sonya,' he says, and grins.

Not going to dignify that with a response.

I whisper, 'I think he's nearly asleep.'

He pats the space beside him.

'That couch is too uncomfortable to sleep on.'

'No bother. I'll pull the cushions down on the floor. Can you get me a blanket?'

'There's one on the back of the couch,' I say as I lean over him.

His hand snakes up my thigh and he grabs hold of my flesh, twisting it, pinching. I brush his hand away, but his fingers continue creeping up, trying to find their way in.

'David, don't. Tommy's asleep in the next room.'

'We'll be quiet!'

'I want to check up on him, make sure he's not fretting.'

All the while his fingers are making their way. I'm dry and it hurts.

'That's abnormal, Sonya. You're crowding him. Do you want a codependent son?'

What's abnormal here, exactly?

'Come here, stop talking, and just… come here.'

I lean over him, brushing my mouth against his, wishing he'd remove his fingers.

'Not feeling it tonight?'

'I'm a bit stressed, obviously.'

'This'll help you de-stress.'

He's trying to pull me down on top of him; my body won't let it happen. He drops his hand, looks at me with a hurt-child expression just for a moment before he has time to rearrange his features into a more reasonable, understanding adult face.

'You go on in to the boy. We have plenty of time.'

He stands up, towering over me, holds me, pours into my ear: 'Sleep well, baby.'

'You too,' is about all I can manage.

I go into the bedroom, whisper 'Tommy?', who whispers back 'Yes?'

'So lovely to have you back, Tommy, I can't tell you.'

He hums Sam's theme tune sleepily.

Herbie sighs. I should let him out to do a pee but don't want to open the door. He'll have to wait. I push a chair under the door handle, not knowing exactly why. Dream that night that I can smell skin singeing.

When I wake, the sun's fingers are creeping in under the blind, and I draw my legs towards each other, then cross them tightly, still lying in the bed. Please be gone, I think, before I notice Tommy's eyes open and staring, boring into me.

'Morning, Mr T. How about you catch some of those rays for me?'

He doesn't move.

Herbie is lying on the floor at the end of the bed, trembling.

'Hewbie has wet himself,' Tommy says.

Of course he has, poor thing. Marmie is still curled up on the bed, purring softly, oblivious to her pal's distress.

'Ok, now, Herbie, ok, good boy,' I say as I get out of bed, opening the door a crack to see David's crumpled form on the cushions on the floor. 'Come on,' I whisper. We all creep into the kitchen and close the door quietly behind us. There's a choking smell of gas. Did I leave the ring on? I open the door to the yard, whooshing the rotten-egg-smelling air out. I fiddle around with the settings on the hob.

'Weird. Tommy, did you turn the gas on?'

He looks down guiltily.

'When? In the middle of the night?'

'Couldn't sleep. Jiminy Crickets in my chest.'

'It's not safe to do that, you know?'

He bites down on his bottom lip.

'Did you light the clicker?'

'Couldn't make it happen.'

'So you tried?'

He looks miserable, fighting the tears. I ruffle his hair, go to find the supply button at the back of the oven. Must remember to turn it off at the mains every night now. And hide every lighter in this house.

'It's ok, darling, just don't do it again.'

Herbie goes outside, straight to a potted plant, long dead, cocks his leg and does a loud, insistent piss. Marmie stands by, patiently waiting for her turn to climb into the pot and crouch and permeate his scent with hers.

The kettle is boiling when David walks in in his boxers.

'Freezing in here. Would you mind closing that door?'

'We need the air.'

'What's that's smell?'

'Would you mind putting something on, David?'

'Sorry, half asleep, forgot the little fella was here.'

Oh yes, and what was that display about last night, then?

He goes back into the lounge, dresses.

'Cornflakes, Tommy?'

'Yes please,' he says, all polite and accurate.

'Do you take cow's milk now, honey? David has put some in the fridge.'

He shakes his head vehemently. I haven't lost him completely.

'What's that pizza-man doing here, Yaya?'

'He's a friend, Tommy. Just a sleepover.'

'Can I go to school?'

I struggle for air. I couldn't help but notice his uniform all neatly ironed and folded in amongst his things.

'Lovely day,' David says, walking back into the kitchen.

'Yes. We're going to get ready and visit Grandad,' I say.

'You sure he'll want that, Sonya?'

'Of course he will. He'll be delighted to see Tommy, won't he, Munchkin?'

'Gandad?'

'Don't want to raise the lad's hopes.'

What exactly does he know that I don't? A flash of Father giving him his business card that day. Would David have called him? Has there been money exchanged?

Paranoia, Sonya. Tiredness does this; brings on the big guns.

'We'll call him first, won't we, T?'

David refills the kettle, flicks the switch.

'We're going to go have a shower. Let yourself out.'

'What? Are you throwing me out without my coffee? You know I don't function without my morning coffee.' He winks at me.

I wonder at this display of overfamiliarity in front of Tommy.

'Help yourself,' I say. 'Chat later, ok? I'm sure you've a busy day planned.'

He opens the cupboards loudly, clanging the mug on the counter. Doesn't he have to be somewhere? It's worrying the amount of time he has on his hands.

I look at Tommy, a protective rage rising in me. 'Will we go for that shower?'

'Ok.' Someone must have gotten him used to this.

'Well, lovely to meet you, Tommy. I'm sure we'll be seeing much more of each other.' David salutes at him.

Tommy looks at me. 'Come on, now, darling', and I lead him to the bathroom, where he tells me to wait outside because he's big enough to clean himself. This hurts in a way I don't understand.

I can hear David clomping about in the kitchen, slamming drawers unnecessarily. I listen to the sound of Tommy humming that tune. The door opens; Marmie and Herbie hurl themselves at me.

'I'm off so, Sonya. Might be an idea to get to that eight o'clock meeting later. I'll come back, babysit.'

'Thanks. I'll let you know.'

'It's on in the community centre.'

'Yes. Thanks.'

I push the subconscious of the moment (I always excelled at playing the level beneath) – *just piss off, don't make me have to say it.*

He looks at me. There's an intensity to his gaze that climbs inside me. Find it hard to untangle.

'See you later so.'

'I'll call you.'

He lifts his hand, an abrupt dismissive gesture. 'Those meetings are not optional.'

'See you, then.' And the front door closes. I breathe out.

I speak to Tommy through the crack in the door: 'Don't forget to wash behind your ears, darling.'

I find some bleach in the kitchen cupboards, get down on my knees and scrub the spot on the bedroom rug where Herbie peed, undiluted peroxide burning my hands. Tommy is at the door, watching me, swaddled in a huge bath towel, and I have to stop myself from scooping him up in my arms and cradling him. We still have a way to go yet.

'Where the man gone?'

'He's gone home, Tommy.' Can't stop myself asking: 'Did you like him?'

He shrugs, dries himself off and dresses himself.

'He doesn't like Herbie.'

There he goes with his perfect 'r'.

'No, he doesn't. And Herbie always comes first.'

'Hewbie seems different.'

I can't help smiling, loving his inconsistencies. He'll never know that Herbie was put in a cage.

'It's just going to take us all a little time to get to know each other again, ok?'

'Ok,' he says, a seriousness in his voice that goes way beyond his years. I'd forgotten that old-man-like quality of his, and now it seems even more deeply ingrained. I am determined to make him laugh again.

'What'll we do today, little man?'

He seems surprised by this question, which makes me think of our former relationship, where he was always a hostage to my whims and moods.

'Would you like to go up the hills?'

He seems astounded by this very normal suggestion. A weekend hike, healthy, wholesome, and afterwards we'll go visit his grandad.

More normality. I roll the word around my mouth, savouring the texture, the taste. Yes, I could get used to this: like drinking tea.

42

The hills are cold and mucky, and all a bit much for Marmie, who periodically freezes, hackles up, hissing at something only she can see. It's grey above and underfoot, a monochrome expanse of drab. Herbie circles me frantically, Tommy says he's tired, and quite frankly so am I. Bored. Reminds me of the hillwalking Sundays I was forced to endure with my father and Lara, who togged me (and themselves) out in all the right gear. I hated those ugly boots and shiny, crinkly waterproof pants, but I have to admit they have their place as I look down at my lightweight soggy trainers and sopping jeans. Even when it's not actively raining up here the air's sodden, and I can't help thinking how David would react to that punchy wet-dog smell in the car.

'Ok, troops, shall we head for home?' I say after half an hour of traipsing, stopping, cajoling the cat, being stared at. Bloody weekend walkers. They're everywhere, with their stupid, damp, stinking woollen bobble hats. Tommy shouts 'YES' and runs back towards the car faster than I've ever seen him. A sprinter, a speeder, like me. We trot after him, his voice trailing in the soggy air: 'Race ya, slowcoaches.' And I do what any 'normal' parent would do – I slow down so my son can win. I never used to be able to let him win at anything.

We pile into the car, steam rising, and yes, stinking to high heaven. I roll down all the windows, crank the music up, foot to the accelerator, and this time Tommy joins in with my squeals of excitement, though the animals just press themselves tight against the back seat, quivering.

'Where to, Tommy?' I shout.

'Gandad's,' he says.

'Ok, hang tight...'

I wasn't able to get through to him this morning, of course I wasn't, but I left a measured, polite message saying that Tommy and myself would love to see him, and would it be ok if we called around. It shouldn't be too much of a shock if we all land.

I leave Marmie and Herbie in the car, tell them I won't be long. Press down on the doorbell, start off polite, then leave it a little longer, becoming more insistent. I know they're in there, the car is in the driveway. He couldn't possibly be ignoring me at such an important time in Tommy's life, and mine. The heat is rising, the music an indistinct murmur. Her outline is forming when Tommy interrupts: 'Maybe Gandad is not in, Yaya?'

Patience, Sonya, patience. I roll the word around in my mouth and it's sticky and sweet, like a marshmallow. I swallow. Hard to digest.

Tommy puts his hand in mine, and I feel myself flow back down inside myself.

I look at him, wink. 'Yes, you're right, lovie. Thank you for making me see the obvious!'

He smiles, relieved.

'Where to now, Tommy?'

'Time to feed the aminals?' he says.

'Shall we all get pizza?'

'Do cats eat pizza?' He sounds amazed at the idea.

'Probably not, but we can get some and then go home and open her can of yack.'

'Yackety-yack,' he says, and holds his nose.

The thought of seeing that rude little madam at the pizzeria again charges my body with adrenalin. I haven't forgotten how she publicly humiliated me. And suddenly my mind is focused only on one thing: revenge. Displaced, maybe, but still.

There's a different person behind the counter. My mood plummets, I really needed to let off steam with that little so-and-so, but this is undoubtedly a young man, and from his back, he's broad and well muscled, probably a gym addict. I'm just about to give him a piece of advice about 'all things in moderation, sonny' (as I'm in no doubt he's a steroid guzzler), when the boy turns and looks into my eyes. *Mr Kittens/Black sacks/Stones.* The boy from the cafe. He smiles, snarky, provocative. What's he doing this side of town?

'Well, if it isn't the banshee,' he says.

How dare he, and in front of my son?

He leans over the counter. 'And is this your poor little fecker?'

I look around the room. Only two other teenagers, waiting on their garlic dough balls, heads lost inside cyberspace. What is it they're looking at? Porn – of course it's porn. I walk over to one of them, peer over his shoulder, but can't see anything, the light is glaring. The boy glances at me distractedly, walks away, doesn't disconnect from his sordid fantasy. Probably one of those games where they go around in white vans, picking up prostitutes and murdering them. The thoughts start building up, crowding me, each one darker and more extreme than the last. Shake my head. The boy behind the counter is studying me with interest.

'What can I get you?' he says to Tommy, kindly, I think.

'Anything vegetawian,' says Tommy, my brilliant boy.

'Coming right up,' the boy continues. 'What do you like? Evwything?'

Did I just imagine that?

'Just cheese and tomato, please.'

'Lovely manners, young lad. Did your ma teach you those?'

Do not lose it in front of this impudent little pup. Do not give him the pleasure a second time.

'Does your boss know your story?' I say.

'What story's that, then?' He speaks very loudly to alert the others in the room.

'He might be interested in hearing it from me...' I continue, knowing I should stop but in the grip of something much more powerful than myself. What is it about this boy—?

'He already warned me about you, but I didn't know it was *you*,' the pup continues, his smile catapulting me right back to that awful moment in rehab. The flapping sound, creatures already in flight, already on their course. White mist is rising. No, please, not that. Not now, not in front of Tommy. *Please help*. And I do what I have to: I summon Jimmy's face, Sister Anne's, the words of the rosary, and invoke them over and over, over and over, *Hail Mary, full of grace, Mary, Mother of God, giver of life, Divine Mother with the bleeding lips and the flaking smile, the mother's smile, the mother's sacrifice, blessed art thou.* I allow myself to be filled. This is it. I feel her. Arms around me, holding me steady.

'Yaya?' Tommy's voice cuts through.

'Is your ma ok?' the boy asks.

I feel the pressure of Tommy's little hand squeezing mine.

'Perfectly fine. Now can you get us two Margheritas, please.'

I think of meeting David in here for the first time all those months ago, how sober, how safe, how in control, how *kind* he seemed, and I can't square any of it with the man I now know or don't know or don't want to know. I lean down to kiss Tommy on the forehead.

The boy looks spooked.

'Get a move on, will you?' I say.

'The boss told me to make sure you paid before serving you,' he says.

I look at Tommy, hand the twenty-euro note over the counter.

The boy takes it, holding it away from him as if contaminated, and puts it in the till, handing me back fifty cents.

'Keep the change,' I say.

He puts the order through and backs away from me. I study him. He looks better, the muscles suit him, though they did come on rather quickly. Where is this boy heading? I think of the man in the meeting who watched his father throw himself into the canal on his fortieth birthday.

He speaks low: 'Glad to see you're ok, you know, after that day 'n' all...'

I pretend I don't know what he's talking about, but then add, 'You're looking well yourself.'

He nods curtly, calls out the teenagers' order, which does in fact include garlic dough balls, and I wonder what else was I was right about. The porn, no doubt, the vicious games, probably, but this boy and the canal? I look at the boy's solid physique, the fact of his holding down a job, earning money, and can't help feeling hopeful.

He hands me the box, lowers his voice again and says, 'God bless you,' as I leave.

I don't think it was ironic.

43

'Last one in is a pooper.'

'Pooper scooper,' Tommy says.

'Want to join us, Mrs O'M?' I shout when I see our treacherous neighbour peering at us from behind the safety of her well-pruned hedge.

'No, Yaya, not Witchy Mary,' Tommy says.

'It's ok, Mr T, she wouldn't dare.'

Just what did the 'little mite' endure in that house, and how many nights was he there before he was moved on? I won't allow this thought to take hold, burrow down.

'Hello, Tommy,' Mrs O'Malley says. 'So lovely to see you all back home together.'

You bitch. I'm filled with the shape, the taste, the smack of the word, which sounds satisfactorily like it should. I grab Tommy by the arm and pull him through the front door.

'Ow, hurt.'

'Sorry, Mr T. Sorry. We all need to eat.'

'Yes, Yaya. Aminals too.'

'Yes, Tommy, I know that.'

Tommy is watching me closely. He opens the fridge, sniffing, eyes darting anxiously around.

'Owange juice, Yaya?'

I pull a bottle of MiWadi from the cupboard. His tense body visibly relaxes. Jesus, is this how it will play out from now on?

'Don't forget Marmie and Herbie's yackety-yack.'

'After us, T. I'll feed them after us.'

'No, now. They're stahving. And they need water.'

'Here.' I hand him the bowl, lift him up, careful not to hold him too close, turn the kitchen tap on.

'Enough, Yaya,' he says, the bowl overflowing. 'Yaya?'

'Yes, darling. I'm right here.'

'You don't sound blurry.'

Christ. 'Thank you.' I articulate the words carefully. Can I do this? 'Do what exactly, Sonya, what?' Something is missing.

'Who are you talking to, Yaya?'

I didn't know I'd spoken that aloud.

'My guardian angel,' I say, trying to smile.

'My guarding angel sat by my bed sometimes when you were away.'

'What did he or she look like?' I tread gently, aware this is the first time he's spoken of our time apart.

'Sometimes like Herbie.'

'Do you hear that, Herbie?'

The dog's tail thumps on the kitchen tiles.

'And sometimes like Gandad and that pizza-man.'

'Giant versions?'

'No, people-size.'

'Oh. Do you think they look alike, T?'

'They have the same voices.'

'Yes, they do sound similar.'

'I hope Gandad comes to see me soon. He pwomised.'

Did he? I find that almost unbearable. Who makes false promises to someone so little? I serve him his pizza, which he eats methodically, chewing carefully. I make myself swallow two slices.

'Tommy?' I speak pretend-casually, not wanting to spook him. 'What did you set on fire in Mrs O'Malley's house?'

'Nothing, Yaya!'

'And in Clare's?'

'Only Mr Candle and Ms Matches.'

'And did you try to set the house on fire?'

He looks at me as if I've truly lost my mind, left it somewhere else, as if only someone spectacularly stupid could ask such a thing.

'But did you want to?' I can't help myself.

He ignores me, bends down to pat Herbie.

'Just going to the loo, Tommy,' I say.

He doesn't answer.

I close the bathroom door behind me and look in the mirror, see a blur looking back at me, which is not unusual. What is unusual is a bar of carbolic soap still in its wrapping. I'd never buy that shit. *Wash your mouth and your thoughts out, Sonya.* A disembodied voice.

'Yaya?' Tommy shouts from outside the door. Was I talking out loud again?

'It's ok, Mr T. Just doing a poops,' I say, hoping to make him laugh, but then I remember our previous open-door policy. Jesus, the booze really lowered the boundaries.

'All done!' I say as I come back out.

'Stinky-stink, Yaya!' He waves his hand in front of his nose.

I pinch mine. 'Poopy-poop-poop-poop.'

A quiet laugh builds inside him. I can see the effort it's taking him to push it down. I tickle him under the arms. He explodes, tears running down his face. I'm not sure if he's laughing or crying; probably both.

'Tommy, would you like to tell me something about your time with Clare? Anything?'

'Poopy-pooppooppooop!'

'Did Clare teach you to light a match?'

'Stinkystinkstinkstinkstink!'

'How about school? Are you happy to go back?'

'The colour of seagulls,' he says.

'Are you talking about the clouds, or the building?'

'Grey white grey.'

'No wonder you're so good at drawing! Will we get our colour book out, my little artist?'

He almost bounces on his heels with excitement. 'Yes, Yaya.'

'You know how it's your birthday in ten days, Tommy? Will we have a party?'

He goes to the art drawer at the bottom of the bockety Ikea chest of drawers, which I didn't bother to assemble properly, and takes out crayons, glitter, glue and a scrapbook.

'Who come to the party, Yaya?'

Clare, Maureen, Father, Lara, David? Not much of a crew for a five-year-old.

'What about your pals from school, Tommy?'

He shrugs. 'Miss Maeve,' he says.

'Your teacher? Do you like her?'

'She gave me gold stars.'

He's engrossed in rubbing Pritt Stick glue on a blank page and shaking the tube of glitter in uneven triangular shapes.

'Tommy, that is truly beautiful!'

He looks at me, delighted. I clear my throat, speak low: Come into my orbit. 'Come, gentle night, come, loving, black-brow'd night.'

Tommy looks thrilled. I climb on to the couch, smooth down my dress, engage my full, sonorous voice: 'Give me my Romeo; and, when he shall die... Go on, Tommy... What's next?'

He stands and sprinkles glitter on the paper from a height. 'Take him and cut him out in little stars...'

'Yes? What's next, you twinkly, brilliant boy?'

'Fowget, Yaya.'

'And he will make the face of heaven so fine...' I prompt him.

'That all the world will love Mr Sunshiny and fowget Mr Night!'

'Magnificent paraphrasing, Tommy, you really are my little genius!'

'Bow-wow-wow, Yaya!'

I curtsy and a cloud of glitter falls on my head. Tommy is throwing fistfuls like confetti. A twisting sensation in my guts. I need it to stop.

'Ok, that's enough, now. Are you going to hoover all that up?'

Again, that inherited gift for puncturing any happiness. *Selfish, selfish, selfish.*

'I'm sorry, Tommy, I didn't mean...'

Tommy ignores me and doesn't try to make it all alright, like he normally would.

I continue, 'How about we make your very first party invitations and you can take them to school tomorrow?'

He sticks the end of a red crayon stick in his mouth.

'Yumptious scrumptious blood, Mr Dracool!' I boom, baring my fangs.

Not a trace of a smile. He wipes his mouth with his sleeve.

'This party, Tommy. How many invitations do we need? Ten, twenty?'

Shit, a children's party. How do I do that? I'll probably need to provide entertainment. Musical statues, I can do that, pass the parcel, what else? I can dress up, draw on my past, wear a tutu, dance with some sparklers. A fiery fairy godmother! I'll track down Mr Fire Blower. My thoughts are speeding up.

'Yaya?'

That bloody imp has made a shadowy appearance. If I don't bring any attention to her, she can't climb inside. Exert a little bit of fucking effort, Sonya.

I breathe deeply. 'What do you think, Tommy? We can have all your little friends over on Saturday, get fairy lights, cupcakes, krispies, paper hats, sparklers, Catherine wheels...' Excitement is building. That hazy memory about those spinning wheels of fire catches hold of me. A bright, sparkling moment. There were happy times too.

'Yaya?' he tries to cut in again.

'Who are your friends, Tommy?'

He looks at me blankly.

'Didn't you tell David all about school?'

He lifts his shoulders slightly.

'Why won't you talk to your own mother?' My voice is speedy, high. 'And after all I've given up for you?' A dark shadow is nipping at my heels. I try to kick it off. 'Tommy, I need names. Names, Tommy, names.'

Did I just shout just then? Tommy winces and withdraws inside himself. Herbie growls.

A memory lands, like a smack to the side of my face. 'Wakey-wakey, princess, it's your birthday.' I'm being pulled from my bed, dragged downstairs by the arm and presented with a room full of twinkly fairy lights and candles. Music tinkles, some kind of Abba-style kitsch, and as I rub my eyes I see a woman in a tutu-style dress, covered head to toe in glitter, telling me to 'dance, darling, dance'. Multicoloured snowflakes, tasty snowflakes, sweeties falling from the sky. 'Such a pretty little girl.' Twirled in circles, lifted under the arms and spun high, laughter in my ears. I don't remember anything more except my father shouting, 'Stop it now, stop it, enough.' He brings me back to my bed, wiping off the glitter with a warm facecloth. 'I'll bring you up some hot milk, ok?' He doesn't even wish me a happy birthday. He's forgotten all about it.

This is not the bright place I was chasing. I snap back into myself, take in the scene around me. Tommy looks too stunned to cry. I deposit the tube of glitter in the art drawer and slam it shut.

Tommy has his eyes closed and is whispering something – a prayer? He kisses Herbie on the soft spot between his eyes.

I swipe my father's number; will not stop until he answers. I have to know. What was it about my childhood, the missing parts? Eventually, Lara's voice answers: 'Yes, what is it, Sonya?'

'I need to speak to Dad and if you don't put that man, my father, on the phone right now, I'll come over with the dog, cat and Tommy, and I'll camp out on your doorstep until you let us all in.'

'I think you'd better talk to her.' I hear mumbles.

'Dad?'

'Yes, Sonya. What is it?'

'I need to talk to you about my mother. What really happened?'

He sips in air through his mouth. 'Oh, for God's sake, Sonya.'

'Dad, I think I remember...'

A silence, then an almost-whisper: 'Please don't go getting all melodramatic on me now, Sonya. Be sensible, for Tommy.'

'Did that line work for my mother, did it? Was that all it was? A touch of melodrama?'

'Please, Sonya, get to your meetings. You have support this time. Make use of it.'

'What was wrong with her, Dad?'

I hear him breathe in an exaggerated fashion.

'What did she really die of, Dad?'

'Sonya, why dredge all this up now?'

'Dad… Do you think I am the same?'

His breath catches. 'Oh, Sonya…'

'I want to see you in person. Tommy wants to see you, you promised him…'

The phone is snatched from his hand. 'Your father is not going anywhere, Sonya. He's not well.'

'Dad?' I shout down the phone. 'You have to tell me the truth.'

'That's quite enough now, Sonya,' Lara says.

'Yaya?' Tommy's voice cuts through.

I throw the phone down and sink into the couch.

'Oh, Tommy, I'm sorry, I'm so sorry. I didn't mean…'

He climbs on top of me, strokes my hair, which is sparkling with pieces of glitter. The warmth and heft of his little body. The sound of his breath in my ear: a divine whisper.

44

'Wake up, sleepyhead. Time for school.'

I never thought I'd be saying those words. I lean in to kiss him on
his red-rumpled cheek. He stirs, a slight smile on his mouth, and I
leave him there as I go into the kitchen to get breakfast ready. Today
is a new day, a day filled with the same vulnerability and resolve
that follows a spectacular blow-out. I don't like how I spoke to my
father; how I exposed a part of myself that isn't safe around him. I
also don't like how I made my son feel unsafe around me.

Tommy dresses himself, and I have to admit he's cute in his little
grey slacks and jumper, but oh, those flashing trainers and the
fire-engine satchel. Bite down on the inside of my cheek. We eat
cornflakes and toast. I bundle the animals in the car – we'll have a
nice walk after the drop-off; isn't that what a suburban mother is
supposed to do? We pull up outside the address Maureen gave me,
which is only a twenty-minute drive in thick traffic. She didn't tell
me it was some kind of a religious institution. What is it about this
country and its seats of learning? A looming cross above the arched
doorway – an instrument of torture, symbol of suffering; prefabs
huddled closely around the chapel, hunkered down in its shadow.

Tommy jumps out, waving at us all.

'Do you have my lunch, Yaya?'

Lunch? Oh shit, I was meant to make a sandwich, put in a drink, an apple.

'I'll be back with it, T. What time do you take lunch?'

He shrugs.

'Leave it with me, ok? Go on, now, and have a lovely time. Remember to give out those party invitations!'

I'm still in the driver's seat, the car engine idling. He nods, blows kisses to Marmie and Herbie, then hoists his ridiculous bag over his shoulder. I stay watching him until he disappears inside the door, then look down at my phone. Eight missed calls from David. I put my foot flat to the floor.

'Time for a run, guys.'

Pull up outside the gates of the local park, and even though I'm wearing jeans and boots I hit the ground running. I leave Herbie and Marmie off their leads. Lots of stares. Do my best to ignore them but can't resist sticking my finger up at a particularly nosy old bag. 'Those animals should be safely at home or that dog should be on a lead.' The woman's words are tracking me down. I run faster. Finally I stop, hold my side, retch a little, attach the leads to the cat and dog and hobble back to the car. My shin splints are pretty acute after smacking the pavement with my boots.

Drive to the Spar, buy a cheese sandwich, should be ok, an apple, Tayto crisps – are they ok? – and speed back to the school. I pull into the grounds this time, take in the small cluster of prefabs, insignif-icant and flimsy, so like the sanatorium and the drying-out wing in the rehab. How many of these little people will make their way there later in life? Some, but not Tommy, I'll make sure of that. 'He's young enough to bounce back from this' – Jimmy's voice rings in my ears.

'Ok, guys, you hang tight. Won't be long.' I speak through the car window, press my nose against it. I'm sure I can see Herbie do his dolphin smile. I'm winning him back.

I press the bell on the door and wait. A disappointed-looking woman with a sunken mouth opens the door. Hear the guys: 'If life gives you lemons…' I know I'm smirking.

'Hello, can I help you?'

'I'm Tommy Moriarty's mother. Here's his lunch.'

The woman takes the bag, holding it a safe distance from her body.

'What class is he in?'

'I don't know… The littlest. He's four, five next week.'

I'm jabbering, feeling judged. Crap mother with her cheap Spar lunch, late.

'Oh, is that little Tommy who arrived on his own this morning? We were trying to call you.'

'No, you must be mistaken. I drove him here myself.'

The woman stares at me, really stares, probing. I look away.

'What time is he finished?'

'Do you have any ID?' the woman asks, looking suspiciously at the bag.

'Excuse me?'

'Just something to tell me you are who you say you are.'

The woman continues with her scoping, which is starting to feel invasive. This is exactly the feeling I had in the days after my mother's death, when the whole school's eyes were on me, pinning me, a rare and dangerous species. I stick my tongue into the healing welt in my cheek. Breathe, ground, pray.

'I'll go home, get my passport,' I say. Ms Sanity in the starring role.

The woman nods, all the while burning me with her magnified glare.

I turn to go. 'Make sure you give Tommy his lunch, ok?'

The woman says, 'Did you not get the list of acceptable food?' I won't turn around, will myself on, back to the car, to the sanctuary of the animals. 'We don't allow crisps, certainly not Tayto.' The voice chases me down. 'The sandwiches are fine, though.'

I pull up outside my front door and see Mrs O'Malley outside, watering her plants. In November? Does the Man Above not piddle down enough? Rage rips through me, grabs me by the throat, rattles me around a bit.

When I open the door, the smell of bleach is overpowering. Did I leave the top off, let it spill?

'Hello, Sonya.'

He's wearing the frilly apron that Tina gave me. Is he trying to be ironic?

Herbie and Marmie follow me in, tails down, hackles up.

'Aren't you surprised to see me?' he says.

Something about the absurdness of the moment makes me play its opposite.

'Should I be?'

'You didn't answer your phone. I was worried.'

'All good.'

'Your father doesn't think so.'

Ah so.

'He asked me to come check in on you.'

'That's nice.'

'How was the little fella heading off to school?'

How does he—?

'I have to go back for him at twelve thirty. Going for a quick shower.'

'Have you eaten, Sonya? You seem a bit jittery.'

'How did you get in?'

'You gave me a key, remember?'

I don't remember, but try to convince myself I do, even as I know I'd never do such a thing.

He opens the back door and says 'Shoo' to the animals.

A chill creeps in. No one moves.

'They're not used to being spoken to that way. Please close the door, David. It's freezing.'

'Better than stinking.'

A quality of silence that holds within it the beating of wings.

'You ok, Sonya? Bit pale. Sit down.'

'When did you speak to my father, David?'

He ignores this, pulls up a chair, pushes me down by the shoulder.

The sound of the flapping intensifies, creating an impression that I'm standing inside a wind tunnel.

'I think you might be about to have one of your episodes. Here, I made you a cheese sandwich, got you some Tayto, an apple.'

I look down at my plate. The exact same lunch I gave to Tommy. I look at David, try to conjure the whole of him, but only get a blurred outline.

'Do you want me to pick Tommy up?' he says, voice even as he sets the tea down in front of me.

'What? No, no thanks. I have to go back with ID anyway.'

'ID? Why? What did you do, Sonya? Have you got them worried already?' He smiles warmly. A shared joke. He closes the door on the animals.

I sip my tea. It's lovely. Comforting and ordinary.

'Let's go together.'

I think of the look in that woman's eyes. Her judgement, her anxiety. It might not be the worst idea; I may be Ms Moriarty, but that doesn't mean I have to be a single mother.

'Eat up,' he says as he draws up a seat beside me and cuts my sandwich into neat triangles.

'I don't like crusts,' I say, not sure what part I'm playing exactly.

He shakes his head, but then good-humouredly trims the edges of the bread. 'Now, madam, to your liking?'

I take a bite, chew.

He moves in to kiss me on the cheek. 'I missed you, Sonya.'

I smile, swallow.

'Right, time for you to take your shower,' he says as he clears the half-eaten lunch things.

'Yes,' I say, having settled on the role of submissive 'Wifey' in an arch, modernist, feminist production.

'And after, we'll both go and collect Tommy, ok? Best to make a good impression on your first day.'

'Probably not a bad idea.' Knowing as I say this how much Tommy will hate that David is there, and not Herbie and Marmie.

'Do you have a car?' I ask while driving.

'DUI,' he says.

'Oh, how long ago?'

'Three years now.'

'Must be up by now, then.'

He shrugs. 'Was never much of a car man myself.'

Think of how, when I first saw him, I'd imagined him driving the latest BMW, regularly serviced, all polished chrome and leather. I know the other guys pictured him driving some lean machine too. Impressions, instincts, off whack.

'Don't you miss your old job?'

'Rather not talk about that,' he says as he turns the radio up loud. *Rainy with showers, temperature falling below zero at nightfall.*

I can't believe I let him leave the animals outside.

After parking up, I turn to him. 'Actually, probably better if you don't come.'

'Jesus, Sonya, talk about not knowing your own mind!' He gets out, closing the door behind him. 'I honestly think it'll look better if there's a man in your life. Trust me.'

We walk to the back gate, where other parents are waiting, mostly women on their own, their husbands at work.

'Do you have your ID to hand?' David whispers.

The children tumble out the back door in groups of twos and threes. Tommy emerges last, the same woman from earlier shadowing him.

He's staring at David.

'Where's Herbie?'

There he goes with that perfect 'r' again.

'Ah, there you are.' The woman trots up to me.

I hand her the passport in silence.

'I hope you understand it's only for the boy's welfare. We hadn't met you before. It was his previous carer who used to bring him in…' She trails off, then offers her hand to David: 'Mrs White.'

Heat rises and crawls across my skin.

'Thank you, Mrs White, for your concern. Have you had a good look?' David gestures at the passport unopened in the woman's red, raw hands, which look like they've washed too many dishes unprotected.

She opens it, flustered, pretends to read the front page, then hands it back.

'I'd have thought you'd have been made aware that Tommy is back with his mother?'

The teacher regains her composure and studies David carefully for a moment. 'I'm sorry, and you are?'

'David Smythe.' He speaks his name as if she should know who he is.

'I hadn't been informed of a partner.'

'I'm a family friend.'

I hate myself for this, but I start to blurt, wanting the woman's approval: 'David is a solicitor and a trained counsellor, Mrs White.'

He hands her his business card, smiles. 'Now, come on, Tommy. We've a birthday party to plan.'

The teacher studies the card a moment, then says in a strained, forced manner: 'Ah yes, lucky boy, Tommy. Who's a lucky boy?'

'Come on, now, Tommy.' I take hold of his hand.

David looks at me, winks, and the two of us move to hold him under each arm and swing him high in the air. It feels so *natural*. 'One, two, three, wheee!' Tommy's body goes hard. I know that signal and I want to tell David to stop, but the teacher is watching us closely.

Mrs White pretend-laughs. 'My, that's mighty high you're flying, Tommy.'

Tommy looks at me, crosses his eyes, rolls his tongue so the sides touch off each other. Clever little boy; he could never stand being patronised. When I look at the teacher again I see conflicting emotions play out on her face. A part of me wants to confide in her, ask her what she thinks of this man. How does he appear to strangers? That bloody resolution to never trust anything my instinct tells me hasn't exactly set up a reliable inner compass. Ok, so God, what do you think? God? Where are you, God?

Back in the car David turns to Tommy. 'Hey, dude. Not cool to make that face about your teacher.'

I look at him in the rear-view mirror. He sticks his thumb in his mouth.

'Bad manners not to answer, son. Did your mother not teach you anything?'

His words stir a familiar reverberation in me. Lara saying something similar to me and my father standing by, letting her.

'Only babies suck their thumbs, and you're not a baby anymore, are you?'

'No, he's not.' I stop him. 'He's a big boy, an almost-five-year-old! Tommy? How many of those invites did you give out today?'

Tommy continues looking out the window.

'Did you hear your mother, Tommy?'

I elbow David, without looking directly at him, my concentration on the road ahead. I whisper, 'Back off him.'

David leans in and puts the radio on. Some rapper is *motherfuckingwhore*-ing down the airwaves. I turn it off. 'Jesus, that stuff should be rated, not played during the school run.'

'Do you hear your mother, Tommy, pretending to be all responsible and concerned?'

'I *am* concerned,' I say, a flash of anger erupting.

'Ok, now, calm down, Sonya, don't go getting all dramatic on me now.'

Did he swallow my father's words? I press my foot to the floor.

'Jesus, Sonya. Slow down. Small person on board.' David is trying to make his tone sound jokey, but much as he spouts on to me about needing to 'let go and let God', I know he's not able, not for a second, and being a passenger in a car driven by a wired, out-of-control woman is challenging every aspect of him that needs to be in the driving seat at all times.

'Wheee, Tommy!' I say, winking in the rear-view mirror.

'Wheee,' he says back, a watered-down limp response, unsure.

'Wheee,' says David, trying to join in.

Tommy looks at him with that look I saw him give me the first night he came back: appraising, cold.

Once inside, Tommy goes straight to the back door, opens it and lets Herbie and Marmie in.

'They're animals,' David says. 'Better off outside.'

'They're domesticated animals, though, David. Not some wild creatures that were reared in the outdoors. They're used to heat and home comforts.'

'Well, they can just get used to their natural habitat again.'

'Natural habitat... a yard?' I hear a pig-like grunt come out of me.

'Are you snorting at me?' he says, and I'm not quite sure what mood his tone is suggesting.

I decide to try to play it for laughs. Make a piggie sound.

'That's wubbish, Yaya.'

'Hey. Don't be rude to your mother, young man.'

'He's not being rude; we're only playing,' I say, and then wonder what I'm doing justifying my relationship with my son to this man, who only yesterday I determined to cut loose from our lives.

'Right. Time for homework.' Relish this, weirdly.

'I'm very good at maths,' David says.

'Don't you have anywhere you need to be?'

'Nowhere I'd rather be! How about I make us all some food while you guys get down to it?'

Tommy is on his knees, whispering something into Herbie's ear.

David sneezes. 'Shit, my allergies are acting up. Really need to stick the animals outside for a while, alright, soldier?'

'We'll go in here,' Tommy says, and moves with his entourage into the living room, closes the door behind him.

'That'll tell you!' I say, laughing.

'Seriously, Sonya? Have you any idea how rude that boy is?'

A sensation like a kick to the thorax; I almost double over with the force of it. 'Excuse me?' I manage.

'Ah, only joking. Go on in, now, and get his homework out of the way. I'll rustle us up an omelette.'

'You're ok, David, we've all only had our lunch.'

'I'd feel better knowing Tommy has eaten properly.' He's already got the eggs out and is cracking the first against a bowl.

'I don't think he'll want to eat again so soon.'

'It isn't all about what he wants, it's about what he needs.'

The kitchen suddenly seems too small for us both, walls closing in. I feel clammy. Open the door to the back yard. Breathe deeply. He watches.

'Not feeling too good, Sonya?'

My thumb is doing its spasming thing.

'You don't have to do this all alone again, you know.' He starts to whisk the eggs.

I contemplate his words. See Linda cocooned inside Mark's arms, her face blissful and trusting.

'You have trust issues, Sonya. We both know this.'

'Yes, I do. And with good reason… And now Tommy and I need to spend some time together, alone,' I say in an even voice, surprising him, surprising us both.

'Just let me finish this omelette for you.'

'Really not necessary.'

He shakes his head, trying on a light jokey tone. 'What woman would turn down such an offer?'

'Thanks for all your help, I'm sure you've other things to be getting on with.'

He is trying very hard to maintain his reasonable, adult demeanour as he puts the bowl into the fridge. 'Just add cheese, mushrooms, maybe some spinach later…'

'Yes, I know.'

'And call me when you're going to a meeting. At least three a week. You have to stay on top of this, Sonya.'

'I know that, David.' I study him closely. 'When did you and my father first make contact?'

'He gave me his card.' He begins to gather up his things.

'I saw that, but why did you think it was ok to call him?'

'He gave me his card for a reason.'

'How often do you talk?'

'You're deflecting, Sonya. We're discussing the need for you to stay on top of your recovery and here you go firing questions at me. As is your way.' He puts his coat on.

'And you never answer. I didn't think I was your *client* any longer.'

'You were never officially a client of mine. You made sure of that, Sonya. You knew what you were doing.'

He looks really rattled for a moment, then changes tack.

'Sonya, your father worries about you.'

'What stops him checking in on me himself?'

'I'm sure you know the answer to that one.'

I really want him the hell out of my home now.

'We must go out for dinner again some evening, find a babysitter for the little man.'

I don't say anything. He's at the door, waiting to see if I reply, debating whether to say anything else, when suddenly, abruptly, he opens the door and slams it behind him. I think he's hurt.

As soon as he's gone I realise I didn't ask him for the key back. Did my father give him one? Our last conversation didn't exactly convince him I'm a capable, coping single mother.

I go into the living room, where Tommy moves with speed and stealth away from the door back towards the couch, a sylph. I bet his ear was pressed to the door; he's had plenty of opportunity to hone that particular skill of late. I have to fight an urge to ask him what he thinks of this situation, have to fight even harder not to ask Herbie.

'Hey, Mr T, how many of those invites did you give out today?'

Tommy reaches into his bag and pulls a full complement of envelopes back out.

'None? Why's that, then, Munchkin?'

His shoulders move towards his ears.

'Tomorrow, then? How about you hand them out tomorrow?'

'Don't want to go tomorrow.'

I should be pleased.

'Ah now, come on, Tommy. It can't be that bad.'

He sticks his thumb in his mouth.

'Did something happen, Tommy?'

He looks at me like I'm a complex puzzle. How to put the pieces together so they fit, and then stay together? Superglue, a frame.

'Yaya, we can stay at home together, just us. Like before.'

And just what did we do all day, before? Watch crap TV, make up games? No, he's going to have a different life from here on in. A life made up of structured, ordered, productive days.

'Darling, you'll have to go – I'm going to get a job.'

I don't know where that came from, but as soon as I say it I settle on it. Of course, I need a job, interaction with the world, money in my pocket, a purpose. What could I do? Retail? My fingers itch at the thought. Receptionist? The weight of boredom at the thought of it almost crushes me. Perhaps I could think about setting foot on stage again? Tommy needs to see his mother happy, thriving, in her element.

I adopt my best Shakespearean stance: feet firmly planted, shoulders back, head aloft, back slightly arched, demanding attention from my captive audience. I start in a whisper: 'Gallop apace, you fiery-footed steeds, towards Phoebus' lodging...'

Tommy claps. 'Hewbie, come here.' He climbs on top of the dog. 'Giddy-up, Hewbie Howsie, giddy-up.'

Herbie's tail is wagging vigorously as he circles the room, barking, the kitten mewling, a rousing underscore to my spotlit monologue.

My voice builds in volume. '... such a wagoner as Phaethon would whip you to the west, and bring in cloudy night immediately... What's next, Tommy?'

Tommy abruptly dismounts Herbie and looks out the window. He's not playing. 'Dada's up there, Yaya.'

The sky has faded from daytime grey to early-evening pewter.

A cold feeling lands in my stomach. Water on fire, a dousing. I too look out, shiver.

'Can't see him, Yaya. Too early for stars.'

'Too cloudy for stars, Tommy.'

The day will come when Tommy's old enough to understand, and I'll tell him, I'll have to – I'll let him know he has a father who's alive. For now, though, the lie, the kindest of lies, continues.

45

I wake, the sheets tangled, cold and damp. Open my eyes, take in the scene around me, all my babies sleeping on the bed. Move my hand from one to the other to the other; like the different textures of hair, fur and skin.

Tommy opens one eye, looks at me fiercely, sniffs.

'I didn't mean to, Yaya.'

'What, Tommy?'

'I used the clicker and Mr Fire got caught in the curtains and eated Pizza-man away.'

'Oh, darling, only a dream. Remember I told you strange things can happen in the Land of Nod? Is Pizza-man David?'

He nibbles the top of his thumb.

'Tell me all about it.'

His face is flushed, his eyes glassy, as his nightmare tumbles out of him: 'Meanie bottle at my mouth and bad fairy flew into me and jumped, giddy, sick, doing hopscotch in my tummy. You growed wings, big black wings, and flapflapflapped in the air and in my head and all my inside. Pizza-man went green like a grasshopper and snot and mould and smelled of yuck.' He comes up for air, before he plunges back in: 'Clicker in my hand and I pressed and fire happened and I bringed it to Mr Curtain in the room where Pizza-man was sleeping. Whoooosh! and fast, fast, fast, hot, hot, crackle, sizzle, spit, lickety-spit, so fast, up it goed, up and up. And nee-naw-nee-naw little yellow men and jaggedy orange fire and changing colours yellow-orange-red, red-orange-yellow, Pizza-man was melting, smell of dripping cheesy, and the bad fairy was dancing and Pizza-man was burning, and the smoke shapeclouded away. Fireman Sam…' He stops, exhausted.

Jesus. My whole body is shaking. Such a terrible dream for someone so little, but then I think of my own livid nightmares, which used to have me hiding under my bed. It's ok, it's ok, it's ok. Time will make all this go away. Time and stability. He needs to see that I won't ever leave him again. It has to be good that Fireman Sam made an appearance at the end. Right?

'That sounds like a really scary dream, darling.'

I clap the air around his head. 'All gone away now. Remember I told you it's all in the imagination?' I brush his damp hair off his forehead.

He pushes me away.

'And Fireman Sam saved the day!'

His eyes dart around him, not sure of anything.

'You're here now, Tommy, you're here. This is real.'

He pinches the skin on the back of his hand.

'Ok now.' I gently stroke the red mark. 'Look around you, Tommy, what do you see?'

He looks dazed. 'The colour of creamy ice.'

'What do you really see? Herbie, Marmie and Yaya, yes? We're all right here.' I speak softly.

He swats the air in front of his eyes. I take his hands in mine and kiss his fingertips.

'You're safe now.'

He looks at Herbie and Marmie, still sleeping soundly on the bed, and starts to breathe more evenly.

'How about we get you ready for school and you can see Miss Maeve and paint another picture?'

'No, Yaya, no. I won't go.'

Exactly like I was at his age. I remember my father walking out of the room, saying: 'Enough of the dramatics, we are leaving in twenty minutes, end of.'

'Is this because of the bad dream?' He shakes his head vigorously.

'Ok, Tommy, how about I go with you?'

'No no no no no no no.'

'Why, Mr T? What happened yesterday? You can tell me.'

He continues shaking his head. Herbie stands unsteadily on the mattress, shakes himself off and pads over to Tommy, lies beside him and lays his big heavy head on his lap. Tommy leans in and hugs him, now inconsolable with grief, his whole body racked and convulsing.

'Ok, darling. It's ok. You don't have to go today.'

He sniffs, looks at me.

'Maybe you can tell me later what happened, ok?'

He clamps his lips tight. I'm not happy with that school anyway, that busybody, that cross, that image of distress, emblem of martyrdom. I'll scout around, find somewhere close to my new workplace, wherever that might be, somewhere more progressive, Educate Together or something, although the thought of all those little people saying prayers together, words they couldn't possibly understand, is strangely sweet. A room full of children imagining the

Mother Mary in her pearly blue gown, with her luminous face, the babe in her arms. Their little nodding heads. Baby Jesus. Nod. I'm back in the room with the monstrous Mary, all those men, Jimmy's bald head, up and down, up and down, clearing itself of its clamour. I look at my son. He is my priority now, and for ever.

'What would you like to do today?'

'Beach, Yaya!'

I'm relieved to see he's got used to this question so soon. Surely other remnants of his chaotic conditioning can just as easily be undone. Such a clever little thing; an outing is exactly what we all need right now. Sea, sand, perhaps even a smile from Mr Sunshine.

I put on my swimsuit underneath my clothes, just in case the urge catches me.

In the car my phone starts to ring. An unidentified number, followed quickly by my father's, then David's. David calls and calls again, and again. The knocking sensation against my ribcage starts. I listen to my voicemail: Where are you?… Your father is worried… The school called him, wondering about Tommy… Call me…

Pulsing eyelids. Twitching extremities. Think of Jimmy: 'Flooded with adrenalin, pissed with fear.' Think of the glitter all over the floor, and in my hair, sprinkled on my cheeks. Think of how pretty I must have been.

I put the pedal to the floor. Careen and swerve my way to the beach. Crave the sea air, the smack of the salt. Space, perspective, that's all. We tumble out into the car park, run as one to the water's edge, Marmie careful not to get too close, myself and Tommy wading in, 'Pull up your trousers, Tommy!' – Herbie starts to whine.

'Ok, old boy, ok,' I say. 'Mind Tommy, ok?' – face towards the wide expanse of sea and sky. 'Tommy, Yaya won't be long; stay there with Herbie and Marmie, and don't talk to any strangers, ok?' He nods, I pull my dress over my head, and stride in. I look back, he's waving, I wave back, then dive under: it's been too long – this, this sensation I've been chasing, the cooling, the stilling. Head under, silence, a real silence, a calm, pure silence, down in the depths of me. When I emerge I check on my trio, all ok, waiting patiently, I turn on my back for a moment, just a moment, allow myself to float. The sea and sky are the same glacial grey, all as one.

I turn my head and see Tommy wading in towards me. Flip my body back over, move faster through the water than I ever thought possible. 'Stop, Tommy, far enough.' Herbie is howling. My son stops, waves at me. He splashes me as soon as I'm within reach.

'Hey, what you doing, little man? It's freezing!'

'Splish-splosh, Walter Wave!'

I come up level with him, shin-deep, and grab his hand, the two of us running towards the shore, and as soon as we hit dry sand I propel myself into a cartwheel. He copies me, legs akimbo, little tumbling clown. We laugh and continue to spin, arms first, legs following, arms, then legs, Marmie and Herbie running alongside, yowling. I collapse first, he throws himself on me, face down, rat-a-tat-tat, our hearts an erratic percussive score.

His skin breaks out in tiny little pimples; his teeth are chattering. How long have we been lying here?

'Ok, now, Mr T, hup, let's get you warmed up.'

I pull off his sopping clothes, retrieve my dress, use it as a towel to dry him off, even though my own skin is marked with blue circles. Wrap him in it and run back to the car in my wet swimsuit. Déjà vu, except this time I'm not in my sopping bra and knickers; this time there's no one there watching me, judging me, and I have a jacket and cardigan on the front seat. I put the heat on full-blast, wrap Tommy in my coat, myself in the cardigan. There are no voices in my head, no directive to steal, to glug, to soothe. I buckle him in, kiss him on the forehead, drive home at a moderate speed. Carry with me the sense of being underwater: cold, clean and clear.

'Are you ok, Tommy?'

I look in the rear-view mirror, my trio all leaning into each other.

'No more Mr Fire in the head?'

He shakes his head. 'Walter Wave put it all out!'

'Clever Mr Walter Wave. I told you he was a magician!'

'Silly Yaya. Water always wins the fight with fire.'

'Yes, Tommy, yes, I guess it does, if you get to it on time.'

46

When I open the front door, the smell of curry hits my nostrils. I hate curry; Tommy does too. The sound of cupboards opening and closing in the kitchen; the radio is on. Herbie growls.

'Hello, guys! Hope you're hungry.' David comes into the hall to greet us. 'Jesus, Sonya. The state of you.'

'What are you doing here, David?'

'Just as well I am here, by the looks of things.'

'I don't remember saying it's ok for you to come into my house when I'm not here.'

'You forget a lot of things you tell me.'

Not rising to that one.

'Why are you all wet?'

He opens the back door as if to usher the animals into the yard.

'Not having them get cold,' I say, closing the door firmly.

He sighs, like I'm being pathetic. 'Where have you been? Your father has been on to me, frantic.'

'Why isn't he here, then?'

'You mean you don't know?'

'Know what… ?

'I thought you knew.'

'It seems he speaks to you more than he does me.'

'He's in hospital.'

'What? What is it?'

'They caught it early; they say he's going to make a full recovery.'

I don't have to ask anything else. I know. That recurring childhood nightmare come to roost. The big C. What does that say about me? I look towards the ceiling, divining nothing.

'Where is he?'

'Lara asked that they be left alone.'

He's talking to Lara? This is ridiculous; an absurd farce.

'I'm sorry that this is such a shock. I thought you knew.'

David turns to Tommy. 'So, young man, big day coming down the tracks. What would you like to do on your birthday?'

Tommy is also looking up, searching.

'We don't want Mummy doing anything silly, now, do we, ruining it?'

'David, what are you doing? What is this?'

'I promised your father I'd keep an eye.'

Tommy's hand reaches towards mine. I enfold it: so tiny.

'Is he paying you?'

He ignores this. 'Look at you both. You'll catch your death.'

'I doubt very much my father is aware of the perks…'

I push past him into the kitchen, Tommy's hand still inside mine, the animals following, take the pot with the curry in it and scrape it all into the bin. I pour water for the animals, get a glass for myself and Tommy. Run the tap, fill the glass, tip it out, fill it again, sip, then tip, then fill.

'Can't be that hard, Sonya, pouring a glass of water.'

I turn to look at him. 'It's my house, I'll pour my water whatever goddam way I like.' There's something about the way he's standing, taking up so much space, being all proprietorial and *invasive*. I wasn't making it up – it happened, right here, in this spot.

I say what I should've said then: 'David, this is my home and I'd like you to leave.'

He fixes his jumper around his shoulders, making sure each sleeve is dangling evenly. I don't feel the urge to laugh.

'She doesn't really mean that, does she, Tommy? Mummy never really knows what she means.'

He moves to pick Tommy up.

'David, put him down.'

Tommy is all harsh angles and held breath.

'David, I said put him down, NOW.'

'Ok, ok, less of the dramatics, Sonya.'

He laughs, puts Tommy down, tickles him awkwardly.

Tommy wraps his arms around his sides.

'For all your talk of *boundaries*, you really don't have a clue,' I say.

He fixes his shirt collar.

'Are you listening to me?'

His hand moves reflexively towards a worn spot on his jumper sleeve, his thumb circling.

'I am asking you to leave.'

He makes no move. I look at Tommy, who's kneeling, his arms around the animals. I speak softly.

'David…'

He leans in closer. I know exactly what needs to be said and in what tone. Slow and deliberate, clearly articulated, space between each word.

'We – Don't – Want – You – Here.'

He draws back as if smacked. Something in his bearing has shifted. I have done it. It's not the first time he has heard those words and they almost crease him in two. That flash of insight, almost blinding, and I see him as a boy, wearing someone else's clothes. *We don't want you here.* I have to stop myself jumping in there to make it better.

'Sonya.' He moves towards me.

I turn my face away.

'You're confused.'

'No confusion.' And it's true: there are no warring voices, no conflicting impulses. There is no denying or minimising what happened. Instinct finally on track, intact.

'I'm going to take Tommy for his shower, and by the time we're finished I'd like you to be gone. Leave the key on the front table.'

'You're making a big mistake, Sonya. I will have to notify the authorities.'

A low humming sound buzzes in the air.

In front of my eyes, a spilling shadow, a shifting of form, of substance. I blink hard.

'Yaya?'

'It's ok, darling.'

'Sonya? Are you going to have one of your fits?' David says.

I rub my eyes, turn to look at Tommy, who sticks his thumb in his mouth.

'David, you know the authorities are never a good idea. You, more than anyone, should know that. You don't want that route for Tommy.'

David puts his hand to his stomach as if to protect himself. All my creatures start to stir. I don't try to stop them. I open my mouth to give full vent. They are silent, released peacefully. David looks about him, sensing a shifting in the atmosphere, confused. 'Right, well…' He goes to get his coat and bag, which are by the front door.

'If you're sure this is what you want.' He stalls. 'Not that you're ever sure about anything.'

I pat Herbie, who's making low grumbling sounds.

'Bye, soldier,' David says, saluting rather pathetically at Tommy.

Tommy looks at me. I bend to kiss him on the top of his head, remove his thumb from between his lips. David starts to thread his arm through the sleeve of his coat, which gets caught in the lining. I move to help him, then pull back.

'If I leave now, you'll never see me again.'

'The key,' I say, in a voice I wish I could have found with my father, with Lara.

He reaches into his pocket and throws it on the table. 'I really hope you know what you're doing, Sonya.' He looks at me then, like that lost little boy. His voice is young. 'You know where to find me.'

As he opens the door, a kind of turbulence, a sound of beating wings. He steps into the wake, following dumbly. At the gate he tries to wave but his arm seems weighted down. He turns again, shifts the bag on to his shoulder and walks away. 'I only want what's best for you,' I think I hear him say.

I put my hand to the base of my throat and swallow easily. A lightness in my body. I look at his retreating back, and at the empty space around him. Another turning away, another ending, another failed relationship, yet more emptiness, a vacuum waiting to be filled. Or. Something else entirely. I find I wish him well. I really do.

I look at Tommy, who's running around the kitchen chasing and cupping the light.

'Sippies,' he says, offering me his hands full of sunlight.

47

'Happy birthday, darling boy.'

Tommy wakes, one eye still glued shut, and looks at me, sleep-crumpled.

I whisper, 'Make a wish,' and intertwine my little finger with his.

He screws his eyes tight shut; his lips move as he mumbles. I think I see the words Gandad, Yaya, Herbie, Marmie forming. Not a trace of the shape it would take to form the name David. The locks were changed last night, pushing me into overdraft, which I was surprised to find was still operating on my account.

'Pull, Yaya,' Tommy says, exerting pressure on my pinkie.

I lean in to him, kiss him on his cheek with my eyelashes. Think of the slogan: 'Just For Today'. Just for today my little man will be prioritised. My every day will be made up of this daily mantra, that will be enough.

I track down the whereabouts of a dodgy party warehouse, call around the three main hospitals, locate my father. I walk the motley crew, feed them, stuff an invitation into my bag, then buckle Tommy into the back seat. We drive to the party shop first and stock up on sparklers, spinners, streamers, balloons. My body jangles when I find a box with 'Catherine Wheel' on the front. I pick it up, hold it, elation building, that hazy, happy childhood memory still tugging at me. I kiss the package. 'Thank you,' I say to the Woman Above. 'Tommy, come here, this is Ms Friendly Fire Spinner I was telling you about. She won't hurt anyone!' He comes to me, holds the package, inhales, nods happily, a new light in his eyes.

'We're going to have our very own fireworks display!'

'Crackle, sizzle, whoosh, Yaya!' He skips away down the aisle, lit from within.

'Do you have any Fireman Sam suits?' I whisper to the shop assistant, who backs away, shaking his head, giving me that look.

We arrive at the hospital half an hour later, find a parking spot easily in the multi-storey car park, no sense of panic, when usually I'd have broken out in hives by now. I remember the ticket, put it in my pocket, pat it, repeat 'Ticket, ticket' over and over as we walk towards the entrance. Green germ-killer hand gel for Tommy and me. I find the shop, where I buy grapes for my father because I can't think of anything else, and because it's what you're meant to do. I make sure that Tommy eats a cheese sandwich, force myself to eat a banana. Need to maintain my equilibrium. Breathe deeply, ground. Announce myself at reception and am told St Michael's wing, room 8.

The private wing is bright and clean, the smell of disinfectant smacking the back of my throat, bringing water to my eyes. I locate the room, stand outside a moment, put a hand on my heart, close my eyes and ask for guidance. Something bigger than me, wiser, some force for good, conjure Sister Anne, call on the Divine

Mother, hear the soft rumbles of the rosary, feel the stillness of being submerged, being held, go deeper, inside, an inward leaning, listening.

'Ok, little man?' I open my eyes and look at Tommy, who's watching me with that familiar anxious expression. I tuck a tendril of his hair behind his ear, push the door open.

Lara is sitting by the bed reading. She looks up, puts her finger to her lips, 'Shh, he's sleeping,' and gets up as if to herd us out of the room. I stand steady, Tommy's hand in mine. Walk over to the bed, lift Tommy on to it, place the grapes on the bedside table.

Lara says, 'I thought I told David we need our space.'

'I think you've taken up enough space in his life.'

I can feel my fury building but manage to contain it, just.

'What were you doing talking to David about me, anyway?'

'Your father and I feel he's a good influence.'

No point in even trying to explain. Think of all the times I tried and failed to make this woman see my side of things, how I'd just get more worked up and lose my temper and she'd win.

I lean into him and whisper, 'Dad.'

He opens one eye, which alights straight away on Tommy. 'Well, if it isn't the little birthday boy.'

Did he really just say that?

'Please, Sonya, we need to keep him quiet, no shocks.'

I look directly at Lara, this woman who barrelled into our lives at a time when my father was still grieving, when I was grieving. For the first time I wonder what happened to her that she felt so desperately threatened by a child.

'Help me sit up,' my father manages.

Lara and I reach for the pillows at the same time.

'Lara, please.' My father lifts his hand in a dismissive wave, a shock to us all. It's as if the hand made contact with her right cheek, which flares. I imagine it stings.

'I'll go get a coffee. Anyone want one?'

No one says anything.

Lara's wide gait, which usually takes up so much space, contracts to a tight thin line, as if she's balancing precariously on a high wire. She leaves the room in this manner, unsure, slippery satin underfoot. I help my father sit up, plump up his pillows. His body is soft, his skin slack and mottled. He seems so small.

'So, young man. Did you get any nice surprises today?'

Tommy nods his head vehemently, a little Chinese plastic nodding puppy. I think of Jimmy. Jesus. Nod. Jesus. Nod. My heart constricts, then expands.

'Fireworks!' Tommy says.

'Christ, Sonya.'

I attempt a shrug. Yeah, and so what?

'Only sparklers and a spinner.'

'Fwiendly Ms Fire!' Tommy says.

'Are those things even legal?'

'We're having a party.' I hand him the invitation.

'Did you make these, Tommy?'

He nods. 'And Yaya.'

'Yes, I can see your mother all over them.' He shakes the card, tiny silver and gold stars falling on the sheets.

'And *my* mother?' I say.

He doesn't answer, just stares out the window at the bare branches of a tree, which almost touch the glass, long fingers probing.

'Dad?'

He looks at me, really looks at me. 'Yes, Sonya, yes, ok...'

He sits back, exhausted, slumps.

'Your mother wasn't well for a long time.'

Something inside me starts to dissolve, a coiled, hard mass in my stomach.

'None of it was your fault. I didn't think you'd remember. I thought it best if you didn't...'

'But what if I'm the same?' I look at Tommy.

'Sonya, you're not the same.'

'But what if I am?' I whisper.

Tommy looks from me to his grandfather, who reaches across and gently wipes a speck of glitter from his cheek.

'Believe me, you're nothing like her.'

It's as if my father has turned to face me for the first time.

'How can you be sure, Dad?'

My father looks pointedly at Tommy. 'Another time, Sonya, ok?'

I nod and brush my son's hair away from his eyes.

'Who's going to your party, Tommy?'

'Yaya, Herbie, Marmie and me.'

My father's face, usually so hard and held, is as open as Tommy's. Sunshine to tears in an instant.

'What about that nice man, David?'

Tommy's head moves side to side so fast it's as if his neck might snap.

'Ok, ok.' My father looks at me. 'What happened?'

'You know the way you were always telling me not to trust my instinct around men?'

'Sonya, this was different. He's solid, good for you.'

'Dad, you said yourself often enough that appearances can be deceptive.'

'The rehab trusted him.'

'Nuns really don't have much experience of that kind of man.' I try on a laugh.

He looks at me and then away out the window again. I wonder if he's remembering things he's tried so hard to forget. I see it now: how Lara has been a part of that forgetting. No wonder everything about me irritates and inflames him.

'Dad?'

He looks at me, warily.

'Nothing.'

My father turns to my son, relieved. 'Young man, I'm honoured you came to see me on your big day.'

Tommy is basking, his face angled towards him like the sun.

'Tommy, have you ever been to the zoo?'

'No, Gandad.'

'Would you like to go when I get better?'

'Are there woos there?'

'Roos,' I say. 'Kangaroos.'

'You know, sonny, I think that might be the only animal they don't have there.'

'No matter, Mr T. We have our pictures at home and one day we'll get on an airplane and fly to the land of the roos.' (I don't feel the need to mention man-made infernos and burnt-out habitats.)

'Sonya.' *Don't go filling the boy's head with nonsense.* I am grateful to him that he doesn't say it.

'Dad? Do you remember bringing me to a fireworks display? A really spectacular one?'

'Yes, Sonya. Yes, I do, not long after your mother died.'

'It was really beautiful.'

'You always liked bright, shining things, Sonya.'

'Yes, Dad. I guess I always did.'

I look at my son, who's still staring, enraptured, at his grandad.

'I think I'll go for a walk, leave you two to catch up, ok?'

My father looks at me, nods. Tommy doesn't take his eyes off his grandad.

I lean in to kiss Tommy on the top of his head. 'I won't be long, darling.'

I leave them then, noting on my way out how both their smiles have the same crooked aspect. I listen, for a moment, outside the door.

'Gandad?'

'Yes, son?'

'As soon as you are better, will you come to our homey own?'

'I think that can be arranged. It seems your mother is going to need a new babysitter.'

'And for Herbie and Marmie too.'

His voice contains a suppressed sigh. 'Yes, the dog and cat too...'

In the corridor I lean my forehead against the cool wall, then turn around and see the new delicate Lara, almost suspended in the air, waiting on the other side, back to the wall. I walk towards her. 'Would you mind leaving Tommy and his grandfather alone for a while?'

'He's been very sick.'

'Even more of a reason.'

I don't trust myself not to say the wrong thing, even though my mind is clear, free from static, space between my thoughts, which aren't chasing, circling, contradicting. I know what I'd like to say.

'Sonya?'

Lara's voice trailing me.

I turn. 'Yes?'

'He'll come through this; he's going to be ok.'

The two of us, grown women, look at each other as if seeing each other for the first time.

'And Sonya… ?'

Lara hesitates, plucks some fluff off her top, pulls her sleeves down. She looks up at me as if she is about to continue, then looks back down and shakes her head in silence. At last: a shared understanding.

48

'What do you see out there, Tommy?'

'The colour of happy.'

'And what else? Real things?'

'Sky and fluffy clouds and hard clouds and marshmallow mountains of clouds.'

Such an imaginative little thing. I start to sing, contained and clear, 'Happy birthday, dear Tommy...' He pushes his face against the windowpane, squashing his nose and cheeks. He doesn't stick his hands in his ears, which makes a bubble of happiness swell inside me.

'I see the colour of happy too, Mr T. Mine is pink, what is yours?'

He doesn't answer, which is fine, perhaps there are no words, or perhaps a specific colour is too limiting, perhaps it's a spectrum of colours. His silence is fine. I can leave him with it, and I don't need to make it mean that he's being disrespectful, or that he's ignoring me. He's entitled to his silence.

I drive slowly, luxuriating in our new-found ease of saying nothing.

We stop off at our local shop on the way home, the two boys from that day when I lost Tommy slouching behind the counter, a shared recognition, though, wisely, a wordless one.

'It's the little fella's birthday!' I say.

'Happy birthday,' they say almost in unison.

'We need Rice Krispies, cake holders and melting chocolate. Oh, and matches and candles!'

They run down different aisles and return in triple-quick time with the items.

'Thank you, boys. Very kind. We'll bring you in some chocolate krispie cakes.'

I pay, they wave, smiling, in relief. 'Bye, birthday boy.'

Yelps of excitement greet us as I open the front door and let the animals out into the yard, the evening air mellow and kind, not too cold, wet, damp, windy, or anything at all, the kind of weather I'd usually call insipid. Back in the kitchen I melt the chocolate, pour it into a large bowl. Once it's cooled, I allow Tommy to dig his hands in. He goes to feed Herbie.

'Hey, chocolate is poison to dogs.'

He looks at me like he doesn't quite believe me, but says, 'How about cats?'

'I wouldn't risk it.'

He lifts a mouthful to his lips. 'Poor Marmie, poor Herbie.' Closes his eyes, savours.

'Want to pour in the krispies?'

He takes the open packet and pours the contents in. 'Snap, pop, Yaya.'

'Crackle,' I say as we knead our hands into the mix. I lay out little bun cases and we scoop handfuls into them.

'Let's leave them to set in the fridge for a while, ok?'

He opens the fridge, sniffs, looks around, as I place a tray of krispie cakes on the bottom shelf.

'Hey, how about we blow up some balloons, Mr T?'

He squints at me as I pull the packet apart, hand him a pink one, then change my mind, and give him yellow, me pink. It's going to be a pink-balloon night; I'll make sure of that. We both blow, his tiny, mine huge, and I tell him to hold them as I stretch their necks, loop and tie, then throw them in the air.

'Wheee!' I say.

'Wheee,' he repeats back, distinctly unimpressed.

The animals love them, barking and squealing, until one lands on Marmie and is savaged. It pops loudly; Tommy laughs, and jumps on the other one. I don't feel like blowing up any more.

'How about musical statues?'

He looks unsure.

'I'll put some music on and every time it stops we have to freeze, ok?'

I turn the radio on, but the Billie Holiday CD blasts out: 'And after all is said and done / To think that I'm the lucky one / I can't believe that you're in love with me...'

Shit. My son is frozen alright, terrified. That bloody song hurtling us both back to that moment when I was taken over, possessed by a terrible need, when I almost suffocated him with that need. I quickly switch to radio mode, and fiddle around to find something benign, alight on bland retro pop, a nasal high-pitched girly voice, singing about spinning right round, baby... I open my arms, offer him my hands. He doesn't take them.

He walks away into the living room, opens the art drawer and gets the glitter, brings it back into the kitchen. He removes the lid, sniffs, then closes it again. My heart is hammering. I hold my hand out, he places the tube into it, then I open the bin and deposit the tiny winking eyes into it.

The whispers start, yet there is something else there too, a stillness, space to hold it all.

'Messy stuff, Mr T.'

His head moves up, down, up, down. I turn off the music. We look at each other.

'Is it dark enough yet?'

He opens his eyes, looks through the window. 'Hmmm-mm.'

I get the box of matches, offer it to him. He studies it a moment, then shakes his head.

'It's fine with me here.'

He takes the box in his hands, pushes his thumb against the lower lid, opens it, stares, his body trembling.

'But Clare said it's dangerous.'

'It's ok, I promise, it's safe with me here. You know how to, right?'

He nods, removes a matchstick, holds it in front of his face, stops breathing.

He strikes, his cheeks flush, his pupils dilate. He inhales deeply, we both do. A rush.

I hold a sparkler in front of him. We move our hands towards each other and touch the match to the sparkler, which ignites, sparks. And another one.

'Into the yard, quick.'

We are both jazzed by the crackle, the sizzle, the sheer beauty of the things as they dance in the air, arcing and weaving, seemingly of their own volition, our own hands chasing them, the sparklers' light reflected in his eyes. We dance to a soundtrack of the animals' barking and mewling. My imp is desperately trying to make an appearance. *You are not fucking invited, not welcome here anymore, love!*

'The other one, Yaya.'

'The wheel?'

He nods, his eyes glassy.

'Ok, darling, and then bed, ok?'

I offer him the package, all bright and gaudy-coloured, which he takes as if it contains something precious, alive. He slowly removes the outer wrapping, the colour of see-through, and hands the box to me. A whistling wheel of fortune, cheap and tacky. I rip it open, try to read the instructions, my eyesight blurring. I didn't realise it was so complicated, requiring hammers and nails and practical skills I don't possess. I go into the shed, rummage and find an old hammer, covered in cobwebs, which I gently disentangle, leaving as much of the spider's delicate weave intact as possible.

There's a nail and a wooden stick in the bottom of the box, which I presume is meant to be used as a stake. I hammer the stick into the ground and attach the wheel with the nail. The hammer slips, or my hand slips, resulting in a jangling nerve pain shooting through my thumb and forefinger. Bring my finger to my mouth and suck, a splinter lodged underneath my nailbed. The wheel is hanging off its perch precariously. Tommy goes to it and rights it.

'You need to move away, Tommy, while I secure this thing.'

He gives me that look, which is enough to spur me on. Tap, tap, tap. Now: *Straighten fuse, light tip of free end at arm's length and retreat immediately.* I pull the fuse through the centre, watch Tommy watching me.

'Want to light this with me, Tommy?'

He runs back into the kitchen, returns with the box of matches and this time strikes with intent, the flame flickering in his shining eyes. 'Arm's length, Tommy.'

I guide his lit match-tip to the fuse, both hands holding, mine encircling his. We connect, and the Catherine wheel is set alight, blazing. The two of us run to the farthest edge of the yard, cheeks pulsing with heat and excitement. The wheel turns, a whirling dervish casting its hypnotic spell, and I'm there, in the happy scene I've been chasing. I am eight, held high on my father's shoulders. The fireworks display burned so brightly and boomed so loudly, the sound momentarily drowned out my internal hissing and cackling, which I hadn't known had been a constant until that moment. My father pointed at a huge circling wheel of fire. 'A Catherine wheel.' He tilted his head back towards me. 'Named in memory of a beautiful young woman called Catherine, who was condemned to die for her beliefs on the wheel, a medieval instrument of torture.'

I remember the delicious thrill of shivers in my body, as if my father had just shared an illicit secret with me. There's no memory of Lara in the picture. 'But when she touched the wheel, so the story goes, it burst into flames. A miracle, Sonya.' Although I didn't know what the word meant exactly, I knew it had magic attached to it.

I look at Tommy, who seems mesmerised, the spinning an antidote to mine, to his.

'Beeootiful, slinky, sunshiny, lickety-spit, wheee, Yaya, wheee!'

I squeeze his hand as the wheel propels itself faster and faster and with a mighty whoosh lifts into the air and soars above our heads, a silver spinning kaleidoscope of sparkles. Is this meant to happen? I don't think the instructions said anything about it being airborne. The animals howl. A sound of sirens far off in the distance. 'Fireman Sam,' Tommy says, two bright spots of colour on his cheeks, his body thrumming with excitement, speed taking hold of him until he has wrestled free of me and is running to a soundtrack of whistles and flickers, crackles and spits, of engines shrieking rescue.

Suddenly, the wheel explodes, like a fireball, and hurtles directly at him. A noise rips out of me, a gargantuan sound I've never heard before. Tommy stops in his tracks; the animals are hushed. *Please help*, and this feels embodied, a current coursing. Is this it, Sister Anne? Energy pulses through me as I launch myself at him, push him behind me, my body a human shield. I stretch my hands upwards and manage to hit out at the burning wheel, connecting with my right palm, deflecting its path. It throws out sparks.

'A shooting star, Yaya!'

The sirens seem to get closer, a screaming violin concerto, then swerve away until all that's left is a distant echo.

'Fuck, that was close, Tommy.' I look at him, my whole body shaking. What could have happened plays out for a moment.

'Fuck, fuck, fuckety-fuck!'

His hot hand climbs inside my already blistering palm.

'Ouchy, Yaya.' He drops his hand, inspects my palm and traces the blisters with his fingertips, then blows on its surface.

Herbie and Marmie huddle against my ankles.

'Thank you, thank you, thank you.'

'Who are you talking to, Yaya?'

Our four faces tilt upwards, as if under a spell. The navy night sky is lit up. We all watch, transfixed, as the wheel of fire skitters off on its new trajectory, trailing in its wake a cloud of fiery glitter. I bend to him, blow the charred fragments off his face, tuck his hair behind his ear and pick him up. He nuzzles into me, his eyelashes brushing my cheeks, his breath in my ear: a divine whisper. Silence falls like a velvet curtain. Swish.

ACKNOWLEDGEMENTS

Thank you to my wonderful agent, Clare Alexander, without whose support, patience and vision this book would not exist. To Ellah Wakatama Allfrey for introducing us in the first place, I am incredibly grateful. To Lesley Thorne and all at Aitken Alexander, for allowing me to be part of your special team. To Geffen Semach, my most patient reader, my ally and friend, thank you. To the brilliant editor Gillian Stern for helping to unlock the heart of this book with her exceptional insight.

To the Arts Council of Ireland for their invaluable bursary; to Arvon and the Tyrone Guthrie Centre for providing beautiful spaces and inspiration along the way; to Linda Walsh for her generosity and sea view.

To all my early readers: Siona, Emer, Gene, Sonya, Earnan, Beth, Julie – thank you. Special thanks to Brian Langan for his perceptive notes and to Michelle Moran, Seamus Hosey, Hugh O'Conor and Tom Farrelly for their friendship and tireless reading. To June Caldwell, Joanne Hayden and Elizabeth McSkeane for their incisive critiquing and support along the way.

To my fearless, visionary editor, Alexis Kirschbaum, I am so grateful for your belief in this book. To all the team at Bloomsbury for their professionalism and support, in particular Sarah Ruddick, Laura Meyer, Rachel Wilkie, Jo Forshaw, Jasmine Horsey, Sarah McLean and everyone who worked on this novel. To Hermione Davis in the Australian office. To Greg Heinimann for his gorgeous cover design. To Silvia Crompton for her copy-editing skills. An absolute pleasure to work with you all.

To Mum, Dad, Aisling, Shell, Clara and all my friends and family near and far. To my brother Stephen, who I want to thank most especially for his generosity in sharing so much of his journey with me. With love and gratitude to everyone who has stood by me and helped shape this book in some way.

A NOTE ON THE TYPE

The text of this book is set in Minion, a digital typeface designed by Robert Slimbach in 1990 for Adobe Systems. The name comes from the traditional naming system for type sizes, in which minion is between nonpareil and brevier. It is inspired by late Renaissance-era type.